THREE

A Tale of the Bookseller's Children

DEVEN BALSAM

Beaten Track
www.beatentrackpublishing.com

Three: A Tale of the Bookseller's Children
First published 2018 by Beaten Track Publishing

ISBN: 978 1 78645 297 9

Cover Design: Roe Horvat

Beaten Track Publishing,
Burscough. Lancashire.
www.beatentrackpublishing.com

Contents

Shiverer In the Trees

THEY WALKED TOGETHER, the two women, small and slight, their thick, black hair captured above slender, brown necks—the older with pale-blue eyes, the younger with hazel. The wind fled fast off the river, lifting shutters to slap against windows, tossing horses' manes, twirling skirts with muddied hems, and prying the slip of paper from the older woman's hand. She twisted to try to catch it, but it was already across the street.

A man stooped to lift it from the muddy puddle into which it had fallen. He came to her, dabbing the slip on his fishing leathers, and handed it back to Mink, who took it with a kind smile, nodding her head to him.

"Much thanks, sirrah," she said quietly. The wind gusted again, pulling at her skirts so that they billowed like a sail.

The man watched her struggle to calm the unruly garment, and he too smiled.

She nodded to him once again and took her daughter's hand to continue down the street. The man remained where he was, watching them walk away.

The day was that of a cold spring, bright and swift, with the teasing scent of fresh greening in the air, but chilly, comfortless to the bones. Mink glanced up at each building, struggling to determine what the business carried on within entailed. A milliner, she needed. And a grocer.

The clerk looked up to see their faces framed by the small window. She motioned for them to enter.

"Hello." Her voice was soft but scratched from age and pipe-smoke, which the shop did not smell like, though Mink noticed the pipe upon the counter—carved ivory upon a red stone dish. "Newcomers to Delster?"

"Yes, madam," said Mink, smiling and smoothing her hair. "Oh, how good it is to be inside and warm again."

"Don't I know it. I'd love to give the wood stove a rest, but the weather won't allow it."

Mink rubbed her hands together. "My daughter Medie and I arrived this morning from Bran, by the river. A porter will be taking our things up the mountain to my grandmama's home. But I thought to stop here and purchase some fabric, and maybe get some dry provisions if you could recommend a place?" She glanced at the muddied list that she still held.

"I'd be happy to. What're you after?" The clerk leaned on the counter, looking at the list as if to read it, upside down.

"Nothing fancy, just what will suit an adventurous young girl living near the woods," said Mink, smiling. "We're nearly out of tea, and have no fruits to speak of. Some molasses would be helpful." She glanced at her list. "Oh, and...well, I'm sorry there's so much. Flour, beans if possible." She looked up at the milliner. "This must be so dull, to hear me recite my shopping."

"Oh, no, not at all," said the woman, staring at Mink as if she were a butterfly pinned to a board. A man walked out from a back room, carrying a basket that he struggled with. He set it down with a grunt and sighed, stood there a moment as if waiting to speak, staring at the clerk and at Mink with weary eyes, then shuffled back away into the darkness beyond the open door. Mink heard him grumbling, speaking of strange things. *Violence.* She shuddered.

"I'm always happy to meet new folk," the clerk continued. "But about that fabric—you'll likely not want wool, as it seems the winter is finally letting up. It was a mild one, blessedly. Not that it seems so on *this* day. I've got a fair amount of linen. Also cotton. Some patterns, some plain. Dark colors or pale?"

"She fancies green, and patterns not so much."

"Oh, and I do remember my granddaughters' mischief, very well. They've since grown and moved to Warring, but they were raised here. That mountain's watched many a mite skin their knee on Her rocks."

"Yes, well, tell that to my brother and he'll say sorry to anyone on behalf of Huil," said Mink.

The bells of the door jingled, and someone else walked into the shop.

"Oh!" said the shopkeeper. "You're Pastor Bear's sister, then?"

"Yes, madam. My daughter and I are taking up residence here."

"Might I ask why, leaving such a place as Bran? If I'm prying, just tell me to shut up. I won't mind." The clerk winked.

"My husband passed. So…" Mink turned around to see the man from the street, rescuer of the shopping list, standing behind her, and she gasped. "Making a fresh start."

"I'm sorry," said the man, who towered over her. "Didn't mean to startle ye."

Mink nodded to him once again and turned back to the shopkeeper. "How about we come back? I can pick up those fabrics on the way home, after we've seen the grocer? As many yards as two dresses is really all I need."

"That'd be fine. And only but one grocery man in Delster. Hugh Godfrey. He's up the street, in the clapboard building. Just got in some good tea from up river, and plenty preserves still—his wife makes cartloads of apple butter every season."

"That sounds lovely, thank you," said Mink, pulling her shawl closer before walking around the man to find Medie. Her daughter was no longer in the shop. "Oh, I didn't hear the bell."

"Quiet one, that," said the shopkeeper.

"I'm so sorry. I'll come back for my things. Let me fetch her, and then I'll see the grocer as well."

Mink found Medie a block away, looking at books through a window.

"Well, don't those look nice," said Mink. "I'll see next time we're in town if I can't get you a new book."

"Next time?" Medie asked, frowning.

"We'll see. Let's first get what we need before thinking about what we want."

They made their way to the grocer's, and while the man told his fishing stories and Mink watched as he brought out yet another variety of preserves to hold up to the light and examine, Medie again slipped out of the shop.

###

Down the street in the bookseller's window was a field journal of creatures and wildflowers. There was also the history of the inhabitants of this region, such as the *swarthe*—the introverted dwarves who kept to their underground homes. Medie Kieren yearned for both of these.

"Well, there's a *saylie* lass," said a deep voice beside her. Medie saw who it was in the window's reflection—the man from the street, the man from the shop. She glanced up at his bearded face.

"Hullo," she said quietly.

"Hullo, *sirrah*," he said, winking.

"I'll say what I like to." Her voice trembled.

"You'll get slapped across that pretty *saylie* cheek, too. Or across worse places." He moved a black lock of hair that had come to rest over the bridge of her delicate, wide nose and traced the back of his callused hand down her face. "Ye might like that too much," he said softly. "Might make ye fall in love with a fisherman."

"Get away from her," hissed her mother, pulling Medie from the man and hurrying past him, jogging along now with her daughter as the wind again hassled their skirts, then into the milliner's shop, fighting back tears as the woman passed the packages to them and took their city money, and said "of course" when asked if there was a back door.

They walked along the river's banks until at last they reached the road up the mountain and carried their bags all the way to their new home.

###

"Do what ye like to it," said the Voice, ensnaked about the grayish body like a road of worry on a moldy map, a silken, tasseled scarf about a moldering corpse; pointless comforts, endless regrets.

Where is my kingdom. Where is my legacy. What am I becoming...

He twitched; a tremor of paranoia triggered the atrophying muscles and his mind. What if it was playing with *him*, as it liked to do with the things that wandered down into his domain, lost? What if the Voice was twisting him?

"I would do no such thing, for you, master, are my love," said the Voice, as always, a pond-ripple to his thoughts—instant, immediate. He was never alone.

Did he want to be alone?

I do not want that.

"What is that you want?" asked the Voice.

Pain.

The shadow-blight traced a keen spirit-nail across his leathery skin, cutting it, inscribing a fine line of murky red.

Others' pain.

"As you wish, master."

The spiraled room, carved by the king himself in fatter days through the endless tracings of his diamond-sharp talons, led down to a puddle in the floor, a black pearl of gleaming water lit by a sputtering iron star kept fueled by the three remaining sons of the king: Dub, Dother, and Dain. The pool itself was a twisting wormhole bored into the earth, leading to deeper pools and caves, miles and miles down, though no dead body ever floated so low.

A sliding of feet, hitching breath, and wild eyes, and then a prisoner slid down onto the concave floor, scrambling for purchase on the polished, wet stone and looking all around him, desperate for courage in this comfortless tomb of a sanctuary. The man was naked, and shivering with terror and cold.

The king reached his unnaturally long arm down from the ledge, upon which he'd been languishing, to the floor's edge. Then the other arm. Then the short, meaty legs—the only repository of health remaining with him while his spidery upper limbs and bloated, malnourished belly grew more grotesque each season, his milky eyes a little more blind, his rotten mouth still mute, though toothy.

The prisoner stared at the thing crawling toward him and screamed.

Make them stop screaming.

The Voice slid down from the ledge like a rain of black sand, sidewinding over to the man and encircling his body, draping itself across his eyes like a mask.

"What a beautiful sight is this, is that. So terribly do your fingers ache to touch its face, caress its curves."

"What?" trembled the prisoner, turning about, reaching up to his own eyes. To him, the shadow-blight felt like the silken hair of a lover.

"Such ample, perfect flesh. Press your fingers upon it, mold it to your palms."

The man stumbled forward, reaching for the king's face, which was there at the man's shoulder height, waiting, mouth open, yellow fangs saliva-less but hungrily ready.

"So daring are they, they beckon to you. Yes, they want you to do as you will. No shame, this little treasure."

The man laughed nervously, reaching out with a tentative touch, tracing down the king's grotesquely long face with his pink fingers, touching the thin, black lips.

"Tongue darts out, licks at your hand. So wanton."

The man's finger popped into the king's open mouth.

"They close their lips about your finger. They gently suck."

The man groaned.

The king, his white eyes riveted to the prisoner, slowly closed his mouth.

"They suck, harder, pulling your finger in. So very wanton."

The king's teeth crunched through bone.

The man quietly laughed, his head back, eyes closed, beads of sweat all along his brow.

The king chewed, swallowed, and then, with his thin, black tongue, licked down the prisoner's palm as the blood ran freely from the stump.

"Give them more," said the Voice.

"Yes," said the man. "More." He groaned with delight, inserting more fingers into the king's mouth to be bitten off, chewed, and swallowed.

"I am going to remove the scarf, because they are so beautiful and I want you to see."

"Yes," said the man. "I want to see."

The Voice slid from the prisoner's body and curled quickly up around the king's thick legs, up his twisted spine to his neck, draping over his head like a shroud.

The man opened his eyes.

The king had the prisoner's wrist in one hand and was chewing the prisoner's palm, deep into the flesh of it, fingers gone, knuckles bared and exposed to the light, the quick tongue licking the blood as it dripped down in thick, pulsing gobs.

The man screamed and tried to pull away.

The king lovingly let his free arm circle around the man's back, pulling him closer, tracing over his neck, his throat, grabbing a chunk of belly-meat and twisting, twisting and pulling, until the flesh came away in his hands, and he lifted that to his hungry mouth, too.

###

"Well, what do you hope's gonna happen here?" said the boy, sitting atop a rock, eating a piece of smoked rabbit. He'd been watching her for the better part of an hour, and she'd been hard at her task for longer than that.

"What do I *hope* is going to happen?" Medie asked, her accent noticeably of the city, the ends of her words precise as a pocket blade, the middles round as loaves of bread.

"Yes. What?"

"Something," she said, taking a long stick and poking it into the hole in the ground, again.

"Because it's likely that after an hour of nothing, surely something's gonna happen this time."

"Sure I didn't ask your opinion."

"I never need to be asked."

"Obviously." She got down on the ground, leaning on one shoulder as she pushed the long stick deeper. "It took my neck chain, and I'll have it back."

"I'll think positively for you."

"How about shut up?" she said, then gasped, then yipped like a small dog. "Something's got it."

"Got what now?"

"*The stick.*" She was pulling and pushing the stick now with vigor, her hair coming free of its bind and snaking over her shoulders. "Yeah, I'll poke you 'til you're dead—*give me my neck chain, you thieving imp!*"

The ground exploded with exactly one angry badger.

"Whoa!" the boy said, jumping down from the rock and landing a kick against the growling animal's rump before it could sink its teeth into the new neighbor. "Git. Away with you." He grabbed the stick and herded the animal into the trees, tapping its hindquarters as if he was playing sticks-and-eggs. When it finally galloped away into the underbrush, he turned around, running back to her. "You all right? Did it taste meat?"

"No," she said, breathing heavily, leaves in her hair. "Oh. Here it is." She scooped up a silvery thing from the dirt.

"Good for you. Come along now, Persistence. Let's get you home before the tenant of this hole comes back."

Medie scooted away from his grasp. "I'm not yet ready to go home, but thank you."

He stood there, arms folded. "Well, okay. What would you like to do, then?"

"Are you assuming, whatever it is, that it's going to involve you?"

"No, madam. I won't be assuming anything from this point forward…about you."

Medie smiled. "Well, at least, you don't speak like the people around here. Much."

"Of course I don't! My da's my…*da*, and your mum's my aunt."

Medie looked up past him, to the trail that led up through the rhododendron, threading its way up the mountain past moss-covered boulders. "So, you're Asher."

"Yes. Who'd you think I'd be?"

"Wasn't sure, but I never assume. I think I'm going to see what's up there, before they call us for supper." She headed away from the gardens and the yard, reaching down to grab a stick first, then slowly climbed the steep hill.

"I'll come along if that's all right," said Asher, running after her.

"Sure." She stooped to examine a trout lily, tiny and golden among the russet leaves, and reached for it.

"No!" Asher grabbed her hand. "Please—don't pluck it." Medie looked at him. "It's sacred to Huil."

She nodded. Further up the path, perhaps twenty steps from the trout lily, a strange, pale-green, glossy plant, its leaves drooping away from its thick stem like a parasol, had sprouted up from the dry leaves in groups of three.

"And these?" she asked Asher, who was hurrying to keep up with her.

"Never those," he said. "Those are poison."

###

"Her name's Medie," Asher's father told him when he got back to the house. It had been in their family for longer than anyone could remember, and it was the only home that Asher had known. The sun was low in the sky, but it was not yet time for dinner.

"Don't care much for that, I'll stick to calling her Persistence."

"Peas in a pod, then, the two of you, as you do as you like regardless of the mayhem it conjures. You could have yourself a new friend finally, but if you call her silly pet names and cajole her, she'll shun you like the rest of the town."

"Thank you, Da. Appreciate that."

"I'm being honest. I may not pretty up what I tell you, but at least you get the truth."

"I'd be completely fine with you prettying up a thing or two, really. Try it anytime."

"Also, she's your cousin. So there is that."

"I already know, and it doesn't much matter to me. She's as strange as anybody else."

"Strange or not, it's good to have family up here on this mountain again. I suggest you make the best of it and treat both Medie and Aunt Mink with some good amount of respect."

"Why're you all named after creatures, Da?"

"Because," his father examined the blade of the knife he was sharpening, "your grandfather was unusual. Now, how about I try to get you to finish tilling that garden of ours?"

"Now? And how do you figure it's *our* garden?" said Asher.

His father, whose name was Bear, stood up from his seat at his workbench and put the whetstone and his belt blade down on the table. Bear towered over his son, who was barely beyond the age of twelve, and who took after his mother.

"Okay, okay, I'm sorry. I'll till it."

"That's good," said Bear, wiping his hands on the front of his apron and marking his child with a dark stare. "Because last I checked, you ate your share of supper—at our table."

Asher walked out to the quarter-acre plot that was the kitchen garden, now busy with weeds that were quickly greening under the soft, warm days and awakening skies. He began to shovel the compost over the dirt, listening to the chatter of the birds and the wind, smacking the tree limbs together and making the woods groan and squeak.

"Thanks," said Medie, coming around the corner of the garden shed, wearing her once-stolen necklace.

"Uh-huh," said Asher, wiping sweat from his face. He finished with the compost and began to dig a ditch at one end of the plot. "I'm not going to ask how or why a badger stole your trinket."

"It told me it fancied it," said Medie, perching, bird-like, on the stump of the oak that had fallen last summer during a storm.

"Of course it did." Asher looked at her. "Go on, tell me."

"Tell you what?"

"What else you hear."

"Lots." Medie watched a brownwing moth alight upon her bare toe. "Some animals. Ghosts. One time, right before we moved from Bran, I saw an alp sitting on my bed, talking to himself."

"Shit," said Asher, laughing, but horrified. "I'd have died of fright."

"It wasn't pleasant," said Medie. "But I managed to run him off. And then I spent the rest of the night watching over my ma to make sure he didn't come back and go for her."

"I would have done the same, honestly," said Asher. "If my mum were around."

"Is she…lost?"

"Dead. Real bad fever that wouldn't let her go. It's been almost five years."

"I'm sorry."

Asher nodded and finished shoveling the last ditch. "Yeah. It's all right."

"My dad died," said Medie. "It's why we came here."

"How'd he go?" asked Asher, leaning the shovel against the shed and taking up a rake.

"He swallowed poison," said Medie.

Asher looked at her, and they regarded each other in silence for a moment, until Medie's mother called for her and the girl sprinted away across the cold grass.

###

Later on, Asher and Bear sat at supper, quietly eating the potato and rabbit stew his father had prepared. Asher picked a leaf of parsley off his spoon and set it beside his plate.

"Oops, sorry about that," said Bear. "Forgot."

"You always forget," said Asher. His father looked at him with that sad look that made Asher feel uncomfortable. "But don't worry about it."

"Saw you and Medie chatting earlier. Thank you for tilling the garden, also."

Asher nodded, then put his spoon down. "Can I ask you something?"

"Sure."

"Medie told me about her dad. I'm not calling her a liar but—"

"It's true."

"Why would he do that?"

"Ah." Bear pushed his chair back a bit from the table, sighing and fiddling with his spoon before pouring a half-more bit of ale into his cup. "It's a sadness. Something that, sometimes, gets within the heart of the elves. Especially, well…"

"Especially *saylies*."

Bear frowned and looked at his son. "Where did you hear that?"

"Kid in town once."

"Ah, good old town. But yes, for some reason. The melancholy heart, it comes to our kind most often."

"Is it because we've got the moon-blood?"

"Maybe," said Bear. "Who really knows. The legend of the Daughter of the Moon, sure, that's a pretty tale, but maybe it's—" he drained his ale and belched softly "—because we have to take so much crap from both sides, all the time. That'd make a man sad, wouldn't it?"

"Yeah," said Asher. "I felt so badly for her."

"Medie'll make it through. You did."

Asher nodded and gathered the dishes, cleaning up the table while his father, after saying good night, went up to his room.

###

Bear had taken his lantern down the stairs with him, stopping by the hearth where the last of the night's fire glowed. He'd woken from first-sleep refreshed and restless. On the mantel sat a clock that he always forgot to wind, a horn-handled hairbrush, and next to that, a painting of his wife. It was the only image of her that remained in his possession.

He ought to go see his sister, he thought; he knew she'd be awake.

Surc enough, there she was—Mink in her kitchen, sipping a cup of tea, her bare feet peeking out from beneath the hem of her sleeping gown as she perched on her chair like a creature. He could see at least a half dozen candles burning brightly on the shelves and tables, and a small fire crackled in the kitchen hearth in the corner. She was always cold.

He rapped on the back door's window, his wide face grinning meekly at her.

"You can't sleep anymore either?" she asked as she let him in.

"No. Too much on my mind. You?"

"I'm just restless. Anymore I find I don't take second-sleep. Just a good long nap in the lazy afternoons."

"That would be nice." Bear poured himself some tea and cradled the tiny cup in his hands. "Ah, that's good. And oh—" he snuffed at the air like a contented dog sniffing at its master's plate "—the good candles. Fine beeswax."

"Don't tease. I've only so many of them, and then it's likely tallow for us. There wasn't much to inherit from my dearheart." She watched him holding the teacup and asked, "The stiffness back in your hands?"

"Hands, knees, hips—never really left."

"I'm sorry," said Mink. Her eyes were always so kind, and large. Pale blue, set beneath thick, dark lashes. She reminded Bear of their mother.

"Ah, it's what it is, lass. Once I find an apprentice worth their weight in complaints and sighs and eye-rollings, I can lighten my load some."

"Oh no!" Mink laughed. "Terrance didn't work out? I might have missed your last letter, in moving."

Bear made a face as if he'd smelled something sour. "*My* goodness."

Mink got up to pour herself more tea. "What happened?"

"What happened?" Bear chuckled. "Well, what happened… the crops in the village commons died. As in, all of them. Even the sunflowers."

"How do you kill sunflowers?"

"With a sword, or you set Terrance on them."

Mink almost spilled her tea she was chuckling so.

"So there went the temple offerings for the season."

"And are you still giving the offerings to the poorest folk once midsummer's passed?"

"Yes," said Bear. "Except there were none. So Terrance and I brought what we could down from my garden, and Asher and I roughed it a bit off wild plants for a while, and we ate a lot of rabbit. A *lot* of rabbit. Called it grass-pig after a while. I still have a wealth of it smoked. Asher enjoys it, bless him. Never thought I'd be sick of rabbit, and I got particularly nervous talking to Huil most days around that time. Thank the world above She's got a sense of humor, that one."

"Oh does She?" asked Mink, a delighted look on her face.

"Heh," said Bear. "Oh yes. When I apologized for maybe the dozen-most time, She whispered in my head, *it's all right, boy. Rabbits make plenty a-more rabbits.*"

They laughed for a while, then settled down to sipping their tea, each staring off at the night beyond the uncovered circles of window glass, solid black, glossy, and listening to the wind stirring over the roof like a ghost seeking a home.

"I'm glad you're here, Mink," said Bear. "I wish…well…"

"I know, boy," said his sister. "You don't have to say it. But I know. If circumstances would have been better… But they are what they are. And I'm glad I'm here with you and Asher too. Glad Medie can have some distraction from it all."

"Did she take it hard, Mink?"

"It's tricky to say. She's so, *so* hard to read. It's not anything she does on purpose, either, she just…lives in the clouds, always hearing so much, seeing so much, drifting away. She doesn't avail herself of me, at all really, and never did her father. She never complains."

"That's a good girl you've got," said Bear. "If mine didn't complain, I'd be checking for a pulse and a possession."

"Oh, nonsense," said Mink. "Babes their age are much too stubborn to fall prey to a bogie."

"Indeed," said Bear. "Remember when Jack found the salamander?"

Mink looked distant as if she were dreaming; it was the look she got when recalling long-ago things. "I…*yes*. Down by the sewer. During the summer."

"The Year of the Red Wyrm, appropriately enough. And she kept it in the bedroom?"

"I didn't pay attention to it. I was busy with other things."

"Other things, ha," chuckled Bear. "You were busy hunting boys."

"Hunting?" Mink, feigned shock and dismay. "*Seeking* is a better word."

"Collecting an even better one."

"Oh, whatever you say. But no, I never heard a peep from that little creature."

"But Hare did."

"Oh?"

"She found it in her bed." Bear got up from the table, and danced about, mimicking their older sister's horror. Mink nearly spit out her tea.

They sat until their bellies awoke from the long-fasting night, and did grumble, and Bear walked out to his henhouse and brought back a small basket of eggs. Mink stoked a fire on the stove to make some porridge. They ate while playing a game of checkers, eleven rounds, with Mink finally taking the last game in victory.

Medie padded into the kitchen, her black hair a monstrous tumble all down her back. She picked up a clean spoon and began to eat the remaining eggs from the pan.

"Child, you'll burn your tongue," warned Mink, getting up and smoothing her gown, pulling her robe tightly over herself.

"No I won't," said Medie, chewing. "It's almost cold." She licked the spoon clean of fat and added, "But it's tasty. What do you need me to do this morning, Mum?"

"Just get a good lay of the land, girl." Mink kissed the top of Medie's head and handed her a cup of tea. "Don't trouble yourself with chores just yet."

They watched Medie leave the room, shuffling and slumped over like a small, thin ghoul.

"You are so much better at…" Bear gestured widely with his hands. "All *this*."

"Mothers do what they do," said Mink. "Fathers fill a space that's needed, but we all do what we can with what we've got."

"Aye, and I've got to do what I can with what I've got up on the mountain today."

"Oh?"

"Yes. New apprentice named Hunter. Think kind thoughts for me."

Mink kissed her brother's bearded cheek and smiled. "That I will."

Bear left for town as soon as he'd given Asher breakfast. He felt somewhat light in the gut but planned to take a hearty midday meal in the forest. The air was stirring; he felt his goddess awakening, and with that his own body responding in its way. The winter ennui was lifting, and all beneath the sky was striving to grow.

He rode his horse down to the end of the switchback path, where the road broadened and took up the name Delster, after the town. He stuffed a bit of tobacco in his pipe, searched his pockets for the sparker, then, having found it, smoked thoughtfully, watching the skies above and listening to the trees speak upon the bold, stirring wind.

A villager driving a cart behind a pony came by and stopped to talk.

"Hail, Master Kieren," said the man, whose name was Thomas.

"Sirrah," said Bear, nodding.

"Has She spoken to ye about the season yet? And is that my pipe weed you're enjoying?"

"A little." Bear winked. "And yes, it is. She's being a bit coy, but I hear a lot of promise in her tone. I think it will be a good planting year."

"Oh, good!" said the human man, chuckling, nodding his head and slapping the reins against his pony. "Keep doing that good job, my dark friend!"

Bear watched him drive off, and smoked his pipe, his face the practiced picture of congeniality, masking his weariness. He would ignore the deeper stirrings of contempt as he always did. A pastor of Huil served the people, as per the wishes of his goddess.

At the sounds of panting, heavy breathing, he winced and turned his head to regard the road. There Hunter was, hurrying up the incline, grasping his lean side and struggling to breathe.

"You'll need a beast of burden, Hunter, I told you that," said Bear.

"I know," said the boy, sullen. "And I'm sorry. But my dad said he needs to see I've proven myself before he commits to such an expense. We've not had the best year."

"All right. I can understand that. If your dad agrees to it, I can sell him an excellent, good-natured donkey for you. For now, you can ride my horse," said Bear.

Hunter climbed up and patted the beast's broad neck, and the animal started back up the road, Bear walking aside it.

"Not to be ungrateful sir, but—a donkey?" asked Hunter, frowning and looking embarrassed.

"You think something's wrong with riding a donkey, do you? Let me tell you something, boy—a donkey's smarter, tougher, and wiser than ten horses put together. It'll defend you against a pack of wolves if put to the task. Never doubt his mightiness."

Hunter looked unconvinced.

"If you buy an animal because it's showy, you'll end up with naught but an empty saddle and a sore ass before too long."

"Yes, sir," said Hunter, looking up at the sky.

Bear watched the young man, and asked quietly, "See anything?"

"I'm not sure, Master."

"Told you not to bother with that. Bear is fine."

"Okay, Mr. Bear."

The elven man wiped his brow and sighed loudly. "Really, Bear'll do."

"I see quite a congregation of crows," said Hunter. "A very large murder, I reckon."

"Hm." Bear shielded his keen eyes from the glare of the sun in the white sky. "Suppose there are, but that's not entirely strange. Crows do as they'll do, and sometimes they have family gatherings."

"But they're not bothering the turkey vultures at all," added Hunter, pointing to the southern side of the mountain, where great wheelings of the scavenger birds were drifting slowly, riding the thermals rising up from the warming ground.

"Let's agree to keep an eye on both, shall we?" said Bear. "And there's the road up to my house."

The men turned onto the broad, leaf-covered switchback path and began the slow ascent of the wide, twenty-acre ledge that overlooked the town below.

"Your gramma built these homes, then?"

"Aye. Sidni dul Kieren, of Bran. Before the family name lost its nobiliary particle in order to sound more, well, human. There were four homes. The one I inherited, and the one left to whichever of my father's daughters was widowed first. The one our Uncle Tomis used as a country home, which burnt down the summer of the Year of Gates—"

"What was that? Wait—don't tell me." Hunter counted on his fingers, twice. "Eleven sixteen?"

"Very good," said Bear. "And the fourth home rotted into the forest, so they say. It's on the other side of a great run of thorns—an actual wall of the stuff. Never stepped foot through it."

"Do ye all have that same surname, then?"

"We do. Another odd thing about my family. The women always kept their names, same as the men."

"That your house?" asked Hunter, as the road finally met the flat land. The mountain continued to rise behind them, shrouded with bare trees and stands of pine.

"No, that's my sister's. Mine's just beyond. And that's my damned cat, Leiben. Hold on just a moment so I can get him inside the house, otherwise he'll trot alongside us when we go up the mountain, and howl mournfully, and wake every hungry thing in the forest." Bear scooped up the ginger tom under his arm and tossed him into the house, closing the door behind him. "I've got all that we need for a good day's walk. You need anything, Hunter?"

"No, sir, I mean Bear."

"Good. Remember what we're doing today?"

"Visiting the Shrine of Sleep, and then cleaning up the Shrine of Waking."

"Glad you remembered. Mainly a housekeeping sort of day, kind of dull, but being a cleric of Huil isn't always thunderclaps and dragons."

Hunter stared at him.

"Okay, it's never those things, I was merely joking, lad."

"That's a relief, s...Bear."

"Tie Walter up to the post here, by the water but away from the rosebushes. He's got a thing for the new buds. I'll go fetch Alan from the meadow and tie him beside, and we can bring you home atop him so you get a feel for his temperament."

They followed the trail worn by Bear's boots up through the trees, turning west to skirt the lower face of the mountain. Each man walked with a carved wooden staff: Hunter's was plain and not yet given to the magic of the goddess; Bear's was adorned with sigils, stained purple and deep red by chokeberries and thistle bloom, and set atop its end was a large beryl so darkly crimson it was nearly black.

"So, when do the paths up here ever flatten out?" asked Hunter, breaths heavy, cheeks red.

"They do, occasionally," said Bear. "Just gotta get up a ways upon Her. Drink your water. Did you bring some? Tell you what." He stopped to mop his brow and lean against a papery birch. "Let me show you something before we tackle the day's business. Head up there, past those rocks."

Hunter looked at the steep hill studded with great, green-cloaked boulders, and shook his head.

"Come on, lad—what master lets his apprentice say 'no'? Drink, then get to moving. You'll see."

Hunter frowned but took a long pull from his water skin, then began to climb the hill, stabbing his staff into the soft bed of leaves and rich soil. Bear followed him, advising which way to turn and which to avoid, if there were thorns or logs that could unloose beneath a boot and roll down. Beyond a twist of vines that had hardened into wood, Hunter reached a level spot of ground, and climbed up onto it.

Bear soon stood by his side, smiling. "Look at this, then."

There, surrounded by a ring of great boulders, was a grassy meadow shivering in the wind, specked by purple and white flowers beneath a swift, gray-blue sky. The sun eased out from behind a cloud and bathed the meadow in a golden light.

"This is incredible," said Hunter, walking to stand in the center.

"One of my favorite places on the mountain," said Bear. Past the meadow, the ground fell again to the forest, but just beyond that, the second peak in the chain rose, darkly covered with coniferous forest, brilliant beneath the patterns of weather. "We can have a meal here if you're hungry."

"I'm always hungry," said Hunter bashfully. "Da gets pretty cross about it."

"Can't be helped," said Bear. "Men have to eat. Though my sister, when no one's watching, can put away quite the Yule's feast."

"Ay, my mother too, especially if she's baking. She says bread and butter are her weaknesses."

"Simple tastes—" Bear sat on the grass in the sun, pulling out a wrapped loaf and a small tin, as well as a knife from his pack "—are signs of a good soul."

They sat then, watching the sky and eating their supper. The sun seemed to be a racing horse, challenging the storm clouds, darting behind them only to emerge again moments later.

"Seems Donnir's lively this day," observed Hunter.

"I've noticed. He's been quite active for over a week now."

"Why, do ye suppose?"

"It's been a warm winter," said Bear. "Strangely so. There is lore—southern mostly, and mostly of the Branwin valley—that when there's too warm a winter, Donnir gets restless. Of course, He fights with His sister, Huil, and the only time those two have peace is when snow blankets Her forests and most life sleeps. Without that respite of hibernation, life just gets a bit too *noisy* for Donnir, and His anger rolls across the sky."

"How could a god of the weather dislike noise?" asked Hunter.

"He doesn't dislike His own noise," said Bear. "Noisy folks rarely do."

They headed down from the meadow as the day was growing late, and regained the path they'd departed from, switching back across the mountain's darker southern face until they came to the rocky stream that wound its way down from beneath the mountain's bald head. They stooped at the water's edge, and there, Bear led his apprentice in prayer.

For She that waits
For She that sleeps
For She that wakes
and gives to thee
we bow our heads
as children do
at sleeping mother's bed
and say
hail, vibrant one
hail She so strong

hail shiverer in the trees
soil-stirring witch-queen.
Allow us passage
among your halls
this day.
And take our
work as payment made.

In the distance, a great tree cracked and began its slow, noisy descent to the forest floor. Bear and Hunter both stood and turned toward the sound.

"Odd timing that?" asked Hunter.

"Mark it, and keep your eyes and ears open," said Bear.

They reached the Shrine of Sleep just as the sun began its descent toward the edge of the world, though it would still be several hours before nightfall. Bear gave Hunter articles of sacrifice to place upon the stone table, all before an old, twisting black tree, where forsythia and briars were already greening.

"Always place the libation first," reminded Bear.

"Oh, I'm sorry. Will She be angry?"

Bear laughed. "No, lad, not at all. Stop for a moment. After you place the dish of honey, stand up and look around you."

Hunter did as he was told.

"Do you see many straight lines in this place?"

Hunter shook his head.

"No. Do you see order—as we know it? No, you don't. You see what man would call chaos. Except it's not chaos. It's true life, which has an order so ineffable, rarely a man—human or elf or otherwise—will recognize in his lifetime, should he live to be two hundred. Don't fret about our behaviors not being so precise. Huil knows what's in your heart, and that's what matters to Her."

"That somehow makes me more uncomfortable, if ye don't mind my saying so, sir."

"It's natural to doubt yourself. But your heart is steady and true, even while the mind skips across the consciousness like a leaf across a path." Bear turned to look toward the mountain's bald head for a moment, cupping a hand to his pointed ear. "Let's get back. Wouldn't mind an early day for a change."

They threaded their way east now, away from the steeper face of the mountain and towards the leaf-covered floor of the open forest, then slowly traversed back to the north face, forgoing the switchback trails to save time. At one point, Bear stopped, holding up his hand, and Hunter looked where his master was pointing. There, further down the mountain, a flock of twenty wild turkeys were traveling up the steep hill to their nesting place, just below the bald.

One turkey took flight, flapping loudly past Bear and Hunter, then three more, then seven more, and finally the rest of the flock.

And suddenly the mountain was shaking, rumbling, and the men fell to their hands and knees, clutching their staves and looking wild-eyed with terror.

When the tremors stopped, Bear and Hunter stepped and slid down the mountainside to Bear's home, leaping over twisted roots and snagging their cloaks and trousers on thorns.

"What is happening?" Hunter yelled, his voice high and strangled.

"She moves," said Bear, panting to keep his breath. "We will examine why another day. Right now, we must see to the road and the town."

They reached Bear's house and ran past Mink, who was standing in her doorway, her face pale as a winter's cloud.

"Find the kids!" Bear yelled as he untethered the animals. "Then come back to your house with them and each of you take a threshold to stand beneath until She finishes Her shaking."

The men turned the beasts towards the road and hurried along, trotting quickly, glancing up at the mountain as if it would explode in a rage any moment. They were halfway to the main road when the tremors began once more, and Walter and Alan danced in terror, neighing and tossing their heads, rolling the whites of their eyes.

"Control him!" bellowed Bear. "His right side's his good side. Cover his left eye with your hand 'til he calms. We must gain the road and hold the mountain in Her power so that She does not spill down upon the town. You lift your staff and you hold it back, boy. You can do it."

"I don't know if I can. It's just a walking stick—"

"You do not have a choice, Hunter. You must!"

The men raced along the trembling ground, horse and donkey kicking up their legs in fright, and finally the quakes ceased, but a thundering sound of moving earth and colliding rocks was coming from the mountain. The men raced down the road, staves held high, Bear shouting words in elven that Hunter did not understand but he shouted with words of his own. Then the forest floor was coming at them, sliding in a wave of leaves and branches, rocks and soil, loosing widowmakers to roll as if water moved beneath them to smack against standing, living trees.

Wide orbs of red light gathered before Bear's staff, then slowly drifted up the mountain side, slamming silently against the wall of earth and holding it there like an invisible fortification, all the dust of it rising up.

Hunter gave the donkey free range of motion and closed his eyes, mouthing words made silent by the roaring of the avalanche. Soon, pale, golden orbs were emanating from his own staff and holding back the earth just below Bear's wall. The men continued in this way until they met the river and the docks of Delster, and turned about to face the mountain. The avalanche had stopped.

Huil had resumed Her stillness and Her quiet. Their magic had held.

###

Bear accompanied Hunter to his family's home and told him to take the next few days to rest and acquaint himself with the donkey Alan. Hunter's father had come out of his workshop to stare at the mountain in shock and disbelief, as had many of the other townspeople. After he'd come to his senses, he'd turned on Bear, grasping the tall elf by the shoulders and gasping, "Did my son do this?"

Hunter looked mortified.

"No," said Bear sternly, moving the man's hands away. "I will discover what is the matter, but in the meantime, you might thank your son for doing his part. Also—here's a donkey, name of Alan. See to him and make sure he gets excellent care. He's my reward to Hunter for such good work today."

The man looked at Bear as if he'd just told him the sky was green, but nodded, saying nothing more, and came to take the donkey around back to be seen to.

Bear rode back alone past Delster's pub, a signless, squat building that the villagers called *The River Rat*. He heard conversation drifting out into the street, calm but lively. Someone down the alley yelled at a dog to "*Get stepping before I get my rifle, ye egg-stealing bastard.*"

Bear tied up old Walter to the post in front and opened the door a crack, peeking in. The pub master, an *ounsayle* from a more southern city Bear could never properly pronounce, was there, keeping quiet, his thin mouth shut and his pale hands busy. He'd married a human woman, and their son occasionally helped in the bar, but the boy was absent today. Bear nodded to the pub master as he walked up to the bar.

"Sirrah," said the pub master, whose name was Iar.

"How's the day turn?" asked Bear, using a phrase he recalled was common among the *ounsayle*.

Iar shrugged his shoulders and stooped to pick up a cup he'd dropped behind the bar. "It's fine," he said, hidden from view.

"He don't care as long as we're thirsty," said a man walking past Bear. "How's that mountain?"

Bear turned to look at him. "Well, She's had better days. Tom, right?"

"Talking about a hill of dirt like it was a woman," muttered someone at a table. The man who'd spoken to Bear chuckled.

"To some of us, She is. Very important that Her pastors think so at least."

Iar shook his head at him, with a look that said *don't*.

"Sure," said the man at the table, now walking to the bar with his empty mug. "Everybody needs to believe in something."

"They don't, but some of us choose to, yes," said Bear.

"Well, I believe I'll have another ale. How 'bout you, pastor?"

"Sure."

"Name's Geoff. Just stopping by from off the river. Mine's the *big* boat."

"Pleasure to meet ye, Geoff."

"Yeah, I'll bet. Darkie like you got himself a free drink—that's a good day."

The first man, Tom Brightwater, who had stood and watched the conversation, now watched the fisherman Geoff. "So," he said. "Guests should likely wipe their boots before crossing a man's clean floor."

"Well, if this one's wife comes in with a skillet for my head, I'll be sure to apologize."

"Give my beer to this fellow," said Bear to Iar, and gestured at Tom.

"What?" asked Geoff. "My money's not good for ye? Make the beer taste sour?"

"Something like that." Bear walked away towards four men seated at a table on the other side of the pub. One of them pushed at an empty chair with his boot.

"Hey there, Master Kieren," said the man, whose name was Gailen, and who repaired boats farther down the river, just a short cart ride from town. "Felt Her shake like the devil today, didn't we?"

"Oh yes," said Bear. "I—" He stopped, glancing back at the bar, but Geoff and Tom were engrossed in a conversation about fishing nets. "My apprentice and I managed to calm Her down."

"Well, I thank ye for that," said Gailen. The other men at the table nodded and muttered words of thanks as well.

"Sure," said Bear. "Just gotta find out what's at the root of it. I plan to reflect and pray quite a bit in the coming days."

"Better you than me," said one of the other men. "I don't have much of a head for prayer."

"Aye," said Gailen. "Nor do I. That's why pastors get chosen."

"So Ned," said the fourth man. "Where's Gwinny gone off to?"

"How'd ye know she's gone?"

The fourth man grinned. "Quiet at yer house the whole past week."

All of them chuckled but Bear, who merely sat and listened.

"Yes, well. Pissed her off good again. Took off for her mother's."

"What'd ye do?"

"Don't know. Wish I did know, though," said Ned. "I'd make sure to do it more often."

From the upstairs of the building came a sound of breaking dishes, or perhaps a mirror—it was hard to tell. The men at the table glanced at the stairs, and two of them chuckled.

"I didn't realize your mother lived here, Ned."

Ned shook his head, smiling. "That's not my mother. Maybe it's the poor golden bastard behind the bar's."

"Oh, well," said Bear. "An *ounsayle* woman'd likely never set foot in a—" He stopped again. A shout could be heard, and a man laughing.

"You'd think Delster had its own bawdy house," said Ned.

"I wish Delster had its own bawdy house," said Robert, winking at Ned.

"Just what we need, the clap and another excuse to trade away a day's catch."

"There's a joke in there, somewhere," said Gailen. "I'm just a little too drunk to figure it out."

"Well, I need to get back up the hill," said Bear. "My boy'll be needing his supper."

"How's he doing?" asked Robert.

"Growing like the grass."

"They do that," agreed Ted. "You take care of yourself, Pastor, and him."

"Good to see ye, Pastor," said one of the other men, draining his beer and getting up from the table.

Bear left the pub and lit his pipe, standing beside Walter and watching the goings-on in the street of again-sleepy Delster. He felt someone walk into his shoulder and turned to see Geoff.

"Oh, were you trying to move me out of your way?" Bear's eyebrow raised.

"What, did yer mum fuck a horse?" said the now-drunk man, staggering into the street and patting Walter on the nose before walking away.

###

"Miserable."

"Bear, if you get yourself worked up, you'll likely get one of those headaches again."

"Negative, unhappy."

"Your eyes are already pink as a rabbit's."

"Doubting, distrusting, fearful *mice.* That's not even fair to mice."

"No, it's not. Not that I enjoy mice particularly."

Bear slumped upon one of Mink's chairs, dolefully regarding a bowl of soup she'd placed before him. "I just want to do what I've been called to do."

"You're a pastor, not a healer. There is a difference."

"Not much of one."

"In plain speech, brother, you are not a wet nurse for the humans."

"Mink, by all the gods, why are they so awful? You know what I see? In ten years' time, a rotten, rowdy town of miscreants. That's actually why Solace and I moved here to begin with—to get away from the ruckus of a large city. No matter how many gardens you plant, how many libraries, an overly large gathering of men and women seems to accumulate strife. And avarice. And above all, human trickery and ass-headedness."

"Da," said Asher, coming into Mink's kitchen with Medie. "I can't believe you actually said all that."

"Well, your father's right, honestly," said Mink, putting bowls of stew and spoons on the table. "Anybody hungry, just eat it. I need to lay down after today's excitement."

"What happened?" asked Asher, grabbing a bowl and sitting down. He pushed a chair for Medie with his boot. "I was with some of the town lads."

"An avalanche. After a good, solid tremble. Never seen anything like it before, son. And now the worst part is I'm going to be distracted—distracted by what those humans are to be thinking is the cause, when the actual cause is something I'm needing to find out, and find out quickly."

"What on earth could the humans blame for this?" asked Medie.

"Me," said Bear. "They will blame this on elves."

"No, Father," said Asher. "First they'll blame the dwarves."

Bear left Mink's house and slowly hiked to the Shrines of Sleep in the thick of the twilight, though his sharp eyes could still see well enough as the sun was sitting, bold and red, at the failing of the skeletal branches. He found the outcropping of rocks he affectionately called the winter's bed, knelt beside it and prayed. The wind shivered through the bare trees, stirring the few leaves that had clung on since autumn. Bear looked at these and felt he was becoming the same—once full of life, filled with the nectar of the goddess and all of Her power, now useless, trampled upon, a bag of bones and skin, nothing.

"I will say it though you already know. All I have in my heart for you is love, goddess. I don't have blame, or fear. You are not alone in this world, your brothers and sisters jostle for room at the Great Ones' table. Such cacophony can seem like disaster to the small eyes of men and women."

His large hands clasped, Bear felt a tightness, a single pang of grief struggle to break free of his chest and his throat, but he held it.

"I am not leaving you alone to fight this," he whispered. "I know this wasn't your fault." He opened his lips to say one more thing, but stopped, ashamed, suddenly, of the personal nature of what he was about to share. He looked up at the forest with guilt-filled eyes and found he was face-to-face with a fawn.

"So early?" he whispered. The animal's mother stepped out from behind a rhododendron, staring at him with her nearly black eyes, then lowered her head to graze beside her baby's feet.

"I will take that to mean," said Bear quietly, "you wish me to speak. So I will be bold, Huil. I grew up, blaming everyone for my problems. I blamed my father for being the selfish, short-tempered wretch that he was. I blamed my mother for allowing him to be so. I blamed my older sisters for not defending Crow. But then I became a man, and I saw—there is never anyone to blame but myself. I have the power to change any situation, and if I can't change it to my liking, I can walk away, and that changes it, too."

The deer lifted their heads to the sudden gust of wind, and trotted past Bear, down the mountain.

"Though I know that I will not walk away."

###

The next day, Asher followed Medie all around the grounds between their homes as she whispered to herself, holding a forked stick.

"If you're looking for water, I can show you exactly where the well's at."

Medie hissed a *shh* in his direction and turned abruptly around, hurrying past the henhouse towards the overgrown fields beyond.

"Nothing there but pain and suffering," called Asher. "Brambles, the likes of which…" He stopped by the henhouse and poked a finger between the wood slats to pet his favorite hen, Lusine. "Let her learn, right? That's what I'll do."

His curiosity tugged at him, and he snuck past the hedgerow, finding the hidden trail to the western side of the great ledge upon which his family's country homes were built. He could just see Medie's white skirts and jacket through the walls of briars. Then she was gone.

"Leave her, then, fine," he said, scaling a pine tree to try and see beyond the thorns. He thought about how cross his father would be should anything happen to his cousin, and he dropped down from the pine's branches, jogging back along the path to find where Medie had gotten to.

Once past the hedgerow, he became ensnared.

"Ow," he muttered, stuck through in three different spots, his clothing being pulled in all directions.

"That's not the way you go," said Medie's quiet voice from somewhere among the briar wall. "Get out of those thorns and turn sharply left, then follow the flat stones I've unhidden from the moss."

Asher did as he was told, tearing himself free of the briars, and stepped back, looking down.

"A garden path," he said.

"Yes, and it leads all the way to the house."

Asher turned around and looked at Medie's home.

"No, the house behind the briar wall."

He followed the stepping stones that Medie had revealed with her fingers, the moss torn away and pushed aside each one. It curved around and wound its way through the red-tipped briars, and little birds twitched and shifted their perches amid the wall of thorns, watching him, chittering encouragement or warnings, he couldn't tell.

"They think it's good that we found the house," said Medie.

"Who? The birds?" asked Asher, astonished.

"Uh-huh. You thought it."

"Oh, now, okay." He emerged from the briar wall to stand in a wildly overgrown garden. Steps led up to a square of tumbled-down walls, which might have been a rose garden once, and then another shorter square of walls, completely busy with weeds and rushes all around a choked, stagnant fish pond. Beyond all of this, the house rose out of the grasses, white and stained with mold, windows broken and curtains stirring in the breeze that swept lazily over the mountain. "I don't know if we can get about together if you're going to hear my thoughts all the time, Medie. That makes me truly uncomfortable to consider."

"Oh no," whispered Medie, hurrying up the steps to look into the fish pond. "That was the first time I had. I think, perhaps, it was because of the birds."

"I'll believe you," said Asher. "But if you creep about in my head, I'll have to take steps." Suddenly he stopped, watching the uppermost window, the only one in the house's peaked third floor. "You see that person?"

Medie stood up and looked to where he was pointing. "I don't."

"Well, I do," he said and ran towards the house, gaining the porch in a single step and trying the front door. It swung open halfway, then hung on its hinges, bent and stiff with age. Asher slipped through the opening.

"Wait up!" called Medie, her usually soft voice cracking as she hurried up the stairs to follow her cousin inside.

They explored each room together, looking at the still-luxuriant touches of the woodwork and large glass windows, a wonder if it had been in town, let alone way up high atop a mountain. After a while, Asher grew weary of it, and they parted; Medie kept investigating, continuing up the attic stairs.

Asher sat on the edge of the hearth of the great room, waiting for her to be done with her snooping.

She'd been up there a ridiculously long time.

"Oy!" he called, noticing how dark it was growing outside. "We need to get back. We can come here tomorrow if you like. I don't mind at all."

There was no answer, and no Medie. Asher trudged up the stairs, his boots leaving clods of mud against the still-glossy wooden steps.

He went into each room, blinking his eyes to adjust to the darkness. He found the stairwell leading to the third floor and hurried up to it, searching in the shadows, his gray-sight shifting into focus and letting him get a clearer picture.

The large attic was empty, but something gleamed in the failing light by the far window.

Asher walked over to it and crouched down. There was a nugget of gold, all by itself on the floor, amid leaves that had blown in through the broken window. He picked it up; it was small, but heavy.

He hurried down the stairs and squeezed out the half-open front door, following the porch around, and then saw the tree. There was a great old tree by the side of the house. One of its massive limbs almost touched a southern window of the third floor—a window he'd not been able to see whilst in the garden. He squinted at the tree limb; there was a tiny white scrap of cloth snagged on a branch. Medie's skirt was of the same cloth.

Asher called for her in the forest, but at last, the dark moon's light providing no help for him to see, he gave up and made his way painfully back along the bramble-path to the house.

###

Bear was sitting in Mink's kitchen again, having a late tea.

"I'm worried I'm going to become a nuisance to you."

"What?" Mink laughed, pushing a loose tendril of hair from over her eyes. "You couldn't possibly become one. We've always got on, you and I. I can't imagine how lonely it must have been these past years, after Solace died." Mink frowned and shook her head.

"Shh," he said. "Don't feel bad for saying that. It's absolutely true. I've been a shambles since I lost her. I tried to shove on and be brave for Asher, but every day I just became a little more lost. And sons don't always make the best conversationalists."

"Well you seemed to have tried with Da," said Mink. "But he was too strange to take you up on it."

"Any of us. Genet tried the hardest, and our father wouldn't have a minute of him."

"Crow tried the hardest," said Mink. "And I imagine he shunned her for similar reasons."

"No, you don't remember, Minny." Bear took a biscuit off a cloth-covered plate. "Crow and Da were thick as thieves for years. You were a baby then. Genet had run off with his cohorts, Mum was busy with the other youngers. It was me, Crow, and Jack. And I tried but never got anywhere with him. Jackal had no love for the man at all, and she spent her days with her head in a book, or at Constance's house."

"Funny that it's her own house now."

"Oh? They still married?"

"Still married. Happy life."

"Oh, that's good news, I'm glad for ol' Jack. She never inherited Mum's wanderlust, then?"

"No," said Mink. "They did wander for a time. Let Constance's brother keep the house. But they came back and got settled, and I suspect their adventuring days are done."

"One's never sure of that, Minny," said Bear. "But about Crow. That brat was the only one our father'd let in his study—did you know that?"

"No!" gasped Mink. "She wasn't allowed, that I could recall."

"When you were older, she stopped going in of her own volition. But before, yeah—she sat in there with him while he worked."

"Basilisks and bombs, Bear."

"I know. They'd work in silence, those two, for hours. Mum brought their meals in to them."

"Must have been nice!"

"It was, for a while. Until the day Crow found that book."

"Why do I not know what you're talking about? About any of this, Bear? How was I out of the loop?"

Bear sighed and rubbed his tired eyes. "Crow told me never to tell. But I mean, what's it gonna hurt now? Mum's passed, and nobody's heard from or been to visit Da in years. Crow's out in the world. In true, I might see her again. She stopped by last yuletide, actually, but I doubt she'd be angered now, were you to know of it.

"What happened?" Mink's blue eyes seemed brighter—with concern.

Bear pushed back from the table. "Mind if I smoke, Min?"

"No, it's fine. Just crack that door a bit behind you."

Bear got up and opened the door, and the chill night air blew in. Mink reached back to take up her sweater from the chair and wrap it about her shoulders.

"Sorry," said Bear.

"Don't be—but get on with it?"

"Right. Okay." He looked for his sparker but then lit his pipe off the hearth with a tinder stick instead and walked back to the window. "Da had quite the bibliophile to deliver to. Two towns away, an estate up by the Carrying River. So he'd been gone nearly a week, but he didn't lock up his study, and Crow was in there most days. Then it was a Sunday, and the streets were quiet, and Da came home. I remember being on the kitchen floor, playing with my metal soldiers and steeds, Da's footsteps coming up the stairs from the front door, the squeaky door of his study opening… And then I heard such a shout, I thought maybe a robber was in our home. I crouched in the kitchen, afraid, listening."

Bear closed his eyes. "And then the study door closed. Next thing, I was hearing Crow scream, and Da was shouting at her."

Mink gasped, covering her mouth. "What in heaven and earth! What was he saying?"

Bear's eyes were dark with anger. "*Good! Scream! I'll break them off! You should never have touched it!*"

Mink's eyes were wet with tears.

Bear nodded at her. "Now you know why."

Mink shook her head, her hands coming up to her hot cheeks.

"I went to find Mum, and she came and banged on the door and yelled at Da to stop. She begged him to let her in. He kept doing what he was doing to Crow, and finally, somehow, Mum found the spare key that she'd lost and opened the door, and we ran inside. And there was little Crow, in the wooden chair, her wrists strapped to the arms of the chair, her hands running blood. Da had his cane up."

"*Oh, I hate him!*" cried Mink.

Bear nodded, and his eyes, too, were wet. "As do I. He'd broken her fingers to bits. She was unconscious from the ordeal of it."

"She'd wanted to paint," said Mink.

Bear nodded again. "And all she can paint with now is her sword and a bastard's blood."

They looked up to hear a knock at the door. Bear groaned, easing himself up from the chair. "Why is that child so awfully formal."

"It's good training," said Mink.

Asher stood in the doorway of the kitchen, and Bear saw the panic on his son's face, thus was himself alarmed. "What's the matter?" he asked Asher.

"Medie's gone missing."

Whitefall

WELL, SHE IN fact *could* have gone far, Minny," said Bear, getting his staff and lantern from his study and bringing a pack with rope and some clothing of Asher's. He had brought Mink to his house. "The woods are still bare from winter. Makes it easy to travel. But try not to worry, we will find her. You stay here while we fetch her. Spare room top of the stairs, across from mine."

"I won't be sleeping, brother," she said, her eyes gleaming with tears.

"It'll be all right, girl," said Bear, kissing the top of her head.

He and Asher hurried to the edge of the woods. Bear gave his son the lantern and kissed the top of his staff on the beryl. A dim, golden wave of light came to presence, as if someone had lit a candle with a tiny wick. It was dim, but then burned more brightly, and the forest floor and the trees were illumined enough for the men to find a path.

Asher chuckled. Bear slapped him lightly on the back of the head.

"Come on, jokester. I'll go first. Got your pig-sticker?"

Asher pushed aside his coat to reveal the short sword Bear had given him for his tenth birthday.

"Think you've got the hang of it, finally? Just in case. Most things up there are either scared of us or sleeping."

They followed the trail up for about a mile, then cut across to the western face of the mountain, tracing over a deer path that led down into a thick gathering of pine. Bear stooped to gently move a sapling's branch aside and studied the mud beneath it.

"Tiny boots," said Bear. "This about her foot size?"

Asher knelt to look. "I…think so?"

Bear sighed. "Well, between the two of us, I'd wager you've looked at her feet more than I."

An owl hooted in the distance. Bear stood up and leaned against the sapling, his eyes closed. The owl repeated its call, and again.

"Seems that someone's seen something."

"What have they seen?"

"Hopefully, they have seen Medie."

Bear led them west now, breaking through deadfall and dried briars, past shivering stalks of spring-fed plants that would become green and crowned with purple flowers in another few weeks, if the weather held. The men stood on a wide stone shelf that looked out over the larger part of the river valley, and they could see lights coming from the city of Bran far in the distance. Farther up the mountain, great tumbles of boulders sat, like blocks left by giants' children; beneath these were dug tiny burrows or lay the entrances to long, low-ceilinged caves. Bear turned his back on the valley and took a deep breath, smelling the air.

"Always bobcat here, and foxes. That's all I smell, though."

"Da, where is she?" Asher's voice trembled from the cold, just a bit.

"Time to ask She who's got the answers." Bear pushed his staff into the soft ground beside the rock shelf and knelt, his back still to the valley, his head bowed to the mountain. His lips began to whisper, and Asher knelt, too, listening intently and mimicking the prayer, eyes closed in concentration.

The owl hooted three more times. The men jumped to their feet; Bear pulled his staff from the ground. The owl hooted once more, farther up the mountain, and they hurried past the boulders, following the sound.

At last, they reached a grove of rhododendron, and there amidst it, sitting on a flat, moss-covered stone, was Medie. They heard the sound of fast footsteps crashing away across the leaves.

"Well now, Persistence," said Asher, walking to the stone and crouching beside it. "This is a strange place to find you lingering."

"Why?" asked Medie.

"Because," said Asher, looking at his father, "it's freezing cold? It's not your house? And you didn't even ask me to come along with you."

"I wasn't sure I could trust you."

"Of course you can. You think I'd tell Da anything we get ourselves into? Well, I promise you that I won't."

Medie glanced at him, struggling against a weak smile. "He's about to kick me now, isn't he."

"Not going to kick you," said Bear. "I'll wait until we get home."

Medie got up from the stone and began to shiver. Bear took a small blanket from his pack and wrapped it around her shoulders.

"It was important," said Medie. "That I come. I don't care if anyone believes me or not."

"Da talks to a mountain," said Asher, putting his arm around her as they began to walk back down the hillside. "I think you're in fairly good company as far as believing things goes."

###

"Who were you with?" asked Mink, gently, but with fire in her blue eyes.

"Their name was Kit," said Medie.

"That wasn't his name, but that's what he was," said Bear, smoking his pipe. They were all seated in Bear's kitchen, by the hearth. "Boys are kits, lasses are kats. They're called *reffke*. Native to this mountain, though I haven't seen the last *reffke* vixen in five years. She had two babes, a boy and a girl. Lived way up top, close to the big spring there, just north of the mountain's bald."

"What's a *reffke*?" asked Medie.

"Fox-folk. Not many of them left, I'm afraid. But they keep to themselves. Pastors of Huil are sworn to protect them, but if I could have ten more of me, I'd likely do a better job. Quite a task to protect something that's constantly keeping its distance from you."

"He's not an it! He's a boy, and we spoke."

"How? Did you read his thoughts?" asked Asher.

"No, I told you. I usually can't," said Medie. "And it was dark and difficult to see. There was no moonlight. But he took my hands and made words upon the palms of them."

"Oh, like your friend Kaiden when you were little," said Mink. She looked at Bear. "Kaiden couldn't hear, so he spoke in signs. They'd have the longest conversations."

"Words are longer without sound," said Medie. "I followed the deer path up to the grove because the mountain was telling me something."

Bear looked at her. "Oh?"

Mink met his look. "Is that so strange, brother? Hearing's gifts could run in the family."

"I'm not meaning to diminish the girl's abilities, at all, Minny," said Bear. "But if Medie truly heard Huil, it's remarkable. Unprecedented."

"Why?" asked both Asher and Mink.

"No woman ever has, not in the Hall's oldest reckoning."

After a while, Asher and Medie left the kitchen to sit by the hearth in the great room, on the bearskin rug that Asher's father had guiltily accepted as a gift from one of the villagers for a good year. They could hear the adults debating in the kitchen.

"But if Huil is a goddess herself, why bar womankind from serving Her?"

"I don't honestly know, Minny. I didn't make the rules. I'm sorry, and I'm not trying to be dismissive."

"No, but your goddess is!"

"Your mom's giving my dad the business," said Asher, a slight grin on his lips.

"She is," said Medie. "She almost never, ever gets angry."

"Well, I reckon if my dad's an ambassador of his faith, he'd better have the answers."

"Faith has no answers," said Medie, getting up and walking to one of the tall windows opposite the hearth.

"I suppose you're right about tha—"

"Shh," whispered Medie.

A huge, black face appeared in the window, its amber eyes reflecting the firelight. Medie gasped and stumbled backward, and Asher leapt to his feet, reaching for his sword that lay on the floor beneath the coat hooks. The face regarded them, and then the mouth opened, and a huge tongue lolled out. The face began to pant.

"That's a fucking dog," said Asher.

"Language!" bellowed Bear from the kitchen.

"Uncle Bear, there really is a big black dog outside, watching us through the window."

Bear and Mink hurried into the room, and Bear pulled Asher and Medie from the window, then spun about to heft the great axe from off its place above the hearth. He lifted the hewn wooden latch from his back door and stepped outside. The children followed.

"Get in the house, please, now," he said to them, stepping slowly towards the dog. "Away, brute. You're not welcome here." He held the axe in front of himself.

The dog watched Bear for a moment, then lay down, resting its great head on its massive paws. It sighed.

"Don't think it cares for your ordering it around, Da," said Asher, standing beside Bear.

"Thought I told you to get in the house."

"It's beautiful," said Medie, walking to it. Bear put his arm across her and pushed her back.

"Don't you manhandle my child!" said Mink, emerging from the house and pulling her robes tightly about her.

"Minny, please, girl—stop fighting with me. Can you not see that's a *shuck*?" Bear turned to look at his sister and pointed with the head of his axe at the dog.

Medie stepped closer to the animal and began to pet the top of its broad head with her tiny knuckles.

"Okay," said Mink, watching the beast roll over and present its belly to Medie. "Maybe it *looks* like a shuck, but it seems to me that a belly rub is not what your usual run-of-the-mill soul-sucking fiend has in mind."

"Fine," said Bear, looking up to the dark heavens. "Fine."

"Thank you, Uncle!" said Medie, who was now vigorously scratching the dog's belly and causing one of its huge hind legs to kick at the air.

"But it's not stepping foot inside either of these houses. And I expect to be minded on this!"

###

"If in the sky you see towers…" muttered Bear, snipping the tangled ends of the hedge that grew between his house and Mink's.

"One should expect there to be showers," said Hunter, pulling weeds from the garden bed from which was growing an expansive wall of morning glory, not yet with buds, but green. "This is pastoral work, eh?"

"'Tis," said Bear. "If it comes from the ground, it's Huil's business. And we—" he put his boot up on a stone to yank a particularly stubborn, errant root from the ground "—are Her accountants."

The day was beautiful and strange. Gusts of wind sent dead leaves and too-early petals skittering through the sky, rising up like scales of a half-visible wyrm, to fall back down across the ground, a spell abandoned. The sun gleamed upon the houses and vanished beneath a white wall of clouds, and the trees bent their naked necks like elders at prayer, while in the distance, the white elms swayed, dreamy congregants. A constant, softly roaring wind buffeted the men while they worked.

"Quite a dragon day," said Bear.

"Somehow, that makes sense," said Hunter.

Bear tapped his temple and winked. "Beginning to think like a pastor. You must be all these things. A hunter—which your daddy gave you a head start on with that name—a farmer, an arborist, a gardener. And—" he ripped a tuft of grass from his lawn and let it fly away on the twisting wind "—a weather-seer."

"Well, if I had to wager a guess," said Hunter, "even though it's fairly warm, right now, I'd say we were expecting snow."

Bear sniffed at the air and turned towards the north to scan the clouds. "Adders and alps. I think you're correct, boy."

"I'd also say most in town have enough wood, but then…"

"Go on."

"A few families had a really hard winter. A few who didn't have a pair of strong arms to chop much wood at all."

"We'll see what we can do," said Bear. "I can offer some of my own, and we can add a little to that from the mountain."

Mink was outside, beating a carpet.

"I'm taking Hunter into the woods to get some firewood, Min," said Bear.

"All right," she said. "Have we no more in the store sheds?"

"Just about out. This is a rare little late snow I'm expecting." Bear waved his hand in front of his face, squinting at the dust coming off the rug in clouds. "Are you still mad at me?"

Mink put the wicker beater down on the grass and wiped her hands on her apron. "No."

"That was brief."

"Promise me you'll take your niece seriously, about the matters we discussed the other day."

"I promise. I've no intention of not taking her seriously."

"All right," said Mink, picking up the beater and resuming her work. "Then I won't be angry with you."

Bear walked away, axe over his shoulder, and whistled for Hunter, who sprang from the outhouse as if he'd been shot from a cannon. The black dog came trotting around the north side of Bear's house, now keeping pace with the apprentice.

"No," said Bear. The dog woofed, once, and began to pant.

"Don't think he takes to orders," said Hunter.

"Who around here does?" said Bear, walking off into the forest.

After saying their prayers to the spirits of the animals that lived in the dead, hole-riddled trunks of the trees Bear had marked for wood, and to Huil for the bounty they were about to collect, Bear felled each of the three trees, rapping upon the trunks first to scare the squirrels out of their hiding spots.

“I’m sorry, madam, sorry, gent,” Bear muttered, wiping his brow as the warm sun glanced through the cloud cover and shone full on him and his work. Once the trees were felled, he and Hunter got to sectioning the pieces and loading them up on a leather tarp Bear had brought along.

“If I could put a harness on you, you’d pull this easily, wouldn’t you?” asked Bear of the dog. “Isn’t that right, Shuck?”

The dog woofed, once.

“Should I get old Walter?” offered Hunter.

“Walter’s quite frightened of the dog, so we’ll pull this lot ourselves. But if Shuck gets in the way, I’m not against lassoing him up and having him pull his fair share.”

###

“You going to town, then?” asked Mink, coming out from the henhouse with a basket of eggs. Bear had hitched Walter up to the wagon.

“Aye,” said Bear. “Always a fun little trip going down that road with a laden cart. But the money I spent last year getting those brakes was a good investment. Last city money I’d held on to, and put to sensible use. Most of the wood is light. Just took a few dead trees down—still going to be a smoky mess when it burns.”

“It’s better than nothing, I imagine,” said Mink. “See if you can do me a favor, when you’re in town?”

“Sure. Anything. Where’s that dog gotten to?”

“Took off with the children just now. Here.” She handed him a slip of paper.

Bear frowned.

“Oh. I’m so sorry! Never mind that.” Mink crumpled the list and stuffed it into her pocket. “Two books I need, for Medie. Just ask the merchant for the two in the window, bottom right.”

###

Thunder pealed across the ragged, storm-gray sky.

Bear drove the cart down the mountain, Walter taking his time at a steady pace; Hunter, on Alan, rode beside him.

"I feel we're going to look a bit foolish, showing up with firewood and all it does is rain for a week. It's supposed to rain for a week around this time of year," said Hunter. "I'm sorry I said that it smelled like snow."

"Don't doubt your instincts," said Bear, reaching out to Alan's bridle to slow him down a bit; the screeching of the cart's brakes was spooking him. "There, there, boy. But no, Hunter. First of all, when we get to town, you just go on home. I'll take the wood to the commons. And second, I think your instincts are correct. I feel it too. I only hope it starts to snow either before the rain, or a good while after the rain that comes has had a chance to soak into the ground, else we'll have a nice coat of ice under the snow, and that'll take at least a week to thaw. Nearly broke my tail slipping on the path between the houses last winter after such a thing."

As they reached the beginnings of the town, the wind had become biting and cold. On the river, amid the mists, a boat's horn blew, and the men pulled up their coat collars and stuffed unbusy hands into pockets.

"Well, hullo, Pastor Bear. When'd ye get into town, then?"

Bear nodded as he drove past Timothy Wayne, the cartwright, who was standing outside his shop having a smoke. "What? Did you not hear the brakes squealing all the way down the mountain?"

Tim laughed. "You're not complaining about my work now, are ye?"

"Nooo, sirrah. Saved my fat arse once again. Tell the missus hullo for me."

"Will do. Take good care, Pastor."

Hunter rode on ahead as Bear bade Walter circle around the town commons and tied the horse at the center, then walked up the steps to the shouting floor and rang the heavy bell. Within moments, villagers began to gather.

"I know you don't want to hear this, everybody," said Bear to the crowd. "But it seems that Donnir wants a bit more from us this season—likely be a bit of snow before too long. I brought some deadwood, not too punky, just in case anyone's run low. Feel free to take what you need."

Bear patted Walter's neck and walked down the street, towards the bookseller. He stood in front of the shop and squinted down, away from the white sky, waiting for his sensitive eyes to adjust to the darkness that waited within the bookseller's shop. He went inside and mentioned the books Mink had described in the window; soon enough, he was leaving the shop with a small, neatly wrapped parcel under his arm.

"How's it ye know Donnir's mind now, Huil-talker?" A man stood outside the shop and began to walk alongside Bear.

"Donnir's the brother of Huil, actually, son."

"Don't call me *son*, saylie."

"I didn't call you *my* son. But sure as you're standing there, you're somebody's," said Bear, walking past the man. "And no doubt causing them much regret and disappointment."

"No dark faerie wretch is going to speak to me that way."

"Maybe not all, but this one is, yeah." Bear continued on, his shoulders squared and the package of books tucked beneath one arm. He felt the thick, cold end of a flintlock pistol against his temple. He stopped. "That would be a foolish choice, mister. Think of all the other things you could be doing other than growing old and forgotten in one of the constable's cells."

"I won't be put in a cell. I'll be pissing on your grave."

"Hey now!" called Tim Wayne, hurrying towards the men. "What in the cat's nine graces are ye doing with that gun, Alfie?"

"Showing this *saylie* who's boss."

Bear watched Tim walk around them, to Alfie's right side. Bear turned his head to the left and reached for the barrel, and Alfie fired, but the shot sent up a clod of dirt just past the men's boots. Bear dropped the parcel of books and swung his large fist into Alfie's face, crushing the human's nose and dropping him to the ground like a sack of hammers.

Bear stooped to pick up his books. Tim stared at him, his mouth open just a bit, his gray eyes wide with shock.

"You can't go doing that," said a fourth man, ruddy and bearded, as Bear unhitched the wagon from the post. All of the wood had been taken.

"Shouldn't aim a gun at a man who's standing right in front of you."

"You ain't a man." said the redhead. "You ain't a fucking man, *you're a goddamned elf.*"

"What's gotten into you all today!" said Tim, hurrying after them. "Have ye all lost yer minds? Go back to your house, Hals, and sleep away that stink that's comin' off ye. For pity's sake."

"No, Hals is right," said a fifth man, and Bear regarded him. "He sits up there in that pretty house, now with his sister in tow, and what does he do? Strolls among the woods. Talks to the birds. He's a ne'er-do-well living off this village, that's what he is. He tells us it'll be a good year, but this year *wasn't a good year.* Not for me."

"I'm sorry you lost your wife, Ben," said Bear, his voice soft. "That's not my domain, however. The goddess of the mountain had naught to do with that. You know this to be true."

"I don't know squat, that's what I know. Except that when there's a bad egg in the cake, it tends to taste sour."

"There's a storm coming, sirrahs," said Bear, slapping the reins against Walter and driving the cart past the villagers. "See to your houses, and I shall see to the mountain."

###

Asher went downstairs, his breath forming clouds in the air of the house. He opened the front door and blinked at the world turned white, the tilled garden now blanketed with at least a foot of snow. He walked to the kitchen door, pushing it open against the drift that had piled against it in the night. "*Well.* That's something."

The blossoms on the tips of the trees were encased in ice. An icicle dagger as long as Asher's leg hung from the eaves over the back step. He reached up and snapped it off, carrying it inside.

"Da," he said, standing by the foot of his father's bed. "Look." He held up the icicle, which was melting in his warm hand.

Bear opened his eyes, blinking. "Well. Guess we've got some work to do."

Asher held the icicle like a rifle, butt end upon his palm, business end against his shoulder, and exaggeratedly marched out of the room.

"Don't go disappearing," called Bear. "Snow shades in the shed."

Asher was tending the fire in the kitchen's hearth, his boots on and his heavy jacket slung over the back of a chair, when his father came in for breakfast. The men ate the last night's porridge quietly, each hunched over their bowls. Asher looked at his father.

"You doing all right today, Da?"

His father nodded, and his kind eyes changed as Asher watched, retaining again something of their usual, merry spirit. "I'm okay, son. Thanks for asking."

"I know you're worried about the snow and all, but I think… I think it's just a weird, random bit of weather. I think it'll blow over soon."

"Well," said Bear. "I'd like to believe that. And I appreciate your trying to cheer me with your encouragement, really, I do. But we haven't yet discovered your talents, lad. Other than a quick wit and a smart mouth." He laughed, and so did Asher. "But I think weather-telling's likely not one of them, beyond the average person's grasp of things."

"Okay, but still. Whatever happens, eventually, logic dictates that the weather's gotta turn, right?"

Asher noticed a fleeting shadow on his father's face, as if he meant to say something, but Asher let it go and didn't pester about it, instead gathering the empty bowls and putting them in the bucket in the wash sink. Together, they dressed in their coats and scarves and stepped out into the day, blinking against the stark, bright landscape.

###

"Mum," said Medie, coming into the house. "You about?"

"In here, girl," said Mink from the kitchen. "Trying to warm it up enough so this bread will rise." She turned and looked at Medie, still dressed in her coat, her boots wet from the snow. "You've been out?"

"I have. It's so wonderful outside. I went up to the house, also."

"Which house?" Mink sat and folded her hands. Her pale eyes were wide with confusion.

"The house I found. Up through the briar wall."

"Oh?"

"Asher and I were in just the other day. That's when I heard the mountain talking, and I climbed on the bough through the window."

"Girl," said Mink, rubbing her eyes. "You're too grown to be this uncareful."

"I'm sorry, Mum. There's just a lot to learn." Medie took something out of her pocket and put it on the table. "And to see. Like this book."

"Oh?" Mink reached for it, opening the faded and cracked leather cover. "This isn't either of the ones your uncle picked up for you. This is a diary."

"Yes. By a girl. Who used to live in the house."

"What?" asked Mink, carefully turning the pages. "Was never a girl living there, not that Bear told me."

"She lived there. With her father. But then she wrote some strange things."

Mink gasped, having turned to the last entry.

###

"Walter's good, chickens are good. Can't find the goats," said Asher, sitting on the back steps, his cheeks red from the cold and the bright sun.

"Probably wandered into the woods to scavenge. They'll be back," said Bear.

Suddenly Mink's scream pierced the quiet of the noonday.

Bear and Asher hurried through the knee-high drifts to the other house's back porch.

"Oy!" called Bear as he stepped inside, tapping his boots against the doorframe to knock off the clods of snow. "Are you hurt?" Asher followed him inside.

Mink came down the stairs. "Oh, I must've screamed louder than I thought for you to hear me outside."

"It was pretty loud, yes," said Bear. "What's the matter?"

"Thought I heard rats, in the attic," said Mink. "A rowdy herd of 'em, actually. Scared me half to death."

"Well, the sudden cold is what likely drove them indoors."

"Wish I'd still Mr. Tin."

"Who?" asked Asher.

"Our old cat. He passed a year ago. I would have brought him with us from Bran. Such a good mouser. Leiben, on the other hand, I once saw taking a nap, with a mouse napping right alongside him."

"Auntie Mink, Leiben's all right," said Asher. "How about him, though?" He pointed to the window behind him. Shuck was sitting there, his breath fogging up the glass.

"Thought I said never, and no," said Bear.

"It's cruel to have him out in the cold," said Mink.

"Look at him. He looks fine."

"Da, he'd probably tear up those rats in a minute. Why not try?"

They climbed the stairs to the entrance to the attic, which was at the top of a narrow, creaky stair, and watched Shuck sniff along the walls, wagging his stump of a tail, stopping in places to sniff overly long, until he finally stopped at a boarded-up fireplace and barked.

"Well there you have it," said Bear. "Coming up through the basement, I reckon."

"I am not going down there," said Mink.

"My poor city lass," chuckled Bear. "That's your root cellar. Might as well use it if you've got it."

"I'll stick all I've got in the cupboards and be glad of it."

Bear shook his head, laughing as he stomped back down the stairs, whistling for the dog, who blundered past him.

"Those two are a pair," said Mink, guiding Asher away from the boarded-up fireplace. "Out now. Back down the stairs so I can lock this door. This place gives me the weeloos."

Bear went back to his house to fetch his staff and a lantern, then opened the heavy outer doors to Mink's basement, blinking at the ripe aroma that wafted up as he did. Shuck stared into the darkness and let go a low, wet growl.

"Well, that I don't like," said Bear. "What's got you spooked, old boy?" He kissed the top-stone of his staff and shined the light into the cellar. The golden glow illuminated heavy cobwebs and a dirt floor, but little else.

"What's down there, Da?" asked Asher, coming outside from Mink's kitchen.

"Don't know, but the dog doesn't approve of it, whatever it is. Fetch my gun."

"Da. Seriously? You hate that thing."

"I hate what gets the jump on me, too," said Bear. "Just hurry up and get it and come back."

Asher jogged away to the shed.

"All right, Grimlock," said Bear to the dog. "Let's have ourselves a look-see." He climbed down the ladder of hewn beams and turned, tearing the webs down with his staff. He heard a scramble of claws and a heavy weight, and chuckled to see the dog beside him. "Was wondering how you'd manage that." Shuck looked at him, his amber, nearly red eyes comically sad.

"Okay. Wonder if she's got a chute, like we do." He cast the staff's light against the walls, looking up at the ceiling, stepping over puddles of water that had seeped up in the dirt floor. "Don't see one."

A sudden clamor caused him and Shuck to turn about; the dog started to growl again.

"Da?" called Asher. Bear hurried over to the door.

"Toss it down, son," he said.

Suddenly the dog started barking and jumping at the wall behind a row of rotten, wooden shelves.

"Fuck," said Bear. "Well, beastie—" he set the staff against the wall "—let's have a look at you." Bear examined the rifle, and the shelves began to rattle and buck. "Son?"

"Yeah?"

"It's not loaded." Bear hissed a curse beneath his breath and tapped his pockets, knowing there wasn't a powder bag in any of them.

"I don't know how to load it."

"I taught you. You forgot."

"I'm sorry!"

The wall exploded, and the shelves collapsed on poor Shuck. Bear staggered backward in surprise, then brought the butt of the rifle down atop the gnashing thing of shadow until it lay still.

###

Standing in her brother's kitchen, Mink looked at Bear's clothes, which were covered with a viscous, brown splatter.

"Uncle Bear," said Medie. "What's all over your coat?"

"The remainder of an alp," said Bear.

"You mean to tell me…" said Mink. "You honestly mean to say."

"Fucking house is lousy with them," said Bear.

"Uncle!"

"Da, really! Language."

"I'm sorry, boy," said Bear, sitting in his long johns and a fresh shirt, the tails sticking out of the back of the chair. "Ruined my coat. My best coat. Have to wear last year's now, and it barely closes around my belly."

"How is this possible?" asked Mink.

"On a diet of rabbits, I've no idea. What, you don't think alps are real?" A teacup nestled in Bear's huge hands; the families had retreated to his kitchen. "Alps are real."

Medie stared at Asher, lifting a finger to her lips.

"Many things are real," said Bear. "I've just never honestly seen a bloody *pack* of them. In a house. Together. The rest of 'em ducked back into that hole after I bludgeoned the first."

"A pack implies togetherness," said Asher. "I doubt alps have a social hierarchy of any sort."

"I knew sending you to town school was a mistake."

"Oh, yes. It was horrible. But at least I can read from Medie's book on wild creatures of the Branwin Valley that alps, *do*, in fact, seek shelters in houses when a late-spring snow falls heavily enough."

Bear blinked at his son. "What?"

"It's true," said Asher, getting up and leaving the kitchen. They could hear him running up the stairs.

"Smart boy," said Mink.

"Smart mouth, maybe," said Bear.

Asher hurried into the kitchen with the book in question. "Here you go. I borrowed it from Medie." While he flipped through the pages, he said to his cousin, "You've got about a fair army's worth of moth cocoons all up in the corners of your room. Did you know that?" He set the book open to the referenced chapter, in front of Bear. "Oh I forgot, Da, I'm sorry."

"It's no bother," said Bear. "Medie, what's that say?" He stabbed at the book with a thick finger.

Medie leaned over, standing next to her uncle. "*Should the skies release a late enough snow, so much that the mountains lay still beneath a heavy blanket, that life that has already begun to stir becomes chilled to sleep once more, or even death, the alp will gather in droves and chase into the houses of man and elf. Only the dwarf knows the remedy for this phenomenon and must be consulted quickly, before the alp-infesting begins to poison the household with their...*" Medie paused. "I don't know this word."

"Let me," said Asher coming around to that side of the table. "*...hateful contagion.*" He slid the book closer to him. "*The alp is a collection of negative thought and spiteful spirit, and as he feeds on the dreams of his victim, so does he also infect them with his filthiness of soul.*"

"And that is *lovely.* So what now?" asked Mink, looking as if she'd weep any minute.

"I go have a consult with the *swarthe,*" said Bear.

###

Bear left at dawn the next day, his rabbit-lined gloves gripping his staff, the light pack across his back hung with bright trinkets. He pulled his snow-glasses over his eyes and went out into the glittering white, as the sun's red fingers slowly bled between the trees.

The woods were still and warm despite the snow, the sun gilding the air and stirring the life within that refused to be daunted by the weather's tricks. Birds hopped from branch to stone, following Bear, until he came nearly to the mountain's peak, and there, in a broad clearing, stood three rocks, each as big as his house. Where the rocks met, a narrow, mossy canyon dripped water into the beginnings of the spring below, running along in a deep black vein amid the sparkling ice.

As Bear stepped over this, he squeezed through the entrance to a great cave and followed the slippery path down, casting the light of his staff upon the cave floor and walls until he reached a stony floor. Amid the chunks of granite and stark, white quartz, he slipped his pack off his shoulders and removed two of the trinkets from it. He shook these things, cleverly braided and sewn with simple, stone beads and brightly ringing bells hung with crow feathers and carved bones of rabbits and chickens, and waited.

Time fluttered on and out. The sun leaked down from the cave opening, growing brighter but still barely touching upon the floor of the cavern.

Bear shifted sleepily in his boots. "Not a bloody seat or dry rock in this place."

"There is, just not right here," said a friendly, sonorous voice from the darkness. "We shall endeavor to improve the décor upon your leaving."

"I'd care very much to stay, if you and your brethren would allow it. I have things to discuss. And aid to request," said Bear.

"I know," said the voice, and a man emerged from the tunnel. He stood as high as Asher, and his hair was shorn close to his finely chiseled skull. His nearly black eyes were grave but somehow also kind, set in a face so dark it mirrored the shadow of the cave. His long beard was braided and set with simple jewelry. "You wouldn't be here, only to visit."

"Alaric," said Bear, smiling and pointing a finger. "I'm a very busy man."

"Always excuses," said the dwarf. "I'm glad to see you, just the same." Alaric reached for the trinkets and smiled in kind, turning to place them on a shelf carved into the rock. He withdrew two disc-shaped stones from his pocket and slid one across the other. A tiny flame danced there where they met, and with this he lit the stub of a candle on the shelf. The light shivered and jumped, and behind it, the somber face of a statue regarded the offerings before it.

"Do the ancestors approve?" said Bear.

"They seem to enjoy your presents as well as your presence—yes," said Alaric.

"That was terrible."

"I know." Alaric came closer to Bear and examined the snow-glasses that now hung from the elf's neck. "These are interesting."

"Soft wood, heat-tempered, carved. Set with sheets of mica. Covered over with resin. Took a week to make them, but well worth the trouble."

"I'd like a pair, when you have the time. I'd wear them even in summer."

Alaric led Bear down the tunnel, which snaked and wound about so often that Bear soon lost his mind's map of the place. Then they were stepping carefully over a broad, shallow river as wide as the road into town but nary as deep as the puddles in Mink's basement. Overhead, the shadow lights were glowing—tiny, ineffable magics of the *swarthe* set to life long ago, gently milling and gathering in the gloom like fireflies of a summer's dusk. At last, the men crossed the greater neck of the river and came to wide steps, dug and smoothed from the cold earth and leading up from the great cavern.

At the top of the steps, another corridor, and another mile of walking, and finally the men came to an expansive hall—empty but for a *swarthe* maid sitting at a long table, carefully transcribing a book.

"Quinne," said Alaric to her. "Forgive the interruption, but would you happen to know the whereabouts of Master Ygull?"

The dwarven woman tapped the bridge of her delicate nose and stood from her work, shaking her long, snake-like braids all about her shoulders, gathering them and smoothing them as she thought. "Last I saw, after his breakfast, he was going on about meeting with some of the brethren to discuss the frozen spring head. But I'm not privy to where this meeting was to occur or even if it was definitely scheduled. I apologize, Master Alaric. I try very hard to keep out of Ygull's way these days."

"I know, Quinne, and I know it must be difficult for you. My condolences also, to your family."

Quinne bowed her head, her long lashes resting against her cheeks like the wings of a dove.

"We'll find him without getting you involved. Be of good hope, maiden."

Alaric motioned for Bear to follow him, and they exited the hall through a corridor on the opposite side.

"Mind if I ask what happened?"

"When?" said Alaric.

"What?"

"Many things happen all the time."

"I meant with the lady."

"Ygull is the oldest scribe in our community. He's getting on, and if I say that, I mean truly, his age is dogging his steps in such a way that it's affecting his mind. He challenged Quinne's father—who has been one of Ygull's apprentices for nearly forty years—to a duel, because he claimed Hara was 'stealing his secrets.' And Hara could not refuse or he would shame his master. Hara tried to go easy on the old man, and that was a mistake he paid for with his life."

"For all your courtesy and civilized ways," said Bear.

"This was unusual, Ursoon. This sort of thing hasn't occurred in nearly two hundred years."

"What does anyone plan to do about it?"

They had come to the end of the corridor and a wide, wooden door set in the rock. The door opened, and a dwarf with a silvered crown and beard stared at them. "Do about what now, exactly?"

"The frozen spring head, Master Ygull. And also, this *saylie* has matters to discuss with us."

Alaric fixed Bear with a stern look as they entered the chambers of Ygull the Master Scribe. Bear nodded.

"It's true, things strange and ungodly have touched the goddess's sleep this winter, and I believe that's why She's awakened so early."

"And what of the late snow?"

"Perhaps Her brother seeks to shield Her, grant Her more rest."

"I would guess that the snow is a bane—a symptom of things gathering up beneath a wound," said Alaric.

"I agree, exactly," said Bear. "And that wound's just broken and released a shit-storm of pus in my sister's basement and who knows where else."

"A shit-storm, eh?" chuckled Ygull. "Of alps? That's quite a problem."

"I know," said Bear, sitting in a small chair, his hands resting on his knees. "I feel the problem should be met at its source, so that I can seal up the rupture and begin the arduous work of cleansing the house. It's been in our family for many generations."

"As has this mountain, ours, for centuries. What has She told you of her troubles, cleric?"

"She's been quiet," said Bear. "Which concerns me."

"That would concern me as well. It means Her energy is depleted, and She's not got enough to reach out to Her faithful. I fear for Her. But not, to be frank, for us. As in the dwarves."

"Master," said Alaric. "If we help him, we help ourselves as well."

"Well, then you don't need me, gentlemen," said Ygull. "And regardless of what I think on the matter—because what I think on the matter is that solving this cleric's alp problem is neither a bane nor a boon, for us—but if *he* wants it solved, we need to deliver him to the Wayfinder, and she can help him hunt these fiends where they've been gathering."

Alaric bowed his head to Ygull, and motioned to Bear.

"And if it pleases the ancestors, kind Master, these gifts for your altar." Bear placed two more trinkets on the desk in front of Ygull, who examined each one, clearly delighted.

As they hurried down another corridor per Ygull's directions, Alaric said, "No idea how you manage to get those giant hands around a sewing needle."

"In some things, one must have faith and resign to relinquish logical understanding."

"That is you, my friend, in a sentence." Alaric stopped for a moment to smooth out his jacket and trousers. "A fair warning—try to avoid excess speech with Mistress Kárum. She's a very busy woman."

"I can understand that. How much is your population expanding nowadays? New paths to forge."

Alaric chuckled. "We're not the most prolific folk, you know that. But we discovered new lodes far south, among the mountain's roots. We're considering a trade road with the southern *bahai.* We need space to further explore and utilize these things."

"And you'd not consider an aboveground site?" asked Bear.

"Ha!" scoffed Alaric. "Never aboveground. You know as well as I that the humans' greed would quickly overtake their courtesy, of which they have very little towards us already."

Bear frowned, and Alaric glanced at him. The shadow lights had followed them down the widening corridor, casting their arcane, aqua-hued glow about the walls.

"It's not your fault they are this way."

"I've tried so hard," said Bear. "To win them over, I suppose. To care for them, because that is my oath. And yet I cannot help but think, in light of recent events, that I have failed, utterly."

"Learning is a constant path," said Alaric. "Not a steady incline, for one falls, often. That is the nature of it. The nature of wisdom, however, is to climb back up after falling down. You keep doing that, Bear."

"I feel I've lost the desire to climb."

"It will return. All things return," said Alaric. "And this is her quarters. You realize how great the odds are against her being at home?"

"Well, then let us have faith," said Bear. He knocked on the wooden door, and waited.

The door opened, and a keen, sharp face appeared in the opening.

"Good day, Mistress," said Alaric. "What excellent luck to find you at home."

"What is good about it, exactly?" said Kárum, yawning. "Come in and put your trinkets on the altar by the door."

"My friend has a problem with alps that I would like us to help him solve."

"That was to the point, so thank you," said Kárum. "But beyond that, I'm not entirely sure what you'd like me to do."

"You're a wayfinder," said Bear.

"I am."

"Find us the way to their nest so I can kill them."

Kárum walked toward the far edge of the room, a perfectly square room carved into the rock itself, and stood at a small table, flipping through a book, quickly and with agitation.

"I've a question," said Bear, studying the walls, which were covered in beautifully even lines of language. "How do ye get the walls so perfectly straight without powder or stick?"

"You're holding a staff of Huil and you ask me this?" said Kárum in a contemplative drawl.

"He occasionally fails to see the biggest picture that he can," offered Alaric. "So what do you think, Wayfinder?"

“Many things, all the time. But for your friend’s particular problem—the road among the roots,” said Kárum. “And this is not safe, nor is it proven. So if you venture forward with me, you agree to be spoken for, of your own lives, and will bear no regret or revenge upon me for leading you toward death or ruin.”

“Thought you said she preferred plain speech,” said Bear.

“Apparently, this is important,” said Alaric. “I think I can safely say for both of us, Mistress Kárum, that we’re aware of and accepting of the risks. Fine details would not be unwanted, however.”

“The ground can give way beneath your boot,” said the Wayfinder, gesturing for them to stand beside her. She placed a stone against a hollow in the wall, and the wall parted, slowly releasing on pulleys into grooves at each side, until a great, wide doorway was revealed. Past the opening was a forest of roots and of soil. “It can drop you into holes from which you’ll not be recovered. There are great insects herein. They are voracious, quite large.”

Kárum tapped the stone in her headpiece, and a light emitted forth, illuminating the slender path ahead that snaked through the roots and over the rocks. The tunnel was barely as tall as Alaric, and as wide as two of Bear, standing shoulder to shoulder.

“And worse things,” Kárum added.

“Worse?” asked Bear.

“Such as they that you hunt.”

Kárum went first, taking a step, tapping the floor with her stick, then taking another step, so that the progress the three made was slow and cautious. The door closed behind them.

“Try to step atop rocks when ye can find them,” the *swarthe* woman advised. “And shake not loose any clods of earth above you.”

Bear’s and Alaric’s eyes were spooked and wide, watching everything around them as they followed Kárum. One great tap root exposed by the tunnel was covered, every inch of it, with swarming beetles. The men were careful not to bump against them. Fat-bellied spiders sat amid their funnel webs, watching the dwarves and the elf pass, raising their arms in defiance at the travelers. One red-colored spider hissed at Alaric, and the dwarf withdrew a small blade from his pocket to quietly run the creature through. Kárum stopped, and looked behind her, and Alaric looked at her in kind. When she turned back to lead on, Alaric glanced back at Bear, a finger to his lips.

"Aye," said Bear, looking around, his courage fighting within his fear like a bird trapped within two hands.

"Up ahead it widens," said Kárum, "and there we have a choice to make."

The tunnel gave way to a small room, and from this, two more tunnels branched. Alaric stepped upon a flat stone and gasped as it fell straight down from under his boot. His foot followed and he sank into the crumbling floor up to his knee. Bear helped him back to his feet, and they stepped away from the pitfall, looking all around in terror.

"Steady yourselves," said the Wayfinder. "If you panic in here, you'll not live long."

Bear took a deep breath and cracked his knuckles. "Aye, Mistress. This is not easy. My respect for you deepens."

"We will need to pick a way," she answered. "I am not all-knowing. I thought a moment of consult would be best. As in—you, with your goddess."

Bear nodded, and slowly lowered himself to one knee. He bowed his head and began to pray.

###

"Do you feel like helping me with some housework today, sweet girl?" asked Mink of her daughter, who was sitting in front of the hearth in the great room, staring at the flames and fiddling with Shuck's small, folded ears.

"Sure," said Medie, not moving.

"What's wrong now?"

"I haven't seen Asher. It would be such an excellent day to play outside."

"I'm sure he's got work of his own he has to attend to. Or, he might be in town, visiting his friends there. There'll be time enough to play yet."

"And I wanted to get some of my things from my room, also."

"I know, but you really shouldn't be in there until your uncle's sorted out the issue with the…" Mink paused, running her hand across the back of her neck.

"Alps," said Medie. "I know. They won't bother me, though."

"Maybe *one* wouldn't bother you too terribly much. But a whole raving pack of them? No, I'd rather not risk it. You're staying out of there, please promise me. I'll be in to clean up a bit. Just tell me what you want fetched and I'll fetch it for you."

"It's okay. It's not important. I'm going to look for Asher, though. I'll help with housework later."

"Later never comes, Medie," said Mink.

"It does come, Mum. It just becomes now. I promise I'll clean now, later."

Mink nodded, her brow lined with concern, and watched her daughter head outside. She stood there for a moment before going out to Bear's porch. Medie was already out of view, somewhere in the cold wilderness, and Mink could hear her laughing. Mink hurried across the frozen lawn and into her own house, kicking the snow off her boots as she made her way upstairs. She opened the door to Medie's room and gasped.

The air was filled with moths, all fluttering about in the light of the curtainless windows. Some were crawling across Medie's dresses, which the child had strewn across her bed. Mink took off her apron and began to beat the insects, brushing them off the clothes and the bed linens to the floor, and stomping them with her boot.

"Well, that's a lovely mess," she said, looking at the collage of tiny bodies and powdery wings scattered across the floorboards.

After sweeping up her daughter's room, Mink stood at the window in her kitchen, watching the day wane to that terrible, sad, deep blue cast that happened in winter, hours before the sun set. Bear wasn't back yet, and she needed more firewood; both hearths were close to guttering. She was afraid to be outside and so unused to being alone. But it needed to be done.

She stepped out into the bracing air, her breath escaping in plumes. The dog trotted over, clumps of ice clinging to his shaggy fur. She patted his broad head.

"Poor thing. I'll let you back in, lad. Follow me to the woodpile."

She made her way through the snow drifts, many nearly to her hip and covered with a hardened rime so that her booted foot had to break through the tops, but only some. She was too light in weight to fall through most of them, so she slipped and skidded across the snow, with Shuck bounding and crashing alongside her, struggling as well but unbreakingly cheerful as the dog always seemed to be. At last they reached the woodpile. Mink heard the sound of smashing glass.

She looked to her house.

Mink ran to the window beside her front door, peering in. Shuck steamed the glass beside her, panting. "It's breaking my things," said Mink in a trembling voice. "And I have had enough of that," she added. "But I am too afraid to do anything." She looked at the dog. "What a misery this is, to be always afraid!"

Shuck whined at her. The sounds of breaking crockery came from within the house.

"I choose to be unafraid." Mink dropped the bundle of wood, keeping one stout stick in her hand as she opened the door. She raced into her kitchen, stick raised above her head, and began to swing at the hunched bodies of the alps tearing at her cupboards. The stick thumped them on their sinewy backs, bashed them against their bony skulls, ruining the milky, bulging eye of one as Mink swung, screaming, cursing, and shouting at them, kicking their strong arms away as they grabbed at her legs and tore at her skirts and her hair, and then Shuck was there, sending broken dishes flying as he leapt about the room, tearing at and rending the bodies of the alps.

###

Great mother, Huil, stony and deep, crested with green and with brown, eyes of gray, all-seeing, fingers of earth, touching everything, please give to me a sign now, that I may find the prey I seek and rid the land of its poison. Show me the way, Huil.

Bear looked up from his prayers, catching Kárum's gaze, but her face was immediately obscured by the explosion of soil beneath them as the floor was torn asunder by dozens of twisted bodies and pairs of clawing hands.

They fell, the dwarves and the elf, in silence, because the soil was all around them, in their faces and in their mouths, tangling their hair, and they held onto their implements, sliding down, getting hooked by roots or smacked by rocks in the shifting dirt, until at last they dropped upon a soft floor below and covered their heads with their arms as more soil fell atop them. Bear leapt to his feet, though blind, and cursed the foes around them, turning about and casting the light of his staff against the ugly faces and grabbing hands. Finally, he brushed the detritus from his head, wiped the dirt from his eyes and mouth, and looked around. He shifted his weight from foot to foot; his bones were unbroken.

"Are you hurt, you two?" he whispered. "How are your legs and feet?"

"Sound," said Kárum. "Alaric?"

"Ankle's sore, but unbroken." Kárum's light shined against his face, and he reached up to touch his nose. "Might have taken a nasty smack across the snout, it seems."

"You'll still be as handsome," said Bear. "But at least we can still walk. Where's your stick?"

"No idea," said Alaric.

"I'll help you."

"I think," said Kárum, "your prayer was answered." She stepped into the darkness, filling it with the amber glow of her headpiece. There, in front of her, the twisted bodies of the alps had filled a pocket of the earth, wrapped together now in subdued sleep, breathing quickly and in unison, their naked skin gray and shining as raw, dead flesh against the lamplight.

Kárum looked up the shaft the three had made during their fall. "There's enough root-fall here to make a decent climb of it. Alaric, do you see the quickfire? I may have dropped it."

Alaric nodded, reaching down and retrieving a tiny brass bottle from the dirt. "Here you are."

"Douse them with it. Bear, how hot does your beryl flame glow?"

"Hot enough for cooking," said the elf, grinning in the gloom.

They watched the bodies sizzle and twist in the intense heat, and then Bear was shouting to them to climb up the shaft lest they, too, be roasted. They struggled up along the hanging roots as the fire burst and crackled below their feet, and Kárum led them back across the dread floor of the tunnel, around the roots and pitfalls, until they reached the safety of the corridors and halls of the dwarven city.

The city was quiet; it was the hours of rest. Bear suggested they continue to the surface and have supper at his home.

"This is a rare treat, you know," said Alaric, as they made their way down the mountain to the houses in the distance. Twilight had settled heavily upon the forest. The half-moon illumined the path ahead, busy with footprints, blue-white, the icy cover glittering. "She rarely goes aboveground."

"I go more times than you think," said Kárum, "I simply go alone."

"How does one cook for a dwarf?" asked Bear, his stomach singing a quiet song amid the crunching of bootsteps.

"Heartily," said Alaric.

"Often," said Kárum.

Bear stopped then as did the others, and suddenly the elf was plunging through the snow, running towards Mink's home. The dwarves ran behind him, knives and staves in hand.

There was Shuck, beside the body of Mink. The black dog lifted his head and howled.

Bear leapt down the remainder of the hill and sped across the snow, his elven grace apparent despite his large form, and knelt beside his sister, ear to her chest, cheek to her breath, his eyes panicked as he gently lifted her and turned to hurry to his house.

"She's alive," hissed Alaric. "Thanks be to the gods."

###

They had brought Bear's feather-down sedan to the hearth in the great room; Kárum had rekindled the kitchen's fire and set about making a strong tea. Alaric ran up the steps to find every blanket and brought them down to Bear who, after removing Mink's boots and stockings, examined her feet. Her hands were also untouched by frostbite.

"The brute laid upon her, I think," said Alaric. "What a creature. Where did you find him? He looks for all the world, like—"

"A shuck, and he found us, and we call him Shuck, and yeah, I've no idea the whys or the hows of it, but at least she'll not lose her hands or feet. That cheek, though," said Bear, and a tear glistened against his own as he looked at the injured skin of Mink's face.

From the kitchen, Kárum brought a bowl of fragrant, sharp-smelling liquid. She set it down beside Bear and pulled a cloth from her coat, then removed a tiny pouch from her pocket and emptied its contents into the bowl. The men winced at the now-noisome scent. "Soak the rag in the medicine and let it sit upon the cheek. It may yet be renewed to health. I'll be back—I want to examine things outside."

"I'll go with you," said Alaric.

The dwarves looked all around the spot Mink had lain and followed the tracks into her house, where they found the bodies of the alps, torn and bludgeoned. They removed those, carried them into the woods and set a fire to them, covering their own faces against the terrible smell and acrid smoke. Then they returned to Mink's kitchen, Alaric with a broom and Kárum with a basket, and they removed the broken crockery and the mud and the blackening alp-blood.

Bear had come to check on them and stood in the doorway. "Well, I'll be a rabbit-sized frog," he said. "*Swarthen* royalty, cleaning up my sister's kitchen."

Kárum raised an eyebrow at him. "Ear of alp?" she said, lifting a tiny flap of skin for him to see.

It was dawn before Mink opened her eyes, and she stared at her brother's face, which was at first serious, then beaming in a broad smile as he gently gathered her into his arms and spoke against her shoulder. "Thought I'd lost you," he said quietly, and she combed her cold fingers over his matted hair.

"No," she said. "I chose to be brave, for once."

"You've never not been, Minny."

#

The day evened out into a pale, bleak sky, and the air was as cold as a keen knife was sharp. Alaric and Kárum left Mink's side to find Bear, out in the yard between the houses, studying the ground.

"Brother, we leave to return, if you feel you and your sister will be all right."

Bear looked at them, his face a chaos of confusion.

"What is it, *saylie*?" asked Kárum, looking at the ground, then following thc tracks up past the houses, to the start of the path that led up the mountain.

"The children have gone," said Bear. "I've checked their rooms and beds."

#

"Mink," said Bear, and his sister roused from the deep sleep she'd fallen back into. Kárum's rag, still damp with medicine, rested on the elven woman's cheek.

"Aye, lad?" Mink whispered, her voice course.

"Where are Medie and Asher?"

"Medie went out to play with him in the snow," she said, and fell asleep again.

"The medicine is strong, as was her trial last night," said Kárum. "She will sleep at least today, through to tomorrow."

"Alaric, I am sorry to ask you," said Bear, his large hands gathering the cloth of his shirt as the worry creased the lines by his eyes more deeply. "But would you stay here with my sister? I need to track them, what, with so much going wrong atop this mountainside."

"Of course, Ursoon," said Alaric. "I will keep an eye on her. You take the Wayfinder and retrieve the children."

"Thank you, thank you," said Bear, grabbing up Alaric's dark hand and kissing it. "There's more wood beneath the stairs, and if you run out, more still near the henhouse. I've bread and tea, and some leftover porridge in the kitchen. Have as many eggs as you like. And also—my rifle is leant up against my bed, which you're welcome to sleep in if you get tired."

"I'll not leave her side but to fetch food or water for us both. Worry not, brother," said Alaric, taking a chair from the kitchen and setting it down beside the sedan where Mink slept.

Kárum jogged along the frozen top of the snow as they went back up the mountainside, a dark shape in her many-tasseled coat of dyed, blood-hued leather. Her hair came to her shoulders, braided in the manner of the dwarven women, but she wore thick woolen trousers instead of petticoats and skirts, and had a pair of binoculars about her neck which she stopped to use every half mile or so. Bear found it challenging to keep pace with her, but his anxiety and fear lent fuel to his steps, and so he loped along, looking to one side of the forest and the other as they gained the first peak of the mountain.

"Here it stops," said Kárum, kneeling behind a small clearing busy with footprints. "And here they meet." She crouched along the ground, lifting her binoculars to her eyes and turning a small dial on one side of them. "A *reffke* child."

"The kit," said Bear. "Medie told me about him, and I saw him run off the first time I'd found her after she'd gone missing."

"Why does she go missing so often, *saylie*?"

"She hears the mountain speak."

Kárum raised a thick eyebrow and tapped the bridge of her nose. She stood and looked to the west, where the mountain was covered in large, glacial rock and dark pines. "They turned here, and walked along the deer path."

"The deer path ends sharply, not but a mile from here," said Bear. They followed the thin trail between the trees and the rhododendrons, and Bear stopped and looked back at Kárum. "This is where the deer path ends, Mistress, and from here, it is not an easy path up to the next peak."

"Children are rarely concerned with what is easy, *saylie*."

They climbed atop the closest boulder and leapt from one to the next, keeping an eye on the sun, which was glowing feebly behind the sky of white, falling now from the mid-point.

"I hope we recover them quickly. This won't be easy to navigate in the dark, Wayfinder."

"I'm aware. But we can get much more out of the day before we must abandon the exercise." Kárum pointed to a grassy hill, visible through a break in the trees, and an old, wide-limbed tree similar to one they'd spotted when they'd begun their journey up from the houses. "That is significant."

"Aye, those are water-keepers," said Bear. "It points to where the spring used to flow the loudest, but no longer. It is an ancient tree, that."

The dwarf and the elf climbed through a thorny embankment and gained the hill, and in the pale light found more footprints.

Bear stooped by the tree's great roots, which were embedded in the rock that sat beside it. "Here," he said, his voice barely a whisper. "By the goddess, she's been here."

It was a tiny, mold-darkened book.

###

Alaric sat beside the sleeping form of Mink, reading from Medie's copy of *Wild Creatures of the Branwin Valley*, his boots off and set by the fire, his legs crossed. He threaded his fingers between his bare toes, as two would hold hands while walking, and chuckled to himself. The dog looked at him, sighed, and rested its wide head again on its front paws.

"Listen to this, pup," said Alaric as he read aloud. "*Swarthen* are clever and bold, and may be useful in trade, for their inventions are worth bags of gold." He held the book longwise, and blinked. "I say. That nearly looks identical to my cousin Sebastian."

There was a noise then, from outside the front door, a hammer driving in a nail. Shuck was up in an instant, padding to the front of the house, a low growl jangling in his thick throat. Alaric set the book down quietly and looked to the axe above the hearth. He lifted it from the wall and crept to the door. There was a face peering in, watching him through the window beside the door.

"*Oy, look at tha' brute,*" hissed a whisper from the other side of the window. "*Black as soot, he is.*"

Another voice said, "*Which one, the dog or the man?*"

"*Run off, come on!*"

Alaric swung the door open and stepped outside, axe ready. Two boys were pelting away, rounding the side of Mink and Medie's house. The *swarthe* turned around to go back inside, and stopped.

Someone had nailed a long-legged hare to Bear's door. Shuck was up on his hind legs, sniffing at it and barking.

Thought and Memory

BEAR FOUND ALARIC on his porch, a bucket of water and a rag set to one side of the front door.

"And?" he asked the dwarf.

"We'll talk about it later," said Alaric. "Come inside—Mink's feeling somewhat better."

She was still on the sedan but sitting up. The brightness had returned to her brown cheeks, and her blue eyes retained most of their usual sparkle, though they were fearful and nervous.

"No, Minny," said Bear, kneeling beside her. "Not yet—but I found this." He showed her the diary.

"She was telling me about that," said Mink. "She showed it to me." She struggled to turn around and reached for the book, and Bear gave it to her. "Yes, I remember." She covered her mouth with her small hand. "Such things."

"What things?" said Bear.

"I'm sorry, brother. Oh, but it's troubling."

"We might need to learn of these troubles now, for later may yet be near as good as sooner," suggested Alaric.

"Well, all right," said Mink, and she began to read.

"Father says the elves won't come back to the other houses. He said they'd gone and died away, and left the homes to rot. But I see he cares for them sometimes. Rips the weeds out, cleans about the place. The briars are growing ever tall; he can't seem to stop them. He told me not to go the cellar either; we're storing the pickles and jams in the shed beside the house.

"He also said we're to go on a great climb soon. He said it was near his birthday, and he wanted a day with his daughter. We'd climb the mountain and find the meadow with the great old tree."

"What's all strange about that?" asked Bear.

"It continues," said Mink.

"I thought I'd been mistaken, but I wasn't. It's not anywhere close to Father's birthday. He seems strange, and he talks to himself. He came back from town with some things: flour, and a new dress for me, and also some rope. He said it's to tie the horse to the fence. I almost told him, no you're wrong. Mama took the horse when she left for Bran, but I didn't say anything. He looks like he's near to tears most of the time. I don't know what's wrong. He talks to himself, especially in the night. I can hear him talking, answering, and he sounds cross. Tomorrow is our day up the mountain. I don't know if I should go. If I run away, who will care for Father?

"Then there's one last thing," said Mink.

"Father said such a strange thing! I don't know who can listen, I'm too afraid to even pray, for fear he listens at the bottom of the attic steps. But he said he was bringing the rope with us tomorrow, to tie me to the tree in case the wind would throw me off the mountain's face. I am so scared. Why would he say that? What is happening? Please, gods in the night sky, protect me."

Bear put his hand over his sister's.

"Whoever lived in that house, before," said Mink, "he killed his little girl, I'm sure of it."

"That hound is returned," said Alaric, gesturing to the window by the back door. Shuck was there, panting as like the night they'd first discovered him, fogging up the glass.

Bear bid farewell to Alaric and Kárum. It was another dawn, and too much time aboveground, the Wayfarer said, but was gracious in parting. She thanked Bear for his hospitality and wished him kindness of the mountain in finding the children.

Alaric embraced the pastor and held Bear's hands as he said, "Should trouble thicken, call to me by way of She, and I will come to your aid, brother."

The dwarves ascended the mountain; Bear watched them from his porch, and Mink watched them from the window by the front door.

"Minny," said Bear, bringing her some porridge. "I'm going to get help, today. You just need to be strong for them. We both do."

"Aye," said Mink, her voice cold and small.

Bear climbed to the Shrine of Waking and with a long branch of pine, swept the table clear of snow and set the dish of fruited bread upon it. He set the heavy iron lantern down and lit the candle within. Then he built a fire upon the rock and looked out over the valley.

He softly sang the Hearken-song of Huil:

> Wild She who bore the earth, the sinew root and granite hearth,
>
> Oh look upon my humble head, it's bowed to you as from my birth,
>
> would I not ask another thing than this life, I'd be happy then,
>
> but I must call you from your sleep, to grace the lives of elves and men,
>
> the winter bites, the winter gnaws—and I've but firewood for days,
>
> the hawk has gripped in cunning claws the last of the hare, and he, too, prays—
>
> that ye awaken from the dark, to stretch your limbs of ivy bright,
>
> bedecked with gold and green and stay, aboveground 'til last harvest night.

In the distance, and in a corner of the white sky that burled with darkness, thunder rolled, and it was an odd thing to hear as the white sun glanced upon the snow, causing it to sparkle like something fine and expensive in a shopkeeper's window. Bear knelt on one knee and muttered deeper words to Her, and also to another, and brought hands that were fists up to his mouth, whispering the message to his sister in them.

He released his hands to the valley and the sky; black feathers wrapped with string hung in the air for only a moment, with a flash and a twitch, these things became two crows flapping away, the brief sun glossing their bodies until the clouds obscured the light once again and the birds were black grains in the quickening gloom.

Late that night, having foregone first-sleep, Bear sat in his kitchen at his table, which he'd pulled closer to the hearth. The dog was at his feet, and Bear's cheeks were deepened in color by warmth as he watched the candles burning upon the table through the amber lens of the whiskey in his glass. He'd rummaged about the cellar and found the last three bottles he owned. A merchant in town had given them to him in the Year of Five Petals, when he'd first been ordained and come to Delster with Solace.

"Lad," said Bear, his voice rough from sitting so many hours in the quiet.

The dog lifted its great head and regarded him, eyes more deeply amber than the whiskey.

"I've had a strange life, Shuck."

The dog huffed, then sighed, then laid his head down upon Bear's boot.

"Don't drool upon that leather, if you mind. No offense to you, as a dog. I'd just prefer it not to occur."

Shuck removed his head from Bear's boot and stretched out in a fat crescent, back to the fire's heat.

"My father, Shuck." Bear drank the remainder of the whiskey in the glass and took up the bottle, turning to lift it to the light of the hearth. More than half-full, still. He poured himself another short glass. "My father, Shuck, is weird. And you might say, 'Weird? Heh, like sisters-in-the-woods weird, like goblins-under-trees weird?' And, Shuck, I would say, 'Brother, my canine cousin, no—*my father is weirder than all that.*'"

The dog lifted his head to turn and regard Bear, then settled back down upon the wood slats of the floor.

"We all had names." Bear took a small sip from the glass and winced, then broke off a piece of hard bread he'd set down on a tin plate, and slowly munched that. "We had proper—" he swallowed the bread "—names. Did you know that? Of course you didn't, you and I have only just met. And I don't even know *your* proper name. Just call you some rude thing because you look for all the world like a hellhound. And for that, I'm sorry. But you've not yet complained."

Shuck belched softly.

"But yes, we had names. Our mum gave us each a proper name. Mine was Alistair. Mink's was Minuet, which is why I still call her Minny. Crow was Rebekah, but we mainly called her Bek, until Da coined her nickname.

"He had ten children. Five sons, five daughters. One is not with us anymore, but for the heavens. Little Madeleine passed as a baby. He still ever referred to her as Mouse.

"You see there, Shuck—Da couldn't keep track of our *names*. He had so many of us, and this was a bother to him. Everything was a bother to him that disturbed him from his books. Even Mum was a bother to him, but that didn't stop the bastard from making more of us botherers, did it? No.

"He hated our names, didn't pick our names, couldn't not have his way in his own house—never mind Mum did *everything*, everything for everybody, except collect the books, and sell the books, and sit and pour over the books, and hoard the books. And give us stinking nicknames of animals as we each reminded him of.

"Obviously he named me for my size. Mink for her straight, silken hair.

"But here's the thing, Shuck. Here's the thing. Da called her Bekks until that very day. The day he broke her bones. But after that day, he insisted on referring to her as Crow. At first, we were confused. We were still kids…well, except Hare. She's the oldest. Then we figured out what he meant, and I remember I squared up to him—I was taller at eleven than he was at sixty-two—and I put it to him. 'Why'd you pick to call her that?'

"He answered, 'For all the squawking she made when I caught her filthy hands on my book.'"

Shuck got up, and shook, and stretched. He sat and looked at Bear.

"And when she finally left her room, weeks after that day, hands bandaged up as Mum had done and cared for her, she walked into the kitchen where some of us were sitting. And she said, in a low voice, deep for her even, 'I'm Crow now.' And then she pushed open the back door with her shoulder and just left the house."

The dog cocked his head, regarding Bear.

"She didn't come back either, until nearly a week later. To this day, I've no idea where she went."

###

That morning, Mink found Bear asleep at the kitchen table, his head thrown back and his mouth open, snoring almost as loudly as the dog. The bottle of whiskey was more than half depleted.

"Ooh," he heard her whisper as he started to wake. "That's going to hurt."

Through unfocused eyes, Bear watched Mink set a kettle to boil for tea and take the glass from the table, still with some of the amber liquor left, and down it in one shot, wiping her lips with her sleeve.

Bear sat upright, accidentally kicking the dog in the rump, and turned to look at Mink. "It's daylight," he said, blinking to bring the world into focus.

"Aye," said Mink and burped softly.

###

"I'm all right Minny," Bear said an hour later, eating a breakfast of eggs and bread, and sneaking bits of it to Shuck who was still beneath the table. "You know I've completely forgotten to milk the nanny goat these past four days, poor thing."

"I've done it," said Mink. "You've had a lot to handle."

"I have," said Bear, "and I've fucked up the lot of it. And thank you, also."

"No you haven't. But now here's Crow." She pointed to the window by the kitchen door.

There in the flesh was their sister, waving one gloved hand.

Bear got up and stepped to the door, then reached out and lifted Crow off her feet, bringing her into the warmth of the kitchen and swinging her while she laughed her rough, deepish laugh, her boots kicking about. The dog barked excitedly, and Mink laughed as well.

"That was fast!" said Bear, his eyes bloodshot but twinkling.

"Oh, yeah," said Crow. "It was. Lucky for you, I was well on the road already, and whoop, what a wallop to my head She gave me, and yours too. Two-handed slap of the goddesses. So thank ye." She dragged Bear's plate towards her and sat in the empty chair, then dragged the whiskey bottle over too. "And thank ye for this as well."

They sat and drank and ate the rest of the afternoon, somber but laughing at times when it couldn't be helped. Talking to Crow involved a bit of laughter, always, as she tended to describe things—even horrible things—in such a way that the humor was always revealed, like drops of garnet in a stone. But then the twilight was creeping over the snow beyond the windowpanes, and the mood deepened, and it was time to speak of the troubles that had befallen Mink and Bear.

"How long they've been missin'?" asked Crow of the children.

"Two days," said Bear.

"Oh." His sister sipped from her glass and looked out the window.

"They're both smart, and I'm sure they brought food," said Mink. "But it's getting hard to sleep, or even breathe, honestly, until they're back. I need them found, sissy. Can you help?"

"Of course I can, Min," said Crow. "That's why I'm here. That, and something else."

"What's the something else?" asked Bear.

Crow looked at them, her sad, yellow-tan face shadowed beneath the eyes and around her dark lips as it always was. She took off her gloves then and winced.

"Let me heat some rags," said Mink.

"Thank ye," said Crow, rubbing her misshapen hands slowly, the one finger on the right hand bent slightly to one side and all the knuckles knobby and wrong.

"What's the other matter, Crow?" asked Bear, gently this time.

Crow looked at him, reaching up and scratching her scalp with one dirty fingernail. "Da's dead."

Mink dropped the plate she was holding, and Bear snatched it mid-air, then set it on the table. He sighed and rubbed his eyes. "How?"

"He just died," said Crow, her voice rough. She took the plate with the warm rags and covered one hand with them, breathing deeply to calm the pain. "Does it matter how?"

"I suppose not," said Bear. "Doesn't mean I don't want to know."

"His heart stopped one night. A woman had been bringing him meals, as he'd become a shut-in. One day she found him—a day many days after he'd passed."

"Among his books, no doubt," said Mink, her arms folded as she stared out the window into the dark.

"Of course," said Crow quietly.

"So now what's to happen?" asked Bear.

Crow looked at him. "We've got to manage his things."

"Fuck. I do not need this, right now. Or ever, honestly."

"I know. None of us do, but there is no hurry. He owed no debts. I've a man at the house, watching against burglars. We'll take our time and we'll go, when we are all ready." She moved the rags from the one hand to the other. "First, we find your children."

"There's one more matter," said Mink. "Slipped my mind, but I haven't been myself the past day. Men from town were up here causing mischief. Reminded me of the first day Medie and I arrived."

"Alaric told me all about it," said Bear, easing himself up from the table. "Let me use my outhouse for a moment, then Crow and I will head to town. I have hopes to get the constable's help in finding the children. Gather a group of men to comb the mountain with us."

###

Crow walked alongside as Bear rode Walter down the mountain, and she smoked her pipe in a peculiar fashion, similar to a man holding a spyglass, her hand stretched along the flute of the pipe and covered in the leather gloves she wore.

"What's Delster like as towns go?" she asked.

"Small and uneventful, despite recent happenings. See all these tracks?"

"I see two sets. What do you see?"

"The same. Not grown men, neither."

"Nope. Barely tall as me. So at least they're not comin' up here with fire and swords yet."

"Hardly anyone in Delster owns a sword, Bek."

"But someone's been running their mouth about ye, and kids always hear everything. And then they get up to mischief when they think no one's paying attention."

"Two concys and a hammer, and some nails   no one's going to likely be missing that."

"You've a cartwright?"

"Yeah. Timothy Wayne. Good man."

"No such thing."

"Oh stop, Crow. I can't agree with you on that."

"I don't need you to agree with me, brother. Just get out of my way if I'm having a disagreement with one of them."

The town lay in a haze of wood smoke ahead, shivering beneath the press of colder, higher air, and the townspeople walked with scarves tied about their faces to shield against the smog. The cartwright's shop was first on the right. Bear tied Walter to the rail out front and knocked on the door.

Tim answered, his face pinched, mouth a tight line. "Pastor," he said quietly.

"I've a weird question for you, sirrah," said Bear.

"That doesn't entirely surprise me. But ask away."

"Are you missing a hammer?"

Tim looked past Bear, to the street, then to Crow. "Come inside," he said.

They walked back through the room and out the back door to the work shed. "Something you mean to tell me, Tim?"

"Well, no, I didn't mean to tell ye. But I suppose I should. Now that you're here." Bear raised an eyebrow at the human. "Look—I'm sorry. It's not your fault, but it's not mine either."

"Well, was it your boy who came up the mountain and nailed a coney upon my door and my sister's?"

"Wh-what?" sputtered Tim, eyes wide. "My child couldn't have possibly."

"Where's your hammer? You're not the sort to misplace a tool you use every day, Tim."

Tim's son walked across the yard, saw the two men speaking, turned and began to jog away.

"Oy!" called Tim after the boy, who ran faster, around the house until he was gone.

Bear stood, his hands folded before him, his eyes sorrowful.

"I'm so very sorry, Pastor," said Tim.

"I know," said Bear. "As am I."

"I'll see to him."

"Be easy on him. Mine's gone missing. If and when I get him back, I'll wish I'd never raised my voice or hand to him. What was the other matter before I go?"

"Only..." Tim looked so nervous Bear thought he might run away like his son. "Folk have been talking. Of forcing you out. Just be ready, if ye can. For trouble."

"Well, that's a minor mystery solved," said Bear to Crow, who was busy watching the townsfolk watch her. The road through Delster was lively for such an unseasonably cold day.

"Good," she said. "So now we're to see the constable?"

"*I* will pay him a visit," said Bear. "You can wait for me here. I have to talk to him about several matters."

Crow pulled a glove off with her teeth and scratched her scalp. "Which matters?"

"Bek."

"Yes?"

"It's best if you don't. At least, I'm going to try to be neighborly first."

"Fine. Delster have a pub?"

"It does." Bear leaned in close to his sister. "Don't be too much in there."

"Me?" laughed Crow, her eyes twinkling. "Too much? Never." She walked away, her slim form swaying exaggeratedly. "Never ever, ever."

Bear sighed and looked skyward, muttering a prayer, then hurried off to the constable's.

###

"Oy," growled a man at one of the tables, his boots on a chair. "What the hell are ye?"

Iar's son snapped his fingers, and the man put his feet back upon the floor. "Mind yerself. This is a respectable bar, not a fisherman's shithole."

"This entire town's a fisherman's shithole," said the man. "And I really want to know—what the fuck is that?" He pointed at Crow again, who slid off her barstool and slowly walked to his table.

"What I am…" she said, reaching over her shoulder with her right hand and around her back with her left. Lifting her sword up and over her shoulder, she pulled on the sheath's pulley and smacked the flat of the blade on the table in front of the man, causing his beer to jump as well as his person. "Is a paladin of *Babcath*." She slowly slid her blade off the table, and the man could see it had an odd, heavy hilt arm, which she let rest upon her gloved thumb as she swung the blade down easily to her hip.

He looked at his beer, then again at Crow, then reached for the beer, lifted it, sipped from it, and set it down again. "Okay," he said. "Please to meet ye. Can I buy you an ale?"

###

"How do you mean to say that Delster doesn't have a smithy?" asked Crow, on her third ale and surrounded by three men of the town and one visiting fisherman.

"We sort of do," said one of them, named Jort. "But mainly he's our cartwright as well as our fletcher. Just he's also got a little forge he built in his yard beside the river. And he's good with payment. Bake him a decent pie and he'll sharpen your blade."

"How many of you have got blades in this town?"

The men looked at each other. "Well," said another, name of Harold, "there's the constable."

"No, he hasn't swung a sword in years. Uses a flintlock."

"Oh, right. Well, okay, and then there's Hugh."

"Think he traded that for his boat."

"How many have flintlocks?" said Crow.

"Lots of men. Had a fellow come through town last summer, selling 'em. Decent make, not unfairly priced."

"How many is lots?"

"I'd say a fair half dozen," said Jort.

Crow chuckled. "Good to know should trouble ever pick Delster for a match."

"Oh, well, I mean," said the third man, name of Mica, "trouble's as interested in Delster as most anybody else in the world is interested in Delster."

"Right," laughed Harold. "As in, not."

The door to the pub swung open then. A red-haired, bearded man walked in, his legs encased in brown fishing leathers. He glanced around the room and his stare rested on Crow.

"What the fuck's this, then," he said quietly, smiling. "Another *saylie* dog in heat?"

###

"Milo, I've lived here thirteen years."

Bear sat at the constable's table, and Milo's wife, Hannah, brought out her husband's supper.

"You hungry, Pastor?"

"No, thank you."

Milo cut through the skin of the trout, and sliced it into neat, even pieces.

"Who was in that house? The one that didn't burn?"

"You don't remember?" asked Milo.

"No. That's why I'm asking you."

The constable put his fork down, and counted his fingers. "Oh, well, that's right. You wouldn't know. Solace's belly was out past her feet when you arrived. Yeah, Asher's twelve, so…thirteen years. And Mack's been in the ground for nearly twenty."

"Who'd you say? Mack?"

"Mack Gunther. I'd say you just missed him, but he'd been missing, so to speak, long before we buried him."

"What do you mean by that?"

"He took to acting strange. Some said he was crazier than a rabbit in a sack."

"After his wife passed," said Hannah, bringing Milo a cup of tea.

"Wife *and* daughter. Remember little Sanandra?"

Bear looked at him, startled. "Did you say *Sanandra*?"

"You've heard that name before, Pastor?"

"Aye. My little niece found her diary. And now both Medie and my son are missing."

"I'm sorry, Pastor."

Bear sat there and sighed, pushing his chair away from the table. "What's been going on in town against me and my folk. You know it isn't right."

"I know, Bear. I know this isn't fair to you or your family. I can't exactly figure why folks are getting so worked up about what-have-you. Why tempers are so short. Old Mack may have been crazy, but it seems anymore half the town's short on sense and long in the mouth about one thing or another. Folks are behaving stranger than cats before a storm. But the best I can say is—for now—just keep clear of them. You do what you need to on the mountain and only come into town when it's absolutely necessary."

Bear folded his arms across his chest. "Milo, you're telling me not to invite trouble instead of talking to the ones who would start it."

"Yes. I am."

"That seems to be the opposite of your job."

Milo put his fork and knife down, again. Hannah stood in the doorway with a pitcher of tea but turned around and went back into the kitchen with it. "Do I tell you, Bear, how to pray?"

Bear stared at him.

"Do I tell you how to invoke Huil for a good season?"

The pastor sighed, and shook his head. "Look, Milo, I can do as you say and not look for trouble, yet it's already come to me. Well, now my son and my sister's daughter *are both missing.* I'm not saying it's the townspeople who're to blame—"

"Do I tell you how to bring an early spring? How to ensure a fruitful summer? How to keep disease at bay? Keep the drought from our valley? Any of these things, Pastor? Have I ever, ever once, told *you*, how to do your work?"

"No," said Bear.

"Then don't fucking tell me how to do mine."

"Did you not hear what I said?"

"Do *not* get loud with me. I did hear it, Bear. We've got infestations of rats, in town. I'm worried about sickness striking us. We, also, have got two of our kids from town missing. And did you know? Almost a year ago, we had a man go missing. Hard-working fellow named Oliver Cook. He went up to *your* mountain, claiming there was gold up there. Wanted to change his life for the better. No one ever heard from him since, and it'd be nice for his widow to have a body to bury. But if I ask you to help with that, I'll be troubling you with human affairs."

"Milo," said Bear, his temper rising, his eyes livid and cold as he stared at the man, "this is your home. And I am trying to be civil. But don't you dare suggest that I *do not care* for humans. That is what I care most for, after the goddess herself. All you had to do was ask and I would've found him for you."

"I'm up to my ears in trouble down here. I can't help ye with yours. Go home. And stop interrupting my dinner."

Bear left the constable's house and watched the storm clouds coming from upriver, around the eastern face of the mountain, and quickened his steps to his apprentice's house. He knocked on the door there, and Hunter's father, Ives, answered.

"I need Hunter's help with a matter, sirrah."

Ives squinted against the brightness of the day outside and frowned. "I don't know if he can be of use to you right now. We need him here at home."

"I understand," said Bear. "Surely I do. When there's work around the house, I try my best to give a fair share to my own son. But we've several things happening on the mountain that need more men to handle. Children have gone missing. And the constable's just told me that a man went astray quite a while ago."

"I don't want my boy to be the next one to go missing. I'm going to have to say, for now, Hunter'll have a leave from his training."

Bear shifted his weight and folded his hands together. "I'm afraid it doesn't work that way. Once devoted to the faith, there are no sabbaticals—unless a pastor be deathly ill."

"Then I suppose you can tell your goddess Hunter's got himself the consumption."

"I'm sure you're not suggesting I pray of falsehoods, sirrah."

"Do what you feel you must. He's staying home."

Bear stood and watched as Ives closed the door.

He walked away, his steps slow and heavy, as heavy as his heart. The snow was falling lightly now, coating the ugliness of the muddy road and the dreary, winter-stained homes. Suddenly a hand was on his arm. He turned, startled. It was Hunter's mother, Zahsie.

"I'll be sending Ives fishing, far downriver, Pastor Bear," she said, looking up at him and smiling nervously.

"Oh?" he said, unsure of what to make of her.

"He doesn't understand such things as gods and magic. But he's a good man. I'm sorry he treated you unkindly."

"He's just frightened, Miss Zahsie. I understand. But then do you mean to say you'll send Hunter up the mountain?"

"I will. As soon as I'm able. Should be before nightfall."

"Well," said Bear, glancing behind him at the Silvers' home. "For that I am grateful. Hoping we can find some missing children not before too long." He looked at her face, the hesitation in it. "Was there something else?"

"Oh," she said, glancing down. "I'm just…sorry for all the trouble, Pastor. You're a good man. And ye do right by Hunter. And we appreciate that."

"Yes, miss," said Bear, nodding his head to her. "And I thank you."

"There's something else," she said. She pulled a small parcel from her apron pocket.

"What's this?" asked Bear.

"A charm. For to put above your hearth or upon your door. You can also carry it on your person, if you aim to travel a path that's dark. Whichever ye like. It's to turn things around and bring good fortune to your family. I'm sorry times have been so hard for you and yours."

Bear smiled, though his eyes were pained. "Miss Zahsie," he said in a quiet voice. "I thank you so much."

She nodded, and hurried away.

Then he heard the shouts of men from the tavern.

He rushed down the street just in time to watch a bearded man run backwards out of the pub's open door, and a chair come flying after him like it was alive.

"You bitch. I'll run ye through," said the man, catching his balance and bull-rushing the door, seeming ready to ram the wood with his head. The door opened, and a sword point poked out.

"With what? Your cock? Before I gut ye with my sticker? Let's see, then!"

"*Crow,*" said Bear, mostly to himself, because everyone else was shouting.

The bearded man slid to a stop, falling to his side so as not be skewered upon Crow's keen blade.

"You troubled my sister. You frightened my niece. I ought to do *to ye* what you were thinkin' of doing to Medie, with my sword *up your arse.*" Crow rushed out of the pub and chased the fisherman up the street, only stopping when he turned to dart between two buildings and make for his boat.

Half the town had come out to watch the goings-on. Bear stood there, wishing he had a hat to pull over his eyes.

The wind was howling now, spinning the air in blasts of snow and sending the townspeople hurrying away to tie up boats along the riverbanks and double-check fastened shutters and barn doors. Bear fetched the ever-patient Walter from the front of Timothy Wayne's shop, and together, he and Crow rode him through the growing storm, back to the mountain.

###

"Well, here it is, then," said Bear, as he brought more firewood from the woodpile to stack upon the porch and covered that with a leather tarp. "A brief, late snow is one thing," he said to Shuck, who was following him to and from. "But this? A full-out storm. That's unusual. I can't ignore the signs anymore, and I don't know what to do with all of these problems happening at once. I envy you, lad."

Shuck barked and decidedly turned to look at the mountain above them.

Bear looked too, and nodded. "Yes I know. I know. She's troubled, and this is what's come."

"Hallo!" called a familiar voice from down the road.

Bear walked past Mink's house with Shuck trotting alongside him. The snow turned sideways on a silent wind, blowing into their eyes. Bear shielded his face from it to see who was calling up to them. It was Hunter, riding Alan, who was slowly turning white from gray.

In Mink's kitchen, they gathered to discuss Bear's intentions.

"I don't care if it's not first of day, Minny," said Bear. "I'm leaving with Crow and Hunter to find the children. Shuck'll stay with you. I trust him."

Mink looked at him with tears in her eyes. "Huil is troubled."

"She's mightier than us, sister. She can deal with trouble and *still* hear her pastor calling to Her."

"I so want you to go," she said, her voice breaking, "but I so don't want you to leave. I am so frightened, Bear."

Shuck laid his wide head upon her lap, and she fiddled with his ears.

"*I know*, Minny," said Bear, kissing the top of her head. "We must do what must be done. You and I must be brave. And we've both proven we can be."

Crow came into the kitchen and took a long, vicious blade from her boot. She laid it upon the table. "Take that, Mink. Slice the fuck out of whatever troubles ye."

Mink picked up the knife, wielding it easily.

"So sneaky, this one," said Crow. "I always knew she was watching me play with my toys."

"Of course I watched you," said Mink. "You were always my favorite."

"Well, thank you very much," said Bear.

"I'm sorry, but it's true!" laughed Mink, with haunted eyes. "You're next-favorite though."

"I'm sure we'll find them today. We'll bring them home, and if I have to find a place for you in town until Medie can stop her wandering ways, I can arrange that. This is just a moment in time. All kids go through things they feel they need to seek out. Especially such intelligent ones as Medie and Asher. This is not a bane, sister, it's a blessing."

"I know," said Mink, and suddenly she was crying, weeping into her sleeve. "I know it is."

"There," said Crow, squeezing Mink's shoulder. "Let it out now."

"It's just so odd. Medie is so, always, in control of herself. And now she's off and running to who knows where."

"Hey now," said Bear. "So were you before you got a whiff of boys."

"Oh, goodness," said Mink, covering her face, embarrassed.

"We all have things that quicken our steps for a moment," said Crow. "It doesn't mean disaster. Well, okay, that husband of yours…"

"Crow, really?" said Bear. "To speak of the dead."

"What? He was a lump. A kind, handsome lump, but still."

Mink wept some more, but laughed also. "He was. A bit—" she laughed louder now, openly "—of a lump. Oh, Crow, how you bring out the worst in me."

Crow kissed the top of Mink's disheveled head. "It's my pleasure. Anytime."

Fool's Fight

THE NIGHT-DAUGHTER, DARK of skin and gifted in many arts, was a scribe, and imagined the saylies, the dwarves and the hidden ones, also called trolls, and she was skilled with blade and with quill, and could communicate with the animals, and with the trees.

She created these peoples, gave them arts with which to defend themselves, and lands upon and under which to live.

Her father was a mighty giant and her mother was the Moon. Her children took after her, graceful and keen.

The Son of Noon, pale of skin and brash of feature, eyes like the blue sky, was ambitious, and bold. He was a huntsman, a magician, and a bard. His songs came to life and flourished, and became the ounsayles and the dragons. But his children fought, and now they are fewer in the world.

His mother was the last of the white queens of Krieve, and his father, the Sun.

And amidst all of creation, it is said, the humans were born of the dreams of these races, the hopes and imaginings, while all the things that torture this world were born of the nightmares and fears of the magical children of Night and Day.

– *Histories of the World's Races*

Asher watched Medie in the darkness. He wondered how he could see in this place where there was no light. Then he thought there must be light, surely, if he could see—just a little bit.

Cats could never see in total darkness; they needed some bit of help—a candle, a slip of the moon—and elves were much like cats in this regard.

Could the moon shine down into this place?

He could hear her sleep, there against the sandy curve of the hole, and he crept toward her. Her breath was just a whisper, like a mouse he'd snuck up on once, which had fallen asleep in his shoe. He'd not wanted to scare it, and so he'd spent the better part of half an hour crawling slowly across the floor of his room until at last, a foot away from the shoe, the floorboard creaked, and the mouse startled awake and ran from him.

"What is it?" she asked, her voice a drowsy murmur.

"Nothing," said Asher, embarrassed. "Just for a second I forgot where we were."

"We're in the deep dark," she said in that weird voice she'd had back at the tree. "In the mountain's heart."

"Okay, well, yes. Obviously we are in the dark, Medie, but I need to find out some particulars about our situation, so that we can get out of the dark, right?"

"We came here after her and we won't be leaving without her, or her, or them."

"Well, there it is again," sighed Asher, sitting down against the sandy curve of the tunnel. He jumped. "I say."

Two eyes glowed in the dark, staring at him.

"Medie. Look."

The eyes blinked, and they became part of a face: a pointed chin, two high, furred cheeks, a small nose-tip, whiskers, and topsy hair that pointed up into wide ears.

"I remember now," whispered Asher.

The face drew closer and cocked to one side, the golden eyes seeming kind, and scared, and looking down to the black, clever hands that moved about in sigils. Asher looked down at them too.

"Medie, I cannot read his signs. Can you, please? I feel rude."

His cousin crept forward and, with a stifled shout, hugged the fox-boy to her, then pushed him an arm's length away to watch his hands.

"Do it again, quickly!"

"Why do you have to boss him so?" asked Asher.

"No, goob, his name is *Quickly*," said Medie, her words sounding more like her usual speech.

"Oh. Okay." Asher watched her, glad of her return to self, and also watched Quickly sign. "What's he saying?"

"That he smells the scent of his sister, Jumps High, here still, though it is cold, and old, and she is long away."

Asher frowned; the weird-speak was coming out of his cousin's mouth again.

"And also that there are deeper ways down, and he thinks we must go these ways to find them."

"To find who?" asked Asher. "Besides his sister, I mean."

"Two others," said Medie. "Two other children." She stood up in the dark tunnel and closed her eyes. "No, I'm wrong." She began to cry, her quiet sobs shaking out of her slowly.

"Hey now," said Asher. "I know it's frightening in here, but we'll get through it, the three of us—more, if we find those kids and the fox-girl. That's a whole gang, isn't it? We can do this."

"No," said Medie. "No, I mean. There's another. *Sanandra*."

"Sanandra is?" asked Asher.

"Not living any longer."

The *reffke* kit tapped her shoulder, and Medie signed what she'd said to Asher so that he could see.

The three decided to take the tunnel down as the way behind them was a solid wall, busy with thick roots, and the very opposite of a door. Asher wanted to know how they'd gotten to the spot where they'd started, but he was afraid to ask, sensing the fear coming off Quickly and growing concerned about his cousin, who seemed to be getting more peculiar by the minute. He had to let things ride, as his Uncle Genet was fond of saying.

The tunnel broadened so that after some time, the three children could walk abreast, and the ceiling was high enough that they could no longer see it. It became colder, and smelled damp, and slowly changed from sand to dark, stony soil. The floor of the tunnel graded increasingly down and was not interrupted by side tunnels or rooms.

Asher realized he was hungry and remembered the heavy pack still strapped to his back.

"Hey there, Medie—care for a snack? I brought all the rations and I've still got 'em." He stopped and slung the pack off his shoulders, letting it drop with a *thump* to the tunnel floor. Quickly crouched near him and signed.

"He says let's light a fire," said Medie. "No one is around."

"Light a fire with what now?" asked Asher, pulling out a loaf of bread wrapped in one of his aunt's table linens, some smoked rabbit, and a jar of apple butter.

Quickly took off down the tunnel, and Asher wasn't entirely sure that he ran on two legs, or four.

Soon, the *reffke* came back with snow shoes and broken slats of a barrel, which he arranged in a pyramid.

"Well, honestly," said Asher. "Good work, mate."

"This place is old," said Medie, "and many have come before us."

"That's good news," said Asher.

"Many have died before us," said Medie.

"Right." Asher looked past Medie and Quickly to the deeper dark of the tunnel beyond.

The fire only lasted an hour. The latter half of that it reduced to glowing embers but didn't smoke much, which was good in the close quarters of the tunnel, and it lent the group a small portion of cheer. Quickly was adamant that he teach Asher some basic signs, and was successful after enough toast and apple butter. Asher now knew the signs for fire, dark, light, *saylie*, and *reffke*.

They sat for a while, watching the embers, all lined up against the tunnel wall, shoulder to shoulder, talking quietly, Quickly tapping Medie on the shoulder to sign to her, and she explaining what he'd said to Asher, and Asher laughing, and Quickly's tail thumping against the ground—a *reffke's* way to laugh—and for a moment they forgot they were lost underground, far away from their parents.

But in time, the fire gave up its fight, and the children stood up, looking back from where they'd come; only Asher seemed prepared to take a step.

"If the only way to go is down, then go down we must, Persistence," said Asher, covering the last bits of the fire with dirt by way of his boot.

"I agree," whispered Medie and signed to Quickly.

The pressing, stifling silence of the tunnel had become a faintly growing whisper of strange sounds, and they were sounds which the children could not make out but grew more aware of with each passing second. Sounds like metal, sounds like laughter, deeper sounds like something pushing through the dirt, startling sounds like a scream, or a small voice crying, and all so faint they felt nearly like memories, playing tricks on the mind to whisper at the ears *these are real; these too, are real.*

"I'm frightened," said Medie, halting her steps after a while. The sounds had ceased completely, and somehow that was worse.

"I know," said Asher. "So am I. I'm sure Quickly is too. As we go along, let's look for things we might use as weapons." Medie signed Asher's words to Quickly.

Quickly leapt away into the dark, and Medie gasped, calling softly after him, for she was too afraid to shout. The *reffke* reappeared, holding something on his palm. It was a small, curved sword.

"See now? Something like that," said Asher, reaching for it. "Good job, Quickly. You really have a talent for this."

The fox-kit relinquished it and sat upon his haunches, his furred knee peeking out of a hole in his homespun breeches.

Asher ran a fingertip across the blade's edge, wincing. "Mother of stone, that's quite sharp. Was there a scabbard lying about."

"How's this?" asked Medie, picking up a long, black seed pod from the tunnel floor.

"Well, I'll be a rabbit in a hat," said Asher. "Biggest honey-locust casing I've ever seen." He chopped the end of the pod clean off and gently slid the sword through the tough skin. It almost fit perfectly; an inch of the blade's end poked out the bottom.

"Good enough." Asher carefully slid the covered sword into his pack and slung one of the straps back over his shoulder. "Okay," he said, heading forward in the darkness, the others following behind him.

The tunnel remained silent, but for their steps and voices.

"Let us keep finding useful things, shall we?" whispered Asher.

"Like, the way back to the surface," answered Medie.

"Yes, just like that."

Time could not be counted in the dark and in the quiet. After what seemed like a terribly long time, the children began to tire, and Medie tugged on Asher's coat that she wished for sleep, and he gently answered he did, too, but they'd only be able to eat from the food they'd brought for so long, so it was better to keep going while they had the energy.

He thought of adding, *while we are uninjured, also*, but thought better of frightening her and Quickly. Besides, despite the oddity of the strange sounds earlier, there was absolutely nothing in the tunnel. What likely had happened was they had grown weary from the cold and slipped down a hole. The earth buried up the entrance behind them, and here they were now. Lost, but far from harm.

They simply had to find a way up and out.

The tunnel seemed to have other ideas, however. It refused to go up and only kept circling down. At least Asher could tell that it was circling—wide and slow, and to the right. *Sunwise*, his father would call it. Asher thought of things that burrowed down; they usually led to at least one room for sleeping, and another for keeping food, and sometimes a last for shitting or for storing the bones. As he thought upon this, he felt somewhat better that Quickly had found the sword.

He wondered how well he'd be able to use it, should the time come.

"Just a little further, and then I need to stop, just for a little bit," said Medie softly.

"Okay," said Asher. "Let Quickly know."

Medie had taken Quickly's hands and was signing against them, when there was a growl. It came from farther down the tunnel, but it was so sudden and loud it felt as if it were right before them. Medie shrieked, then clamped her hand across her mouth. Quickly crouched, his breathing coming in fast hitches, his tail swinging about and his hands digging into the tunnel floor. Asher let the pack fall from his shoulder and had the blade out, the seed-pod sheath on the floor at his feet.

The growl happened once more, closer now.

"I know what that is," said Asher, holding the sword in two hands, the blade point aimed toward the darkness of the tunnel.

Red eyes appeared far off in the gloom.

"That's a badger," whispered Asher.

Medie reached for her throat and gasped. "Oh no."

"What?" Asher watched the eyes draw closer.

"My necklace is gone."

"Oh, for pity's sake, Medie."

The great beast—as big as any of the children—stood blocking the tunnel, his chittering cry echoing loudly, his fat body shaking at times as he postured menacingly at them. Asher stood, knees bent, sword at the ready, with Quickly and Medie behind him, and the four kept at this pointless position for so long Asher felt his hands begin to ache. Eventually, the badger took a few steps back and stopped its chittering.

"Well, honestly," said Medie, sitting down in the dirt.

Quickly, too, sat on his haunches, watching the badger.

"You know what I think?" said Asher. "I think he just means to get out of here, like us, and we're blocking his way."

"So let's let him past," said Medie, her arms wrapped about her knees.

"But what if he gives us a good chomp on the way by?" said Asher, mostly to himself. "He's the biggest badger I've ever seen."

Quickly tugged at Asher's pack, and removed a piece of bread from it, showing it to Asher and Medie. He crept around Asher's legs and showed the bread to the badger, calling to the animal in a similar chittering voice, then tossed the bread behind them in the tunnel. Quickly put his hand on Asher's shoulder and guided him back so the three children were pressed against the tunnel wall, giving the badger room to pass by.

"Put down your sword," whispered Medie.

"Ah, no?" whispered Asher.

The badger looked at the bread, snuffling his big, black nose in its direction, then trundled past them, grabbing the bread and running away into the darkness in the direction from which they'd come.

"That was easy," said Medie.

"It was," said Asher. "Easy but worrisome."

"Why? If all the animals down here are that reasonable, we'll be okay."

"If all the animals down here are trying to flee, as we are, then I worry about continuing farther down."

"Perhaps we can follow the badger," said Medie. "And perhaps he will dig out the way to the surface."

"Yes!" said Asher. "Exactly. We should follow him."

Suddenly, Quickly was barking, towards the direction the badger had come, and then the fox-kit was gone, racing down into the unknown dark.

"Oh no! Stop, Quickly!" called Medie, running after him with Asher fast on her heels. He called to her, but she was already gone.

Asher stumbled forward in the gloom, and then the gloom was a thick, impenetrable blackness, unlike the gray-glint of before. The soil had become a fog, a miasma, and the very air choked him with its foul stench. He pushed forward, fear gripping his heart like a hand squeezing a frog, and then he stumbled a few more steps and fell, down soft stairs onto a stony floor.

He looked up.

There were Medie and Quickly and another *reffke*, its hair gathered up in little knots all about its head, with two long braids framing its pretty face. It was holding Quickly to itself, and his tail was sweeping back and forth. There were torches flickering against the hewn stone walls. The room, though small, was several times as wide and as tall as the tunnel had been, and also led out into three new tunnels.

But the other *reffke* was in irons, chained by one ankle to a wall. There was a grate in the center of the floor.

Asher realized this was Quickly's sister; she was being held a prisoner here.

Medie and Quickly were signing so fast their hands looked like blurs to Asher, and Jumps High was signing as well.

"Medie," he said, and was ignored. He went to the other tunnel entrances, listening at each, hearing nothing, and then sniffing at each. The middle one had a scent like deep water, and the one on the right had a scent like warmth with an undertone of rot, even death. The tunnel on the left smelled the same as the one they'd been traveling through.

"*Medie,*" he tried again.

"What?" she asked, somewhat sharply.

"Can we talk later and see about getting her out of that chain now?"

"Yes, but they are already discussing this. The chain, if hit, will make a loud sound, and the sound will carry to her captors, and they will come, she's already said."

"Well, that stinks. But let me think on it some," said Asher, lifting the chain carefully, apologizing to Jumps High as he lifted her foot and squinted at the manacle around her ankle.

"It's got a seam," he said. "And a hinge." He dropped his pack, setting the sword against the wall and digging around amid the belongings there. He grabbed for something tiny, captured it and lifted it into the light.

It was a nail. He'd found a nail stuck in the old tree, and had taken it for no other reason than it was fun to have a nail sometimes. He stooped by Jumps High's ankle and began to carefully wedge the nail into the manacle's seam.

The other children were still now, as they watched him work.

###

Ygull's steps made no more sound than the moonlight-hued moths fluttering about a glowing stone set in the wall of one of the city's outermost boundaries. He hurried past and into the cruder tunnels of the intricate warrens that sprawled out like veins in a leaf, deeper underground even than the city of the dwarves. Along the way, the scribe dropped a small, glowing pebble. Then another.

Without a sound, he climbed atop, then over, a gigantic root, stopping first to observe its cold, ruddy surface for crawling things, stinging things. There on the other side waited a brutish shape. A hiss made Ygull cover his ears. He watched the shape carefully as it dropped to the floor of the tunnel. "I am here."

"You have heard him—his bidding."

"I have," said Ygull, his throat spasming with discomfort, the proximity of the foul nature of this creature overcoming his own personal protections. Ygull's hand reached up to the pattern he'd painted around his neck—delicate sigils of deflection against harm—in the white chalk paint of ancient magic. "He wanted a thing."

"Do you have it?"

"I've two. Take your pick." Ygull reached into his pocket and revealed to the beast the two altar trinkets Bear had given him. "Made by one who is close to that which your master seeks."

"It is not my master," hissed the shape. "It is my master's advisor." The creature's hand brushed Ygull's as it took the altar trinkets.

Ygull shuddered with revulsion at the slight touch. He forced himself to stand straight, blinking his eyes against the darkness of the creature and the tunnel surrounding it.

"The advisor of your master…" said Ygull, regaining a bit of his own sense of self and walking backwards, then climbing quickly back over the root. "Is your master." He dropped down to the other side, running and retrieving pebbles as he fled. The hissing sound of the creature's words were lost with the distance of Ygull's escape, and Ygull was thankful, so thankful, that he'd survived the trial.

###

The master scribe re-entered the city. From the cover of an ink-dark alcove's shadow, Alaric crouched, hidden, watching him hurry past.

The younger dwarf followed the older, for a time, until Ygull stopped just before the crossroads of the lower-most level of the city, and turned.

"Who is there?" Ygull called.

There was no answer, and he could see nothing. He continued on to his chambers, following the roads leading up into the more inhabited levels.

###

Deeper down, below the warrens and tangles, amid the veins of quartz once thought so precious by humankind but disregarded by the dwarves—for the land containing such treasures was afflicted, made stale and cold by something they could not name—breathed a very old thing. A thing that had outlived its time, but lingered on nonetheless.

"My lord," said the Voice. "I stand beside you."

He to whom the eyes belonged turned, slowly, as slow as the dirt, as slow as a worm amid the soil, rendering his thought to the Voice which spoke, emitting his desire to him. The Voice shuddered with pleasure. The bodies, one of flesh, one of shadow, eased closer to each other, in the dark, in the pressingness of cold and heat, ether and weight.

"I hear you twitch, my lord."

The eyes rolled back, as the body delighted beneath the soothing touch of the Voice's shadowy hands. The body shuddered and ached.

"I am commanded," said the Voice. "Thy will be done."

###

“We’ve been all over this mountain,” said Bear. “What am I missing?”

“I don’t know,” said Crow, smoking her pipe and sitting in the crook of a tree. “Have ye been thinking like a child?”

“Yes,” said Bear. “This whole time.”

“Does your son think like a child?” asked Crow. “Does Mink’s daughter?”

“Fuck,” said Bear. “No.” He got up from his knee and sniffed the air. “They surely don’t. And another storm’s coming, right on the tail of the last one. At least this fresh fall has settled only half as much into the tracks that were made, but after tonight, they’ll be covered up and lost. We need to hurry.”

Crow dropped from the tree and stooped, tamping her pipe into the wet snow. “So let’s hurry, then.”

They struggled up to the mountain’s bald, and suddenly Bear stopped.

“What?” asked Crow.

“I’m a fool,” said Bear. “A blind, old fool.”

“Yer not either.”

“We need to head west and before the moon rises.”

He led Crow to the tumble of rocks by the pine stand and up the mountain to the great tree where he’d found the diary. But the moon had risen already.

Alaric was there.

“Brother,” he said. “Ursoon. Strange things were revealed to me—I see the strands like worn rope. What aid may I lend?”

“All that you can,” said Bear, stumbling through the snow to the old tree where he saw in the moonlight his niece’s silver chain, hung with the single black pearl that had once belonged to his mother.

“What trinket is that?” asked Alaric.

“Medie’s. My niece’s. She and my boy are missing. Children from the town as well. And a human man.”

“There are dark workings below our feet,” said Alaric.

"I cannot say," said Bear. "Or just the foolishness of men and children, seeking riches when they are blind to the richness of the mountain that already surrounds them."

"Master scribe Ygull does not share this blindness, yet he was out, far beyond the borders of the city. On what business I do not know."

"You said his mind grows feeble. Perhaps he lost his way."

"In one fashion or another, you're likely correct. But how may I assist you now?"

"My sister is waiting, and all she has to watch her is that hound. I would ask you to guard her as well, if that isn't too humble a chore for you, my friend."

"I am very concerned with current events and the danger they pose to those I love," said Alaric. "I would be more than willing to keep an eye on your sister and her dog."

"You are so kind, brother," said Bear, embracing Alaric.

The dwarf held him for a moment, then said, "I believe in your strength, Ursoon. It is more than the span of your arms and the height of your legs. You will make this right."

They bade farewell to Alaric, Hunter keeping back from the group with suspicion in his eyes.

The snow began to fall heavily once more until the wind was screaming against the mountain, and Bear made the decision to build shelter until the storm subsided a bit. He found a good spot, between the ancient tree and a large boulder. Where a younger tree had fallen and wedged itself between the arms of the greater one, Bear and Hunter leaned a roof of deadfall, covering it with pine branches. With the end of his staff, Bear dug a shallow trench and drove more fallen boughs into the earth, and there they had some shelter from the storm.

Crow made a small fire in the ground, against a hollow in the rock, and they huddled there, listening to the howling and the wailing of the winds as the night whipped the snow like horses late in a race being whipped by their riders.

"This is the kind of weather one sees after yuletide," said Hunter, hugging his knees beside the fire, jumping each time the wind tried to lift their deadfall lean-to.

"Yes, it is," said Bear. "It's not typical. The mountain is fighting back, but against what, I've no idea."

"If we could find a way to get under, to get closer to Her heart?" suggested Hunter.

"Pardon me if I'm overstepping," said Crow, only her face visible as she sat tucked in her heavy, fur-lined coat and hood, "but perhaps Huil doesn't want anyone to get closer to Her?"

"Perhaps She doesn't," said Bear. "An animal will turn on those she trusts when she is injured, but as Her guardians, we must try."

"Then to the caves?" asked Hunter.

"The domain of the *swarthe* is separated by magic from the goings-on of Huil. They are protected by Her, but they are nearly in a world apart from Her."

"What about the old mine?"

Bear stared at him, then began to laugh nearly as loud as the storm was strong. "You're right! Good boy. I'd not even thought about it. I'd completely forgotten that men had tried to mine here long ago. That's exactly where we should look—first thing in the morning."

"I don't want to wait until dawn, Bear," said Crow, staring out at the night through the spaces between the deadfall. "I feel as if time is pulling at me like a dog would pull at your trousers. Do ye not feel that too?"

"I do," said Bear, "now that you mention it."

"And I feel it too," said Hunter, staring at the fire. "What if they're in peril right now? About to be eaten by some...*thing*."

"Lost is not the same as them tied up in a pot being stirred by a ghoul," said Crow. "Get yer head out of stories and focus on the real world—which is scary enough. They've not the skills to build shelter or navigate this mountain range on their own, and if they'd ducked into the mine—if there is a mine—"

"There is a mine," said Bear. "If memory serves me, it was abandoned because it did not yield, but it exists."

"If they'd gone into it without light, they could have fallen easily into a hole."

"Let's away, then," said Hunter. "Please? I hate to think of them in the dark, alone and afraid."

They left the meager shelter and headed out into the blinding storm, Bear's staff shining against the wall of snow as if that were part of a cave itself. Only their boots below them and their hands before them could be seen in the blizzard, but somehow they made their way across the face, beyond the bald, to where the humans' luck had run out over a decade before.

"And there she is," said Crow, pointing to a dip in the mountainside where stones stood all around like frozen beasts watching the entrance to the mine.

The door looked like a giant's snarling mouth, wrought of ancient water carving at the cold stone. Hunter hurried to it, his staff in hand. "Any footprints have been covered by the snow."

"It's still our best option," said Bear. "We'll press on."

They entered the mine, Bear's staff casting its amber glow about the walls and the floor of the mine. The road down was less a road than a narrow path with crumbling wooden buckets and baskets discarded along the sides and heavy curtains of spiderwebs, some torn in places. Mushrooms sprouted up amid the pebbled floor, and the smell of dark, deep water rose from the darkness ahead.

"I do not like this place," said Hunter.

"Only two places I like are my bed and my table," said Crow. "Get used to it—that's the world."

The howl of the storm gradually subsided as they traveled down into the damp and the dark, and they continued onward for what seemed several miles, the road tapering steadily, the ceiling getting lower, the walls narrowing in. Finally, the three came to a small, wide room where the path twisted around to the right and became sandy, not full of mud or stones.

"This looks like no mine I've ever seen," said Bear.

"How many have you seen, then?" asked Crow.

They walked forward into the sandier tunnel, but slowly, hesitating to look and listen with each half-dozen steps.

"When I left Da's house, I worked for a time in the silver mines at Rudspel. Almost a year. Then, before I was sent here to Delster, I spent time among the monks of Nulhennen, and helped them clear out a spirit that had invaded their ruby mine."

"Sounds awful," said Hunter.

"It was. I will never love being in anything underground that was built by human hands, I'm sorry to say, Hunter. What the mountain builds Herself, or what gentler men and women such as the *swarthe* create, I will gladly walk within, but these mines are a rape of the ground. They do not hold, because She wants them buried."

"*Swarthe*...gentle? I've heard they are brutes."

"So sayeth true brutes," said Crow. "Ye met Bear's acquaintance. Did he seem uncivilized to you?"

"The dwarves are noble people," said Bear. "Their cities are never haunted, nor do they fall. As we fight against the evil that is attacking this mountain, somewhere below our feet, the *swarthe* go about their quiet days, studying, building, cultivating, untouched by our troubles. Huil protects them. She always has and always will."

"So why don't we go seek shelter with the *swarthe*, then?" asked Hunter.

"It takes a very long time and much proof of good character to be granted entry into the lands of the dwarves," said Bear. "Stop now. Listen."

They did so.

"I hear running water," said Crow.

###

"I see someone, Shuck," said Mink. She was at the kitchen window, watching the woods above, semi-illumined by the pre-dawn light. A small, black figure was hurrying through the snowstorm, down the mountain. "Oh, Shuck, I'm frightened."

The black dog growled and rose up on his hind legs, his great forepaws on either side of the window as he looked through the glass. Then he wagged the stump of his tail and barked.

"Well, I suppose that's a good sign, then," said Mink. She went to the door and pushed it open against the snow to lean out and call to the stranger. "Hello!" The wind stole away her small voice. "Who is it?"

The figure jogged through the snow drifts on strong legs, a cloak over their head obscuring their face from Mink's view. They rounded the house and appeared at the door. It was Alaric.

###

"Your brother asked me to come keep you some company," Alaric said, sitting in the kitchen, his cloak hung over a chair before the hearth, his boots below it. Mink had brought blankets to drape over him; Alaric was close to freezing when he'd made it to Bear's door. "Not that your company isn't delightful, or a man would need to be asked overly much." He scratched Shuck's shaggy head. "But it's wild aboveground this day, and I worry for my brother's family."

"Have they found anything of the children? Their tracks or belongings?"

Alaric moved to speak, but was silent. Then he said, "Their path, in theory, yes. Bear and your sister and Bear's apprentice are following them, possibly to one of the smaller caves. It would make sense if the children sought shelter from the storm." He eased out from under the blankets, set them across the chair and walked to the kitchen window to watch the storm outside. "I'm glad to be here, lady. You could use another soul to keep company with you, through this."

"I'm glad you're here as well, sirrah," said Mink, also watching the storm through the glass.

###

Asher opened the manacle and eased it off Jump High's ankle. The *reffke* kat stamped her foot a few times and shook her leg. Her skirts shivered around her as she put weight on the bruised foot, flexing her long, black toes.

"Is she hurt?" asked Asher of Medie, who signed to her, and the kat signed back.

"No, it just didn't feel good, is all." Medie looked toward the tunnels. "Oh no, Asher, I hear something."

Jumps High looked too and turned to flee back into the tunnel from which the other three had come. Quickly reached for his sister, signing desperately to her, *no, the others.*

Asher could hear the voices now too, strange and growling, uttering words he couldn't understand. He took the sword and wedged it between the edge of the grate and the stone.

"Help me lift it out," he whispered loudly, and the other children did. It was incredibly heavy, of the thickest iron, but eventually they pried it up from the hole in the floor and set it down.

"Now what?" asked Medie, looking into the darkness of the hole.

"Now we go down," said Asher as he sheathed the sword and slipped it back into his pack. Medie signed to the *reffke* siblings.

Shouts and growls filled one of the corridors—they couldn't tell which one—and the children stood around the hole, looking into the darkness and at each other, stuck by fear and panic, until Medie at last dropped down into it, and they heard a splash. Quickly and Jumps High followed her, and last fell Asher.

The children looked up from the shallow, cold water in which they stood, and saw the small square of flickering light above them grow dark. There were eyes there, in the space, looking all around—bulbous, staring, leering eyes, turning around independently of each other, baring the whites as if touched with madness or great fear—but the tongues that lolled from the mouths were not afraid as they wrapped around the yellow fangs, and the great nostrils were bold as they sniffed, sniffed at the air below.

A tongue so strange, it sounded as if someone were speaking backwards while gargling water, said soft, hungry things, and Medie closed her eyes.

"I can see the words float by, as if they are tiny ships, on black water."

"What are they saying?" whispered Asher.

"Running…meat…down…get."

"We must away."

They splashed in a direction without question, deeper into the stink and into the dark, away from the hungry faces.

"Keep going," hissed Asher, running, his boots soaked, his socks soaked, the ends of his trousers soaked, and his head pounding because the smell of this underground maze singed his sinuses as if with smoke. He was sick and in pain from the scrapes and cuts of the sharp walls against his shins and knees, and his hands and elbows, but he could hear the howls and the inhalings of the creatures behind them. They had to keep going.

"Don't stop," he urged, until he slipped on a slick, moss-covered stone in the water-logged tunnel and felt his chin hit the floor, and then all was black.

He felt hands upon him, lifting him up, but he could not speak or stand.

"Jumps High has you, Asher," whispered Medie. "They are almost past us. I think they cannot smell us down here, where everything smells so foul."

Asher slumped against the strong arms of the *reffke* kat and nodded. He could hear large, clumsy steps out there in the dark, splashing in the filthy water.

"This tunnel continues on," said Medie. "After they've gone, we're going to make for the surface. The floor leads up, and that's a good sign."

Asher nodded again. He felt a cool hand against his brow and saw it was Quickly.

The steps of the creatures faded away. They had missed their quarry.

As the children headed up through the tunnel, the standing water eventually failed and the floor became dry, covered in places with a glowing moss. The air became warmer. Jumps High sniffed at the air and stopped. Asher felt strong enough to stand on his own.

"What's the matter?" he asked.

Jumps High signed to Medie.

"She feels we shouldn't go this way," said Medie.

"Does she care to say why?" asked Asher, already walking forward, ahead of the group.

"No," hissed Medie. "But I think we should listen to her!"

"I must get us out of this place, Persistence," said Asher. "And that's not going to happen if we stand still in the dark."

The children watched him walk up into the light, then they heard him curse.

"What is it?" Medie asked, running after him with the *reffke* behind her.

They followed the tunnel around to the right, and came out into the room. Asher was standing there, looking at the grate and the open hole in the center of the floor. They were back where they'd started.

"Let's away," said Asher. "Pick one of the other tunnels!"

Medie chose the tunnel on the left, Quickly the one on the right, but the kit backed away, yipping in fear, as the entrance was suddenly blocked by a hideous form. It looked like the twisted *nicht-ogren* from old tales. Medie called for the others to follow her, but she only got a few steps away when two more of the creatures appeared in the left-hand tunnel. One of the ogren grabbed Jumps High and snapped an iron collar about her neck, which was connected to a length of chain.

They were blocked in, and the ogren were herding them down the left-hand tunnel, putting huge hands to their backs and causing them to stumble as they hurried before their captors to an unknown fate.

After a while, Asher unshouldered his pack, slowly and quietly, then pretended to stumble as he fished the seed-pod-sheathed sword. Dropping the pack to the floor, he slashed the closest ogre down its broad, naked back. The beast turned around, roaring in pain and swinging its bulging arm towards his head. Asher ducked and ran the sword across the creature's meaty thigh. The ogre stumbled and snatched at Asher's arm, but not before Asher was able to swing around at the next nearest of his captors.

The other children began to fight also. Quickly scrambled up the back of one of the *nicht-ogren* and tore at his head with his sharp claws, and Jumps High ran about the legs of one to trip it with the chains of her leash. Medie found a sizable rock on the floor and bashed at the kneecaps of the one holding the chain, and that ogre fell to its knees.

"I see the cooking pot!" yelled Asher. "They mean to eat us! Have at them stoutly," he shouted as he spun about in a frenzy of terrified, slashing cuts and desperate hackings, until great arms pinned his own to his sides and a giant hand squeezed his. His eyes flooded with tears from the pain and the clang of the sword falling to the floor. He watched on as other ogres lifted Medie, Quickly, and Jumps High off their feet and slung them over shoulders like sacks, hands covering mouths or pulling at hair to elicit screams, and they were taken away from the room with the great iron pot and down a different corridor.

After what seemed a terribly long time being so close to the foul creatures, the children were unceremoniously dumped into a wide pit. A ceiling of bars was slid across it, and as the dust settled in the air so that the torchlight from above could illuminate the room, the children saw other shapes in the darkness.

There were two human boys; Asher walked to them. "I know you," he said as they stared at him. "Leisel. Gareth. Right?"

The boys nodded, and both burst into tears, throwing their arms around him as he embraced them in kind.

"It's going to be all right, men," said Asher in the deepest voice he could muster. "We're going to find a way to get out of here."

"There is one more," said Medie. She walked to a corner of the pit from which a faint light emanated. "Do you see her?"

The *reffke* children backed away from the light, obviously afraid, but Asher—when he didn't allow his eyes to focus—could just barely see the outline of a small girl. She looked to be a living silhouette, a person standing between the viewer and the sun, but as if their body had been taken and only the outline of the sunlight remained.

"Her name is Sanandra," said Medie. "She told me."

"From the house? From the diary?"

Medie nodded. "She's been here a very long time."

"You know what?" said Asher. Medie looked at him in the gloom-light. "Had this hunk of gold banging around in my pocket for days. Probably got a bruise on my leg because of it. When we get out of here—and we will, get out of here—I'm showing it to Da. Maybe it's worth so much money that we could travel to anywhere in the world that we'd like to."

"That sounds like a dream," said Medie.

Asher pulled the nugget from his pocket and puzzled at it. The thing upon his palm was tiny, and white.

It was a tooth, stained with old blood. With a gasp, he dropped it to the floor and held his hand as if it had been scalded.

###

It should have been dull, waiting and sitting, just the three of them—the *saylie*, the *swarthe* and the dog, yet they could not pry themselves from the rear windows of Bear's great room because the storm seemed to whip itself into a greater level of fury with each passing hour. The snow had, at first, at dawn, lashed the windows as if it were made of sand, so fine was it, and icy. By noon, the sheets of precipitation sped sideways past the house, heading straight down the mountain to the town.

"It's as if She's sending Her rage down upon them," said Alaric, standing beside the chair on which Mink sat. "But why? What have they done?"

Mink breathed out loudly, and Shuck lifted his heavy head to regard her. "They can be wretched."

"All things can be so," said Alaric. "Does that mean they deserve death?"

"Death comes," said Mink. "Death comes whether things deserve it or not." She got up from her chair and walked loudly across Bear's uncovered floors to the kitchen.

"I'm sorry, m'lady," said Alaric.

"No, you're not," said Mink from the kitchen. "And neither am I."

Alaric sat in the chair, scratching the top of Shuck's shaggy head. "Well, I tried to be courteous." Shuck eased himself out from under Alaric's touch and padded away, towards the front room. Alaric watched him go.

"Do I stink?" asked the dwarf, sniffing his shirt. He stared at the windows, the snow obscuring the view of the outside world completely. "Mink," he called to her. "The snow here on the glass of your windows. It seems strange."

"How so?" answered Mink from the kitchen.

Alaric drew closer, his face inches from the panes. "The flakes seem to be changing shape. Elongating. And there are peculiar sounds."

Mink came from the kitchen and stood just behind Alaric. She, too, watched the glass.

The sound from the other side of the window was almost like a mournfully blowing wind, but quieter—so tiny it were as if it came from the snowflakes themselves, not unlike a soft-sighing, then a crinkling, and something disturbingly similar to whispery, tiny screams. The flakes began to look like white spiders, with jointed legs sharp, all stiff-haired, and tapping at the glass.

The tiny, faint screams rose in volume, like waves of a windstorm rising to the sky, until the creatures, or ice-patterns—it was difficult to tell—were emitting howls louder than the gale outside, loud enough that they might break bones with the sound, should they break the glass and enter the room.

Alaric and Mink ran from the windows as they shattered. The tiny pieces of glass moved as if they'd grown legs and followed them, *tinking* across the floor in a flurry of focus, angry, determined, thirsting.

Alaric hefted the door to the basement back against its frame as the snow-spiders slapped into the wood, *tink, tink, tink, tink*. He undid his belt in a flourish, whipped it from his trousers, and spun the thick material about the door handle, tethering it to the banister of the stairs.

"Lad," he said to Shuck. "If dogs pray, do so, now."

The dog curled its lip and growled. Alaric stared.

"What the fuck's your problem with me, then?"

Shuck barked and bared his teeth.

"All right? Let's have it out. I'll not stand on ceremony before a common beast."

The dog lunged at him, aiming for his throat.

Mink screamed and begged the dog to spare him, but Alaric stood there, at once torn between duty to Bear's sister and absolute defiance against such a horridly mannered creature. But then Shuck fell back upon his massive haunches and hung his head.

"Do you smell that?" said Alaric, his eyes fixed on some distant point.

"Smell what?" asked Mink, glancing at the door of the basement, trembling. "What are you talking about?"

"It's a…familiar scent. An absence scent—ozone, black pepper, intent mingled with summation."

"I don't understand," said Mink.

"I know this smell. *I know it.*"

"Please, I'm sorry, I—"

"A condition has been met!"

The dog exploded.

###

Mink saw the darkness flood the already gloomy light of the basement. She turned and ducked behind a short wall that Bear had built to store his tools upon, and gasped as the wall shuddered and leaned; the air popped and expanded outward.

Then there was silence.

She heard Alaric gasp too, through the pounding of the silence and through the wooden wall.

"Well, I say, then!"

"Yes, you might say. I'm sorry, but I needed to get all of that over with, and soon."

Mink crept out from behind the wall and saw a naked man, beautiful of build and firm of form, hair the color of tarnished gold matted and damp upon his head.

She averted her eyes, blushing.

"So?" said Alaric, his back turned to the madness up the stairs, his muscular arms folded. "You're *human*?" He looked all about the basement; there was no evidence of gore, or flesh, or anything that would have occurred upon an explosion of a creature Shuck's size, or even the size of a rabbit, and the dog had been worth at least fifty rabbits.

"Yes," said the person who was once Shuck. "I've got a question too. Anybody got a bit of spare clothing? I'll take anything. I can work naked, but I'd prefer a little modesty if possible."

"I imagine you would," said Alaric, looking at once-Shuck's endowments. He eased off his boots, untied his trousers and tossed them to the man. "They'll be short on you, but take them. I've additional garments beneath."

"That ye do," said the person, staring square at Alaric's inheritance, visible through his clothes.

"Dress quickly," said the dwarf, biting a grin. "Death approaches."

"I have a cure for death. Its name is Wystan," said the human. Mink watched as he climbed towards the faltering door of the basement, the ice-spiders gnawing their triumph through the wood. She felt their abrupt demise upon the blast of the heat and light emitted from Wystan's opened palms.

"Not, sayeth I! Do not be, do not be, you will not be evermore for I am more than thee and I am commanding you to go," he cried, standing on the third to topmost step as the melting, cracking ice-spiders swarmed over him. *"Back to what made you, back to what bade you—go back!"*

Wystan collapsed forward across the uppermost stairs, and Mink came to him before he fell into oblivion.

###

"Where am I?" he asked, less than an hour later. "Who am I?"

"You are Wystan, once-was-a-dog," said Alaric. He held the man in his arms, his eyes darkly fearful, for the stranger had taken many bites from the ice-spiders directly upon his naked chest, and then he had fallen. "What do you remember?"

"I remember…that a bitter witch desired me and I declined their offer. And they laughed, ever much, and cursed me into the form of a black hound, and then said I must do many kind deeds for the children of Night, until I regained my born-form."

"Is your form accurate? Do you feel yourself?"

Wystan looked down at his body, at his arms, and touched his bearded face. "It is, and I do."

"Well, I suppose your quota was filled, last of all by not tearing out my throat," said Alaric, chuckling. "And I do thank you for that."

Wystan smiled weakly at the dwarf and traced a fingertip across Alaric's neck. "The pleasure was mine. Between you and I," his voice lowered to a whisper, "I'd never have bitten you. Not out of anger. Was simply the last of the curse needed lifting."

"Next time, ask," said Alaric, tensing at the man's touch but not pulling away from it.

"I will."

"Meanwhile," said Mink, crouched behind them and staring up at the gaping, ice-covered wreck that was once her brother's great room, "the house is filling with snow."

"Then I imagine we'd best make for your own house, mistress, until the storm calms its fury."

"All right. Then I'll fetch some of Bear's clothes for Wystan, as well as his summer boots. You're shorter and more slender, but they'll keep ye warm just the same."

"Thank you," said Wystan, starting to shake, his skin most pale around the tiny bites of the spiders.

"The day's just begun," said Mink breathlessly as they hurried up the stairs. "And I'm sure that I can't take much more of this."

"You'd be surprised at how hardy you actually are, mistress," said Alaric, waiting for her as she ran up the stairs.

"Bear's going to have an awful lot of housework when he gets back," said Wystan.

"More than just housework," said Alaric. "A house that suffers such an attack of evil—"

"Requires prayer and candles," said Wystan.

"Cleansing," added Alaric.

"And can Bear not do that himself?" asked Mink, returning from the upstairs with armfuls of clothing. "Being a pastor?"

"He's skilled with fighting evil in the domain of his goddess," said Wystan. "I don't think an ill house is within his area of expertise."

"But by the time this is all over," said Alaric, "you'll both need to find someone who possesses such skills. Because this is not chance, and these are not run-of-the-mill creatures. This is a sickness that's pouring forth." Alaric carefully removed the portrait of Solace from the mantel and tucked it under his arm to take with them.

"What could have made Her so upset?" asked Mink.

"I wish I could determine, but here and now, we must resign ourselves to matters of defense. Or escape. Does Bear keep beasts of burden?"

"He's got a horse and a donkey," said Mink. "And somewhere—several goats."

"Well, none of us can ride a goat," said Wystan, "but we might make a good run for it on a horse and a donkey."

"Are you comfortable with riding, Mink?" asked Alaric.

"I, well…I'm not sure."

"Wystan?"

"I am."

"Then you can take the horse and carry her. I'll take the donkey, if it comes to that. Until then, what weaponry does your brother keep?"

"All his tools are back down there, in the basement," said Mink.

"I'll go and fetch them," said Wystan. "I know what to look for."

###

Wystan had been gone for some time, and Alaric and Mink had left for the other house and were now seated on the rug before the fire in the great room, watching the windows and listening to the storm rage beyond the house's walls. As old and well-built as the home was, it seemed as fragile as an egg's shell in this weather, and they could hear the roof being sucked by the wind and the walls and windows rattle. Everything sounded as if it were alive; every moment seemed like some new terror had come to prey upon them.

Wystan came in through the front door, his arms laden with treasures, which he spread out on the floor before the *saylie* and the *swarthe*.

"Apologies to your brother for raiding his cache," said the man. "We've got two swords here, some very sharp knives, sheaths for all but—" he slid one of the knives to the right "—this blade and a flintlock rifle."

"Were that there was more than one powder weapon," said Alaric, "so that we'd not have to get so close to any beasties, but these'll do. Good work, lad."

Wystan winked at the dwarf, who grinned.

"Pick your poison, sirrah," said the human.

Alaric chose the smaller of the swords and ran his fingertip down the length of the blade.

Mink chose two knives to match the one Crow had loaned her.

Wystan strapped the larger sword to himself and walked away with the flintlock to examine it. "Clean as a baby's bottom, this," he remarked.

"Bear's fastidious about his things," said Mink.

"I wonder how he's doing?" muttered Alaric, walking to one of the barricaded windows. "I worry for him, and the human boy."

"And what of Crow?"

"I do not worry for Crow," said Alaric.

"Nor do I," said Wystan. "That one's better than all of us put together."

"And this you observed in your dog state?" said Mink.

"Aye."

Suddenly, they heard the crash of a tree coming down beneath the weight of the storm. Alaric opened the front door of Bear's house to have a look. The whiteout was tremendous; he could barely see six feet in front of him.

"Don't go out there, lad," said Wystan. "In fact, I wonder how we'll manage to find our way to the barn should we decide to make for town."

"I doubt going into town would be the best idea," said Alaric, ducking back inside, already shivering. "It seems the storm is headed that way."

There was another crash, and then a third.

"That troubles me," said Wystan.

"There are so many old trees in this forest," said Mink. "Bear told me they get a lot of rain here, and it makes the wood soft, so when there's a great wind, trees fall."

"Snow and ice would coat such trees, making them heavy," said Alaric, watching out the window.

"True," said Wystan quietly.

"The snow has stopped."

Mink and Wystan watched Alaric leave the porch of Bear's house and walk through the heavy snow that had coated the yard. The drifts were as high as the dwarf's waist in some spots, but with much muttered cursing and struggling, he gained the outer yard that began the road back to town, and looked up to the mountain and the forest.

In between, the trees were shorter, misshapen pillars of snow, and the sky was clearing.

He turned to go back to the house, but Wystan was already behind him.

"Smaller trees?" said Wystan, gesturing to the oddities above.

"That were not there just a half-day ago?" said Alaric, turning back to regard them. "And the storm—she has stopped." The sun was shining in a mostly blue sky now.

"And he burns as if it was the midst of his day," noticed Wystan.

"When he should be setting down to his supper," said Alaric.

Wystan crouched, staring up at the mountainside, and sniffed the air.

"So I've a question," said Alaric.

"Have at it."

"Did you do dog-like things before you spent your time as a dog, or do you do dog-like things now, still, *because* of the time you spent as a dog?"

"I'd growl right now, but no, that's not my habit," said Wystan.

"How long were you cursed?"

"I'm not sure," said Wystan, standing. "The last I remembered as a man, I was fleeing the witch's village on horseback. The moon was red. The air was warm, and the fields were green."

"Last time we had a blood moon in summer was…" Alaric whispered to himself, counting. "The Year of the Lilies."

Wystan stared at him, his mouth ajar and his eyes clouded over as if in anger.

"I'm sorry," said Alaric.

"Nearly ten years lost," said Wystan.

Alaric put his hand on Wystan's shoulder, and the human looked at it, then at him, and grinned—just a small, grim smile, but one nonetheless.

"Should have asked," he said.

"Oh, I am—"

"I'm only joking," said Wystan. "Not had a man's touch in ten years, I'd say—*don't ask*, just do."

Alaric chuckled and ran his hand over his own face, trying to suppress a grin.

The mountainsidc rumbled.

###

Mink had stepped out onto her porch to look past the men talking, out at her yard, Bear's gardens, and the mountainside. She was astounded by the depth of the show—it made the grown men look as little children. Then she noticed the odd shapes among the trees—twisted, lumpen pillars of snow and ice, a hillside of forms—nearly forty of them. The sun cast down now from a too-bright sky, and she stepped out into the trodden path the men had made in the snow, breathing the crisp air, feeling the warmth of the sun despite the horrid cold rising up the land.

She heard Walter whinny, and the donkey Alan bray as well.

Then she heard moaning, as if the wind was whipping through a narrow, stony canyon. She'd heard that sound once before in her life, when she and Medie were taking the boat from Bran to Delster and they'd passed by the phenomenon known as the Viper's Teeth: pillars and ribbons of stone, carved by the river on its way down from icy Herronhorn, a mountain taller than Huil's own peaks and always covered by a cap of snow. The wind blowing through the Viper's Teeth sounded like living things, mournful things, things coming down from the mountain to hunt or, perhaps at night, to haunt the dreams of men and women.

But they were not on the river this day. There was no stone here as there was at the feet of Herronhorn, and the sunlight was suddenly waning as bleak clouds rolled in. The moans became screams—hawk-like, louder, as if the trees were screaming too. The horse and the donkey struck the walls of their stable, braying in terror, and Mink ran to them, her knives in their scabbards slapping her legs as she leapt over and through the snow.

"Back to the house!" the men yelled to each other, and just before she unlatched the barn door, she saw Wystan and Alaric leaping as she'd done, scrambling through the snow to gain the porch, then ducking inside. Her hands shook as she lifted the heavy bar and pulled at the door, but the snow held it fast. She put a boot up on the wall, pulling with all of her might, and at last managed to open it just enough for her to squeeze inside.

Mink untethered Walter and the donkey, and soon after heard rifle shots and the men yelling and that strange, windy scream. She wondered if she'd not be trampled by her own brother's animals on this bright, strange day.

At last she managed to hold Walter still, long enough to mount him, and with the donkey beside him, they ran to the barn door, but then Walter was rearing and screaming, and Mink knew she'd failed utterly. Were she to jump down and attempt to push the door open, she'd be kicked by the panicking horse; were she to remain on his back, they'd be stuck here, waiting for the monsters to tear the wood from the walls and get inside and have at them.

The donkey then beat against the door with his hooves and busted through one board, opening the door a foot more. Alaric was there, wide-eyed, glancing in.

"Get back!" Mink shouted as the donkey reared up again.

###

Wystan ran back into Bear's house just as Mink was fleeing it, and he paused to caution her but saw she was making for the barn, so he continued inside. When he stepped back out into the snow from the porch, wild-eyed, the sword strapped to him and with flintlock and bags in his hands, he set the rifle's stock on a place upon the snowy ground he'd trampled down, loaded the charge, held the cloth over the muzzle, and lined the tube containing the ball. Pushing it down with the rod, he watched the beasts made of snow and ice step towards the houses.

Their movements were jerky and unnatural, and they screamed as they walked, crumbling and trailing ice until the snow around their feet crept back up onto their twisted bodies, again and again. Wystan aimed the rifle at the closest one and fired. Its misshapen head exploded mid-scream.

Wystan was breathing hard and fast now as he loaded the gun again and shot the next nearest one, then again, until the first four were mere piles of snow, but the other creatures were jerking past them, still gaining the house.

"You can't get all of them this way, and I question the efficacy of swords," shouted Alaric. "Can you not cast against them?"

"Against nothing bigger than I am tall, generally," said Wystan, firing again, his face gleaming with sweat. He repeated the process over and over, wincing at a shoulder he hadn't realized—or remembered—was sore from a night in town when a drunken villager had kicked him.

There were still thirty or so snow-creatures shambling towards Wystan when he set the rifle down in disgust—not at the weapon, for it was well-made, but at himself for even thinking he could win this fight.

"You idiot," he growled.

He ran at the nearest monster and cut clean through with his sword so that the top half fell over and sat with a *flump* beside the second half. Before the two halves could recombine or sprout hidden legs of their own, he stuck the sword into the snow and raised his hands at the two halves, calling words of hex and melting them into two small circles of bare grass. He grabbed the sword up and ran to the next monster.

###

Mink tried to calm Walter, who had driven himself into a greater frenzy and was running the length of the barn, turning, and running back again. The donkey looked to be preparing to break his own legs against the stout barn doors, but Alaric, in a moment when the donkey had seemed to take a few steps back, finally hefted the door open several feet with a mighty pull, enough for horse, *saylie*, and ass to thunder through. He leapt up on the donkey as it passed him, and they clumsily rode towards Wystan, who looked as if he was being tackled by three of the ice monsters.

A great flash emitted from the snowy heap that covered Wystan, and the man jumped free of his oppressors and reached for Mink's tiny hand as Walter struggled by. Wystan leapt up behind Mink as the remainder of the snow-horde gained the yard, the animals leaping past them in terror and running for the road beyond Mink's house. Alaric turned to watch the creatures also turn and, to his horror, saw them begin to shamble slowly after them.

The horse and donkey made quick but clumsy, panicked work of the snow-choked mountain road. Finding easier footing on the broad, flat road into Delster, they sped along, the screams of the creatures growing faint in the distance as the road met the river and paced alongside it.

"Where are they?" asked Alaric.

Wystan guided Walter closer to the donkey as they slowed their animals' paces and looked at the dwarf.

"The people?"

"Look at the houses, brother," Wystan said.

"They are covered in ice."

They stopped the animals, and Mink dismounted, struggling over the deep snow to the milliner's where she'd bought the fabrics for Medie's dresses their first day in town. She stared at the door. It was completely covered with ice. Not even the handle protruded from the slick, clear coating, and the windows were covered as well. A thick sheet of ice ran up over the house and around the sides. There was no break in it.

"Chimney's not smoking," said Wystan.

"Maybe they'd gone home before the storm," suggested Alaric.

"She let me and Medie out the back that day," said Mink. "Her home *is* this house. An apartment in the back and rooms up the stairs, I believe. Three stories."

"It could be warm enough in there, with this ice, to not have the fire going," said Wystan.

"But for how long?" asked Alaric. "Eventually it will chill. We keep perishable food in ice rooms in my city. We do that because it keeps things near to freezing."

"Well, let's break through this, then," said Wystan, his face pale.

"I'll try with the blade," said Alaric, first slashing across and down with the sword, then trying to stab at the ice. The sword glanced away with each stroke.

"Did you pick up my brother's rifle?" asked Mink. "I saw it in the snow."

"Yes, ma'am, I did," said Wystan. "It's tied to the saddle." He walked over to Walter, fetched the flintlock and loaded it up.

"Aim for the door handle, brother," said Alaric.

The outermost layer of ice blew away, showering them in crystalline cold before the bullet glanced off the metal handle and buried itself in a porch pillar.

"I might've been more careful with that," said Wystan. "Sorry."

"None of us are harmed so," said Alaric. "Mink, may I have one of your knives?" She handed him one, and he began to chip away at the ice; after a few moments, the handle was completely exposed.

"Now, let us pull," said Wystan, and he and Alaric tried, awkwardly holding onto the handle together. Alaric put a boot up on the slippery wall of the house, but the door would not move.

"Might as well be encased in lead, this place."

"I don't see smoke rising from any place at all," said Mink, looking down the street.

"Only one," said Wystan, pointing. "There."

Mink looked. "I think I see something. On the door."

The men led the animals down the deserted street, and Mink ran up to the house, wiping at the ice that covered the door and staring through it.

"What do ye see, m'lady?" asked Alaric, tying Walter to the rail in front of the porch.

"A posy," said Mink. "A house-blessing posy. This, I'm fairly certain, is Hunter's family's home."

"I can see someone in the window!" shouted Wystan, wiping at the ice and sniffing.

"You can smell through that?" asked Alaric.

"No, I can smell next to nothing," said Wystan. "Bad habit, though."

"Old habit—not necessarily a bad one. I see her, Mink. The lady of the house."

"She's alive, bless us," said Mink. "Wystan, can you not magic the door?"

Wystan mimicked the height and width of the house with his arms, shaking his head.

"Only things smaller than him."

"Ach, how typically manly," said Mink. "But I do think that, perhaps, Hunter's mother can assist."

"How so?" said Alaric, waving at the form in the window.

"She's a witch."

Alaric glanced at Wystan.

"I've nothing against the craft as a rule," Wystan said. "If Bear thinks well of her, I'm sure she's a fine person."

"Last chance, before we attempt to free her from this icy prison," said Alaric.

"I stand firm in my beliefs, my friend."

"All right. Getting back to your ability to bedevil things smaller than you…"

Wystan turned and grinned at Alaric, as the dwarf stood half a foot shorter.

"If you ever try, I'll sew your ears to your eyelids. That's a *swarthe* specialty," said Alaric, trying to suppress a laugh and not succeeding.

"Mean*while*," said Mink, slapping her small, brown palm against the thick ice that coated the door. "To the task at hand?"

"It's not because of my own choice, you see," said Wystan. "It's not for any sort of…*intimidation* thing. It's simply that I've only been out of my apprenticeship just four years. That's not very long. In time, I might have the chops to bedevil a mountain—"

Alaric shook his head and waved his finger.

"Right, I'm sorry. Very poor choice of words. But you get my meaning."

"Why don't you just *try* the door, because it's only a bit taller than you?" said Mink.

"She's got a point," said Alaric. "Perhaps only the door and not the house entire?"

"I can try. Stand back a ways. Motion for the lady of the house to stand back as well."

Wystan steepled his fingers, going down on one knee and bowing his head. He cupped his hands and breathed deeply into them, then turned the palms skyward, slowly balling them into fists. He repeated these movements, then repeated them once more, and stood.

"She's backing away," said Alaric.

Wystan felt the push and the pressure in his forehead, then down through his chest and into his arms, followed by that awkward sizzle of heat and fire that ran both out his hands and to his groin and always made him worry he'd piss himself. But the blasts soon pooled in his palms, which became immediately damp, and he sent the blasts to slap against the ice-coated door with the sound of a hundred knives embedding themselves in wood. He opened his eyes.

The fire he'd let fly was scurrying all around the door as if it were twin gatherings of lightning beetles, and the fire-motes traveled up, then back down and all around, melting the ice until the bare wood of the door was fully exposed.

The door opened, and Hunter's mother stood there, a dousing wand in her hand, her pale eyes wide and frightened.

"Thank the gods you've come," she said.

###

The children huddled in the curve of the odd pit-room, shoulder to shoulder on the driest part of the floor, and talked of things that did not remind them of their current predicament. They spoke of school and laughed at jokes they'd heard there; they spoke of feats of skill and courage and told funny stories or shared strange facts their parents had told them. Gareth told a story of the huge trout he'd caught a summer ago and how it nearly pulled him into a stream. Leisel told them about a glider he'd made of wood and paper wings, and how he'd sailed it through the air from a rooftop and nearly lost it in the river, which was a quarter of a mile from the building by his not yet fully matured boot-steps.

The *reffke* watched and listened to the words, and signed to Medie. They were learning the language of men and women, though their mouths were not formed to be able to speak it. Medie signed encouragement to them, and the fox-kids chirped, slapping their tails against the ground.

"I ain't ever met a fox-kind before," said Leisel, extending his hand to Quickly, who took it into his own. "Feels so strange, like shaking a dog's paw."

"They are brother and sister," said Asher. "Their mum is out there somewhere, worrying for them."

"Our mums are too," said the town-boys.

The children stopped talking then; it was bound to come up eventually, but the mention of their troubles had rendered the group sad and silent.

In time, one of the ogres returned and knelt beside the pit to lift a hinged part in the bars of the ceiling. It lowered a bucket down on a rope, and this was filled with very hard bread, followed by a second bucket filled with water. That bucket hit the ground a bit too hard, and the water splashed up out of it towards the ogre's hand. It hissed and pulled the limb back before the water could reach it.

"Let the bread soak a while," said Leisel. "Just a little while. Pour it into your cupped hand like this." He showed the others.

"Sometimes I will break a bucket and hide the pieces," said Gareth. "And sometimes I kill rats for us, and we cook them down here."

"They don't seem to get cross over that," said Leisel. "I don't think they care."

"What are they?" asked Asher. "They look to be…but they cannot be—"

"*Nicht-ogren*," said Medie. "Sanandra said so."

The children looked at her, astounded, the two town-boys more so than the others.

"You can hear her?" gasped Gareth.

"She hears and sees," said Asher.

"You're a witch?" asked Leisel.

"Not that I'm aware of," said Medie with a sharp look to the boy. "Never cast a spell in my life."

"There's nothing wrong with witches anyhow," said Asher. "Every village should have at least one or two."

"Weren't any when we lived in town," said Leisel. "No one would have cared for that."

"Huh?" said Asher. "Sure. Until someone gets sick and what they're sick with can't be cured by sleep or brandy. Then you're gonna be mighty thankful you've got a witch among you."

"I guess that's true," said Gareth.

"His baby sister almost died once," said Leisel. "Bad fever."

Medie gasped.

"It's all right, Persistence," said Asher. "It doesn't hurt me much anymore."

"What doesn't?" asked Gareth.

"My mum died that way," said Asher. "There wasn't a witch, not that we knew of."

"I'm sorry," said Gareth.

"Sorry, mate," said Leisel. "Didn't know *saylies* could pass from fevers."

"We're just men and women," said Asher, standing up and looking to the barred ceiling. "Men and women who live a bit longer, usually. Men and women with weird-shaped ears."

"They're not that weird to me," said Gareth. "Look at this birthmark on my chest—*that's* weird." He lifted his filthy blouse to reveal a vivid, scarlet blotch that spread across his sternum.

The children admired it for a while, until the heavy footfalls of an ogre made them hug against the walls once again.

"It's talking to us," whispered Medie.

"That I can hear, yes," said Asher.

"Can ye figure it out?" asked Leisel. "He said you hear things."

"I can hear things unspoken, or deeply spoken, and usually of decent folk or creatures. But this thing, I guess—" her voice trembled "—is neither. I heard it thinking before, when we were down in the water, but I suppose its thoughts were stronger then."

"Maybe there's a good reason we're here and he's up there," offered Asher.

"What?" said Gareth. "No, there isn't. There was another boy here, he was older. He'd been here a long time. Poor chap. Then they took him. The night they brought him back, he was all cut up and broken. Then they took him again, and he never came back."

"How, cut up?" asked Asher. "How broken?"

"Like he'd been stomped by things. Slashed by things."

Leisel said, "Like he'd been in a fool's fight at school when the teacher forgets to check on everyone outside and ten fellows fight one."

"But worse than that," said Gareth, his dirt-streaked face stricken with grief.

"Worse than that," agreed Leisel, putting his arm around Gareth's shoulders.

"I have to," said Medie, suddenly in a panic and looking around.

"Have to what?" asked Gareth, looking at her tear-streaked face. "What's wrong?"

"*I have to*," said Medie, and she signed to Jumps High.

The *reffke* kat softly clapped her dark hands at the boys to get their attention and lifted her leg in pantomime.

"Oh," said Gareth. "We use the other side of the pit. We'll all turn around. We use the bucket rim—it's metal—to dig it over if we need to shit. I'm sorry, girl. I promise we'll plug our ears."

"And our noses too," said Leisel.

"I only have water to release, thanks," said Medie stepping gingerly across the shadowed floor to the other side. "Promise you won't look."

"Cross our hearts and hope for death."

"Which I'm sure we'll get anyway, but still, we promise."

#

Hours later, the ogres returned, and pushed the ceiling completely off the pit.

The children trembled, each of them quaking as if taken by a great fever, though in reality they were freezing cold with fear. They huddled together like goats—goats who knew the butcher's knife was for their necks. Medie let loose a single sob, and then all of the children were crying.

The ogres heard this and laughed, deep and wet, like footsteps in the mud at the bottom of a cave.

One of the ogres dropped down into the pit and reached out his hand, beckoning the children with a fat finger, *come.* The children pressed together even more tightly, shaking their heads, their voices pitching up into a panic, sounding like pigs now, little pigs before the wolf.

Asher broke from the group and walked to the ogre.

"Take me," he said, his voice shaking. "Leave them."

"I'll take all of you," said the strange, unexpectedly whispery voice of the ogre. *"Come to my hand."*

"You must give them a guarantee, or they will not come."

"I do not care if they are willing or not. I will grab them, and I will take them."

Asher's heart pounded in his ears and his eyes, and he struggled against the blind fear that wanted to steal his breath.

"If you break their bones, they will not taste as good. If you hurt the animal before it gains the stew pot, the flesh tastes sour."

The ogre laughed again, and the reek from its crusted mouth was tremendous. *"We aren't to eat them,"* it said. *"They are for better things."*

Asher's eyes widened.

"What," he swallowed. "sort of better things?"

"Games of chance. Do you want to leave this place?"

Asher finally got his terror under control, swallowed again, and straightened up.

"Is there a chance that we might, should we play your games?"

"*Yes,*" said the ogre, reaching for him.

###

"My lord," said the Voice. "I hear you weeping."

He to whom the eyes belonged rolled upon his belly and reached out a slender, pale hand to the Voice, grabbing weakly at its shadow-skin, its silken hair. His thoughts were shudderingly lonely, lost.

"What would have you smile again, my twin, my commander?"

The muscles shuddered in a great stretch, and he felt the cold of his domain for the first time. He felt death settling over him like a brine of ice.

"Contests," said the Voice. "We may have them yet again. We can light the fires of the arena, rouse the beasts, squeals of pigs, bloody-bones. The pain of the breaking, of the proud."

The ancient heartbeat thudded in answer, thrilling, quickening. The Voice wrapped itself all around its master, licking the cold skin, breathing out hot spirit-breath to warm that whom it served.

Bloody-Bones

"What is your name, madam?" asked Alaric as they walked around the outside of the house with flaming brands, tossing them upon the ice and hurling buckets of water after to douse the flames once the ice had melted. It was sloppy, imprecise work, and Wystan had questioned the efficacy of it since the ice coats seemed magical, somehow, but they continued working until the home was removed of most of its sparkling shroud and the windows were open to let out some of the smoke that had gathered within.

"I'm Zahsie Silver," she answered. "Wife of Ives Silver, mother of Hunter."

"Have you lived here all your life?" asked Mink.

"No, we came just before Hunter was born, from the North. Town name of Catchery."

"Funny how so many people come here, ripe with child," said Mink.

"Oh?" asked Zahsie. "Now that ye mention it, I suppose that's true. I know Pastor Bear and Solace did as such. Also Reney and Aster, and Martin and his wife Anne. Well…so many!"

"Seems to me," said Wystan, "Huil was calling for folk."

"So why is She trying to hurt us now?" asked Zahsie.

"The others," said Mink, gesturing to the other buildings lining Delster's street, her voice in a panic. "We must be quick."

"I've a big cauldron we can keep the fire in, and if I can get my cart to your mule, we can bring water. If all ye stronger ones can help?" said Zahsie, hurrying inside, followed by Wystan and Alaric. Mink went around back and struggled to pull the cart over the snow drifts out to the street, then worked to get the donkey into the harness. She looked up as the wind howled again from the mountain and saw the figures, far down the road.

When the others came out, they found Mink trembling, pointing, her mouth open.

"What is that?" whispered Zahsie.

"More trouble from the mountain," said Alaric, lifting the heavy cauldron onto the cart with Wystan's help. "One problem at a time, madam."

They made their way to each house, and it was slow work, until finally, Alaric hurried back to the Silver home and found a hatchet as well as Zahsie's dousing rod. Wystan and Zahsie got each door opened first, and Mink and Alaric ran inside to free the inhabitants. They used this method on the remaining houses.

Out of twenty-three homes, sixteen families had survived. The wind had picked up, and the snow blasted through the village, hindering sight and sense, and still they could see the figures coming, slowly, with jerking movements, part of the storm and yet unnatural.

The surviving families filled most of the rooms of the Silver house, shaken, some in tears. Many had hidden in their root cellars while the smoke from the hearth had filled the rooms of their homes. Some had ripped up part of the floors and dug under the walls to release a portion open to the air where they had lain, breathing cleanly. Some had woken to find the rooms filled with smoke, and in the dark crawled about to find their loved ones.

"What do we do now?" asked one of the villagers.

"Is there a constable among you?" asked Wystan.

A man shook his head. "No, sirrah. No longer. He's gone from us."

"Well, you've not survived to give up, have you?" said Wystan. "These things coming down the street—I don't know what they're about, but they're not of the Goddess. I've subdued them by cutting them into smaller parts and then having at them with fire."

"Fire will blow out in this madness," said one man, named Harper. "And if we don't kill these things, maybe they'll cover this house and the others with ice again!"

"We'll destroy them," said Alaric. "We have to."

"The snow will build them back up, perhaps," said Mink.

"Where could we get some empty barrels?" asked a woman.

"For what use, Else?" asked Zahsie.

"To break up the ice-things and keep them in."

"That could work—maybe float them into the river?" said another man.

"Don't know that anyone has so many empty barrels."

"Timothy Wayne. The forge behind his house—he's amounted quite a collection of barrels, used to hold wine, traded with a barge in from Bran for some tools."

"Well, then, let's hoof it over to Tim's," said Harper. "He make it?"

"He's out on the river himself," said Zahsie. "With Ives."

"Lucky," said Wystan. "At least so far as the river's up to no mischief."

The villagers ran to Tim Wayne's, rolling the barrels into the road and leaving them standing, the tops to one side of each. Next, they gathered wood to burn from outside Tim's shop and waited in the road. Many of the brands blew out.

"This will never work," said Alaric, his sonorous voice struggling against the rising fury of the storm. "Get tools that can chop them—we'll have at them that way and lift the pieces and put them inside the barrels!"

The villagers scurried about in the white, some returning to their homes to come back with axes or shovels, even with brooms. They formed a line across the street then, waiting, with Mink and some of the wives inside the Silver home with the children.

The creatures lurched closer, shapes growing ever more distinct in the blinding storm.

###

Bear, Crow, and Hunter had followed the path that narrowed and was dry until it suddenly became hewn stone steps leading down to a rushing river. The cavern through which the water traveled was immense, and they could not see the ceiling, but all along the banks of the river were softly glowing stones amid the sand like stars in a night sky.

"I am so enamored of this place," said Bear. "Forgive the delay, but I must say a prayer."

Crow nodded, and Hunter went down on one knee beside his tutor.

"You may repeat the things that I say, lad, if you choose to."

"Aye, sir."

Goodly goddess
thou art wise
in daylight's brash
and brilliant skies,
in moontide's sweet
and gentle sleep,
in shining rock,
and hillsides steep,
oh come to me,
great Huil and bless,
oh come to me,
fair Huil and guide,
oh come to me,
fair goddess,
do not hide.

The sudden sound of flapping wings shook both Bear and Hunter to their feet, along with the lapping of the waters against wood as a vessel came out of the darkness into view. An old boat drifted close, covered with orange lichen and moss, carved in the shape of a swan, its single oar still sitting over its bow.

"Did we just…" said Hunter, his eyes wide.

"I don't know, lad," said Bear. "The world is steeped in miracles."

Crow waded out into the river, the water rising above her knees, and grabbed at the swan-boat's side, pulling it to shore and dragging it up onto the sandy beach. "How long we've been going at it, brother, would ye say?"

"Nearly a full day by my reckoning."

"Before we get in and seek this river's secrets, I might say a meal and a warm fire would do some good."

"You brought wood with you?" asked Bear.

"Always," said Crow, unshouldering her pack and bringing out a small bundle of dry pieces, which she arranged on the sand. Bear took out a fire kit from his pocket and struck it twice, sparking the twist of fiber that Crow had wedged between the sticks. Soon the fire was crackling merrily, and they sat watching the small flames, eating dried venison and chunks of goat cheese that Bear had brought, and sipping from Crow's flask of brandywine.

"We're gonna find them, right?" asked Hunter.

"Yes, lad," said Bear. "I have no doubt in my heart as of this moment, that we will. And alive."

"Brother," said Crow.

"What?"

The flames had settled, and now the fire was glowing embers, snake-like, beautiful in the dark. Hunter watched them while Crow stared into the black beyond the river's tail. Bear looked to his sister.

"Nothing's certain," said Crow.

"That's a lesson most men still wrestle with," said Bear.

"Why do ye think they do?" asked Crow. "I'll tell you why. Because people lie to them."

Hunter looked up at them each in turn.

"Don't lie to this one. Or to yer son, or to yer niece."

Bear frowned, pushing at the fire with the edge of his boot. "Well, all right. I can't say for certain. But I didn't lie about there being no doubt in my heart." He stood up, stretching his legs. "Because there is none. There's only hope, and I believe in that."

"But when fear comes, you let that in, too," said Crow, also standing. She filled her pipe and lit it. "Don't ever pretend you don't hear fear knocking. You let it in and you give it a place at the table."

"Really, Crow?" said Bear. "How could this be advice—from you? A paladin of Babcath?"

Hunter gasped. "You are?"

"Ye let fear *in*," said Crow, setting her pipe down upon the sand to unsheathe her sword. She pointed the blade towards an unseen foe. "And you let it *sit down.*" She slowly held the blade to an unseen neck. "And you let it get comfortable and think it's in a safe place." Then she mimicked slicing the blade across skin and letting go of a body, watching it drop to the sand. "And you spill its sweet blood like milk from a bucket." She sheathed her sword, chuckling, and retrieved her pipe.

She looked at Hunter. "You stare it right in the face. You say, 'How do ye do, sirrah.' You offer it a meal."

Hunter nodded. "Okay."

"A calm, happy heart is the best way," said Crow. "Death doesn't fear His duty. Neither should you."

"What about when you should run?" asked Hunter.

"Some of us never run," said Crow. "Some of us stand and take the blow. Or sit and think of meadows when the storm is shrieking in our faces. When we hear the crashing footfalls of the fiend in the forest, some of us turn around to the sound, and we wait."

###

Asher called to the other children, and it took quite a while, but in time he convinced them to draw close enough to the *nicht-ogre* that they could be lifted up and out of the pit as well. They found themselves surrounded by the other two creatures, each as tall as two men standing atop each other, well-built, their protruding bellies bare, necklaces of teeth and bones strung around their fat necks, long braids of thick hair hanging from their patchy, balding scalps, and yellow eyes like a snake's. The eyes held no intelligence that Asher could see, but there was recollection; whenever one spoke, the others moved as if the speech were thoughts already in their own heads, as if they were hearing the words but not with their ears. The creatures seemed connected in mind.

The children were pushed to walk down yet another corridor. In the dark, it was troublesome to see well, but after a time, torchlight spat and sputtered along the walls, and sometimes they passed great pits filled with fire, the tops of young trees sticking out of them, burning, the smoke rising up through narrow chimneys, presumably to the land above.

"How's no one seeing that," said Asher to Gareth and Leisel. Mink was up ahead with the *reffke* siblings and Sanandra.

"Maybe we're very far from the town."

"Maybe we're on the other side of the valley?"

"Impossible. What's beneath the valley is just dirt. No caves go down this deep but for under the mountains."

"How do you know?" asked Leisel.

"I read about it. Look at that!"

The boys looked, and they were passing rooms barred, like cages, with groups of wild boars inside them, milling about, grunting.

"Wish I could have some of that to eat," said Gareth.

"Hope they're not aiming to feed us to them," said Asher.

"Aye," said Leisel.

The children were led into a room similar to the cage that the pigs had been in, but this one was larger, and there were three makeshift beds built of tree limbs covered with straw and scraps of uncured furs, which smelled but were dry enough and softer than the dirt floor. There were buckets of water and plates of bread and roasted meat, which the children fell upon instantly, gorging themselves.

"*You sleep, after eat,*" said the ogre who'd spoken to Asher. "*When you wake, you will fight.*"

"Fight?" asked Gareth, having grown more bold by the latest series of events.

"*Yes,*" said the ogre. "*Fight and die, some of you. But the others may win. And then you can go free.*"

The children looked at each other, faces streaked with grease and crumbs, their eyes wide.

A while later, they fell asleep, for the room was warm and their bellies were full.

A long while later, a sound could be heard that was so peculiar, and after being in such still silence for so long in the dark, Leisel roused awake with a start. He shoved Gareth, who, in turn, crept over to Asher and Medie. Medie sat up and looked for the *reffke* siblings, but they were already awake, crouched by the barred door, sniffing, watching.

"Those are drums," said Asher.

"Aye," said Leisel in such a small voice it made Asher angry—angry that such a good, sweet boy should be down here in these horrid quarters at the mercy of such creatures.

Asher brought the boy close and held him, petting his head. "There now," he said. "Courage, lad. We'll make it through this. And won't our parents be proud?" He held Leisel at arm's length and winked, smiled.

"My da would likely give me milk and eggs for the rest of the year," said Gareth. "And maybe my own room."

"I'd get all the books I ever wanted," said Medie.

"Maybe my da would let me skip cleaning the barn and the henhouse," said Asher. He laughed loudly. "What am I saying—that'll *never* happen."

The other children laughed, too, and sat down on the beds. They looked at their hands and feet, and looked up again.

The drums hadn't stopped. They'd only gotten louder.

The *reffke* leapt away from the door and stood beside the other children, crouched still, baring their keen teeth, growling.

"What's gotten into—" said Gareth. "Oh. The lovely ogre-men. Someone ought to recommend them a tailor."

"City boy," said Medie, chuckling. Gareth smiled at her.

The three *nicht-ogren* stood at the door. The one who'd spoken to Asher unlocked it and beckoned.

"*It's time to come and play,*" it said. "*Come and play with the piggies.*"

"Those wild boars," said Asher.

"That's what we're fighting?" said Gareth. "With what?"

"Hopefully more than our bare hands. But you promise me something," said Asher leaning close and looking the younger boy in the eyes. "You keep Leisel and Medie safe. Me and the foxes—we're going to be at the front."

"All right. Promise."

"Good lad."

"And Sanandra!" Asher called out, and he saw Medie look at him. "Be with us. If there's a way to get you out of here too, I'm going to make it so. Lend aid as you can. I am thankful you are a part of our gang."

Medie gasped and closed her eyes as the tears streamed down her cheeks.

"She says she'll do her best and thank you."

"So, who's ever seen their mum or da butcher an animal?" asked Asher as they walked the corridor, surrounded by the ogren.

"I," said Gareth.

"Me too," said Leisel.

Medie signed to the *reffke.* "They hunt for food, so."

"Good," said Asher.

"I saw a chicken that my da bought get butchered, once," said Medie.

"Good enough. Then you'll all be fine with what's going to happen. Because it's not us that's going to be put on plates—it's them. Agreed?"

Asher led the group, and though the three ogren surrounded them, the children held themselves straight, heads high, trying to see around the great backs and shoulders of the creatures. Finally, they were led out into a massive space, round with wet, dripping walls as if a river moved above them. The ceiling was so lofty it was hard to distinguish, but now and again they could hear bats flapping their wings. Medie trembled at the sound.

All above the walls were hewn stone steps, and upon these steps, hundreds of faces in shadow, gleaming eyes, all solemnly watching them. If Asher stared too hard at any of these figures, they flickered like smoke above a dirty candle, but out of the corners of his eyes they all seemed real enough. At the end of the arena was a large stone chair, and upon it a hooded figure, larger than the three ogren and seeming to be of the same characteristics but for their shadowed face and cloaked body. Their legs were bare, the fabric of their garment stopping just before the knees. Their huge, gnarled hands were missing several fingers, and the remaining digits were curled around two stone balls of veined, white quartz set upon the ends of the arms of the chair.

"'Tis a throne—and they're the king?" asked Gareth.

"Or queen," said Medie.

"Regent of ogres—never read about such a thing in all the books."

"Maybe nobody knows about it."

"Except us, now," said Leisel.

Quickly and Jumps High were sniffing, crouched upon the sandy floor, their tails big and swinging from side to side.

"They know what's coming. Medie, please?" asked Asher.

Medie signed to the *reffke*, and nodded. "Yes there are pigs. They are just beyond that gate, beneath the throne. Chair. Whatever it is that the creature is sitting upon."

Suddenly, a thundering *hiss* made the children clap their hands over their ears, and the door behind them slammed shut. The three ogren who'd brought them in were gone. The hiss continued, and the crowd became animated, swinging arms and beating on the stone seats. There were torches lit, and by the firelight, toothed and hungry faces growled down at the children, leering, snarling at them.

The hiss became words.

"You are here to amuse the great one. The ageless king, Bran-Nokken. Do well and you may live to fight another day. Do well again, and you may fight one last time. Do well, during the third and last trial, and you will be set free to walk out upon the world."

The crowd was roaring, hooting, cat-calling.

"Do you understand?" The words ended in a sizzling hiss that hurt the children's ears.

"Yes!" called Asher to the throne. He could just barely see a hunched shadow curled all about the king's right side. "Do we have weapons with which to fight?"

A sword landed on the sand, tossed to the children from the crowd.

Asher ran to retrieve it. A spear landed next to him, barely missing running him through. He stopped.

Suddenly the air was thick with weapons, and the children were huddled together, crying out. Knives and axes, swords and spears landed in the sand all around them. One small blade glanced off Leisel's leg, and blood began to darken his trousers. He shrieked and scrambled to hide among the other children.

Asher saw three shields close to the arena wall; he leapt for them, scooping them up and running back to the others, trying not to drop any. He tossed them to the *reffke* and Gareth, then dodged away, spying four more shields close to the other wall. He grabbed for the closest and held it over his head just as two knives embedded themselves in the wood, *thud, thud*. Taking that and the other shields like a pile of great plates in his arms, he ran to regain the other children, and then they formed a huddle, a tiny shield-mound, waiting until the weapons stopped raining down upon them.

The crowd was laughing. Shrieks and gales, hoots and whistles.

Asher cut the shirt tail off his blouse and tied it around Leisel's leg. "It's not bad," he said. "It'll be okay. You're not going to be fighting, all right? You'll stick with Gareth, you and Medie. Me and Jumps High and Quickly are going to be in it today. Medie, sign to them for me, please."

They all lowered their shields slowly, glancing around with frightened eyes.

"Medie, ask them who's stronger, who's got a stronger bite," said Asher. "Do it fast. I don't know when we're to start and I have to find some spears."

Medie did as Asher instructed. "Jumps High has a stronger bite."

"And who can bark the loudest?"

Medie asked the *reffke*. "Quickly. Also…"

"What?"

"He said they can understand more than half of what you're saying."

"Good! But just to be sure, tell him he's got to scare the pig. We'll go for one pig at a time. He scares the pig, Jumps High'll grab that pig by an ear, and I'll skewer it. Got it?"

Medie's fingers moved fast as lightning as Asher ran around looking for spears. He placed pairs of the ten spears he found at various points around the arena and jogged back holding two.

"Listen," said Gareth, "you know pigs'll run themselves right through on a spear to get to you, right?"

"No, I didn't know that," said Asher. A horn blew suddenly, and the children gasped, turning around to look all about the arena.

"Yes. A simple spear won't protect you. There's gotta be a crossbar or something to stop the pig from gutting you."

"So," said Asher, taking one of the knives out of the shield he'd used to protect himself and then pushing a spear tip through the hole the knife had left. "How's this?"

"Very good," said Gareth. "Good luck, mate."

"Thanks," said Asher. He turned to face the gate beneath the throne.

The great drum beat a second time.

Gareth took a shield, set it down on the sand and positioned a knife, point down, near the shield's center. Holding the handle, he stomped it hard with his boot again and again to punch a hole in the wood, then carefully pushed another spear through.

Asher watched him.

"Might be a stray pig or two," said the town-boy, and Asher nodded.

"Let's spread out," he said.

The gate began to slowly lift, a terrific clanking as the rusty chains holding it were pulled, and Asher could hear the sounds of the beasts corralled beyond, snorting and squealing. Jumps High's eyes were intensely focused, keen and bright, her nose twitching furiously. Quickly stood apart from them, more towards the left side of the arena, and Asher stood his ground in the center.

The other children were backed as far away as they could from the throne and the gate and the fighters. Leisel and Medie each had a shield and an axe; Gareth had his spear and shield.

Four pigs galloped into the arena, rounding the left side towards Quickly, who leapt away, barking and running at a pale boar with yellowed, thick tusks. The *reffke* waited until the two pigs behind the chosen boar had passed, and then the fox-kin hurried after them, scaring the two to run faster and pass the white boar. Next, Quickly was hounding him, snapping at his hindquarters and even reaching out to rake the skin with his claws, barking and snarling. The white pig turned from his group just as they were nearing the other three children and made a straight line back towards the gate, and to Jumps High.

Jumps High crouched on the sand, watching the boar run at her, then leapt, her tail standing straight as a pole. She came down and chased along the pig's side as Quickly flanked his other side, still barking and growling. Jumps High grabbed at the boar and took its ear in her mouth. She pulled until the pig lost his feet beneath him, and Asher stopped his run completely with a spear through the chest.

The pig's feet scrambled in the sand to pull him forward and pushed the spear deeper into himself until the shield pressed against his snout as he finally succumbed.

The three fighters jumped up. Asher pulled the spear from the fallen animal's body and turned as a black boar was thundering towards him, squealing in rage.

Gareth came from the right side, throwing an axe at the black pig. The axe landed with a meaty *thump* into the squealing animal's shoulder, and it turned to charge Gareth, but Asher drove the spear tip into the pig's other shoulder and walked the weapon forward.

The pig danced and stomped the ground, twisting furiously and shaking Asher like a dog shaking a rat. He almost lost his grip on the spear, but Gareth was there, helping him hold on to it, and they slowly walked the weapon deeper into the pig's body until, at last, the boar gave up the fight and moved no more.

Asher turned back to look at Medie. She was weeping, covering her eyes to the violence, but she and Leisel were still unharmed.

The *reffke* had cornered the smallest of the boars, a piebald with one broken tusk. Asher and Gareth ran over to it, taunting it to run at them. The fourth pig, however, an older boar with tremendous tusks, had decided to turn and charge the other children. Asher ran after it, reaching down to retrieve weapons and throw them at the animal, but missing his mark each time. He screamed for them to move, but Leisel was rooted to the spot and Medie had come to stand before him, her arms raised.

"What are you doing? Run!" he called to his cousin.

The ground all around the old boar sprang up in curtains of sand, then fell, heavy as a wave of lake water, and the pig lost its footing as it lay beneath sand and soil, on its side, legs pistoning in confusion.

Asher caught up to the pig and brought an axe down into its meaty flank, then again, and again, until his arms were scarlet with the creature's blood and it moved no more.

Three sharp yips from Quickly, and Asher turned around to see how the others had fared.

Gareth had brought down the smallest pig.

###

"How many knives did you manage to keep?" asked Asher.

They had been brought back to their cell with buckets of water, and hours later, platters of roast pork were brought to them, as well as sweet fruits and soft bread. The children washed and ate, and were resting on the beds while Asher and Gareth spoke in whispers.

"Five," said Gareth. "And an axe too."

Asher laughed, then covered his mouth with his hand. "How'd you manage an axe!"

"I walked funny as they led us out. Pretended I was hurt. Said *'ow'* and *'it's bleeding'* a lot."

"You magnificent knave, you," said Asher.

"Ha! Never been called that before," said Gareth.

"Lots of things never happened before."

"Right?"

"Yeah."

"So what do ye think we're going to be fighting next?" asked Gareth. "I mean, do you even think they'll honor the plan?"

"Not sure," said Asher. "But for now, we should assume they will so we can be prepared to fight. I suspect next time, it'll be some sort of men or women. Something that lives down here or that they've kept."

"Why not more animals?"

"Because we'd have heard them, or the *reffke* would have smelled them? Let me ask Medie."

He asked Medie to sign to the fox-kin, and his guess was confirmed; there were no other animals down below in the domain of Bran-Nokken, at least, not anywhere close.

"So what did ye see in the stands? I could barely make out the eyes," said Gareth.

"Not much more than that," said Asher. "Sounded like growling, hooting."

"Ever seen a goblin?"

"Nope. You?"

"Nope. But I hear they're fierce. Fight like cats, tearing with their hind legs."

"Do they not wear shoes?"

"I don't think so."

"Hey, Medie," said Asher, waving her over. "Ever read about goblins in your books?"

She nodded. "Yes, a little. You think that's what might be next, in the pit?"

"Is that what ye call it, then?" asked Gareth.

"Yes," said Medie. "It's a tunnel that goes down—very, very far, actually. I could feel it. So deep. I don't know how they built that floor across it and covered it with sand, but that's what they've done."

"I don't know, but that scares me more than pigs and goblins," said Gareth.

"Aye," said Asher. He looked at his cousin. "Tell me, if you can."

"Yeah?" asked Medie.

"How did you do it?"

She shrugged her shoulders, looking all around the cell. "I don't know. But I hear, *Her.* Sometimes, down here even louder than aboveground. And She told me to move the sand."

"Her?"

"Huil. The goddess."

"Can you ask Her to get us out of here?"

Medie looked at Asher, her lower lip trembling. "I've tried."

The Vibrant One

Oh ye ice and bladed things
with teeth of mice and tiny stings
your clever crystals gathering –
– come lay the good man down.

We've locked the doors and shut the gate
and given up our lives, to fate –
but even that dark one's gone
missing, in this cursed town.

Come blow across the shadowed eaves
while lonely widows weep and grieve
no finer raiments she will weave
with spinnerets, or fingers.

And we will walk against the storm
all hands across, all shadows gone
and when she blows her heart away
her melancholy lingers.

WYSTAN HACKED AT the nearest lumpen form and struggled to cut through its icy skin; it took several more swings with the blade to cleave the creature in two. He threw down the axe and lifted the twisted, howling head in his arms, running for the closest barrel. As he ran, the snow-thing focused its form, staring at him and screaming, an icy maw filled with pointed teeth.

Screaming himself, Wystan slammed the head into the barrel, where it stuck, being slightly wider than the barrel was across.

"Help him get it in there!" bellowed Alaric, hacking at the sides of the snow-creature's head with his sword. The other villagers followed his example, and soon, the creature's screaming face was muffled beneath the top of a barrel.

"Hammer and nails!" called Wystan. "And when ye chop at them, it's like chopping wood, so be stout about it." Other villagers were rushing at the creatures now, hacking with their blades as the monsters screamed.

"We're running out of barrels. I can fit a whole one in here if I chop him up first," said Thomas. Wystan was yelling into the brutal wind, but the man couldn't hear him or else did not oblige to listen, and the top was sealed with nails.

The barrel suddenly exploded, sending splinters of wood, nails, and shards of ice at the villagers. Martin and Gailen staggered away, their arms and chests bloody, and Thomas fell. Wystan's eyes were wide with horror as he watched the monster, newly formed, move over the fallen man and cover him. Thomas's eyes turned red as the crushing weight burst the vessels within, until at last he was still, and lifeless.

Wystan swung the axe wide and hard, cleaving off the topmost chunk of the ice-creature's body, and he let the axe spin away from his hands so that his palms could slam amber rage unto the creature, whereupon it became a hot mist, then blackened soot. The remaining pieces of the barrel were scorched and the metal rims glowed red.

"Only one barrel left, forgo this plan," shouted Alaric, gesturing at Wystan.

Three of the villagers—Hugh, Martin, and Gailen, the latter two having plucked the larger splinters from their coats to discover the exploding barrel had only superficially wounded them—saw what Wystan was doing and turned to the nearest creature, hacking off chunks and slices. They called to Wystan, and he ran to them, magicking the creature to a hot mist. He took the three down this way; there were still four more to contend with. As Harper and Else rolled one of the barrels towards the river, there was the sound of a pop, and one of the nails flew out of the wood, barely missing Else's shoulder.

"Get away from it!" called Hugh.

Else screamed and ran away between the nearest two buildings, turning the corner around the back of one before the barrel exploded, not as ferociously as the first, but the nails embedded themselves into the porch columns of the shoemaker's shop, and one nail punctured Martin's leg. He bellowed in pain. Else hurried back around the shop to regain the street and struggled with Harper to lift Martin away from the battle and back into Zahsie's home. Hugh arrived as well, wrapping his scarf around Martin's leg to staunch the bleeding.

"He's lucky," called Hugh to Alaric. "It doesn't bleed like the bad one."

Wystan looked back at them after incinerating another creature, his breathing strained, his face dripping with sweat. "He'll live?"

Alaric nodded, running to Wystan. "Missed the conduit of life's blood, yes, he will live. How many more?" The wind picked up again, pushing against them with stinging sleet.

Wystan pointed; there was one more creature, and it stood still as the snow gathered around it, building it up.

"Bring brands!" called Alaric to Hugh and Gailen. "Help him burn it down."

The men surrounded the creature with fire, and Wystan struck at it again and again, until it finally succumbed and revealed the bare, black mud of the road.

The villagers returned to the Silver home, where Zahsie was tending to the wounded as best she could, and her best was excellent, but it was Mink with her tiny, precise hands who was able, with tweezers, to pull the splinters from the bleeding flesh. When the two women had finished their aid, they sat in Zahsie's kitchen, shaking hands holding cups of tea with whiskey. Other villagers lay on the floor in the front room, some stationed at the windows to watch the storm.

Alaric sat at the table with Zahsie and Mink, and soon, so did Wystan.

"You've done well," said the dwarf, bowing his head to them. "Tending to their wounds as you have."

Tears streamed down Zahsie's face, and she shook her head, mouthing words she didn't have the strength to put breath to.

"It shouldn't have happened," said Mink. "How could this have happened to these people?"

Zahsie got up and came to Mink. She hugged her, and they wept together while the men looked at things around the kitchen—the mess of bloody rags on the counter, the stacks of dishes, the bowls of bread covered near the hearth, the hearth fires going steadily but getting low.

"Why don't ye both go upstairs? Take your tea. Get some rest. Is there a spot up there not filled with a villager?" asked Wystan.

"Hunter's room is empty. I didn't want it disturbed while he was away," said Zahsie, her small voice still trembling.

"Go up there, then. I'm sure the lad won't mind. Alaric and I can go get you some firewood after we've done the washing-up. All right?"

Mink and Zahsie nodded and, taking their cups and shawls, made their way up the stairs.

"Coin toss for the dishes," said Alaric.

Wystan glanced down the hall at the front room; all was quiet. They were alone in the kitchen. "I'll get the dishes and the rags—you just keep me occupied. Talk about something."

"Well, I can sweep, at the very least, while you wash," said Alaric.

"Fair enough. Broom's next to the cupboard,"

"Ah," said Alaric, moving the chairs all to one side of the room and looking around for a dustpan. "Where I'm from, it's ill luck to keep a broom in a place of food storage or preparation."

"Okay, then where do you keep your brooms?"

"In a broom closet."

Wystan nodded, dunking the rags into a bucket and wringing them out. "So ye've room enough for brooms to have their own special rooms. Must be nice."

"We've all the space beneath your noisy feet, yes," said Alaric, chuckling. "Our closets could have closets if we deemed such a thing useful."

"Never much found much use for a closet," said Wystan.

Alaric looked at him.

"Being a traveler and such."

The *swarthe* nodded and smiled. "Your closet is then whatever bush you toss your broom into."

"I'm a bit choosier than that."

Alaric pulled the dustpan from behind a china cabinet. "That's good to know." He began to chop at the dirt and dust on the floor with the broom, corralling everything into small piles.

"You're very meticulous," observed Wystan.

"You know what they say—" Alaric swept each pile onto the dustpan "—that the dwarves are neat. They are tidy. They could carve a bas relief on the head of a pin."

"They can? Remind me to ask you to do my stitches, should I ever suffer a good enough hack with a sword."

"But, of course, that's an exaggeration," said Alaric as he opened the back door and dumped the dirt into the snow. "When a society has peace, it is able to nurture its more contemplative side. When a people are allowed to contemplate, they can take more time with their pursuits." Alaric leaned the broom up against the wall and set the dustpan down beside it. "A man who takes his time with things is often more skilled—" he came to stand beside Wystan at the sink "—with things."

"I see. Also, I believe you told me to ask permission," said Wystan, looking at Alaric. The pale light made the darker man's skin gleam like burnished silver.

"Don't worry about it," said Alaric, and Wystan leaned to him and pressed a gentle kiss against his lips.

###

"She's sound," said Crow, steering the swan-boat down the dark river.

"Aye," said Hunter. "So beautiful. If only I could get it back to Da… He'd lose his head."

"Hey now," said Bear. "Let's keep the talk of decapitation and various parts down to a minimum, if you don't mind."

Hunter ran his fingertips along the boat's edge. "How does one even carve such a thing? Seems to be hewn from a solid piece of wood."

"Time and skill," said Crow. "And patience."

"You two," said Bear. "Hush for a moment, please."

Hunter and Crow sat in the boat, still and quiet, listening.

"Sorry, but I might be hearing rushing water. Don't want to get sucked down a hole into the bottom of the world this day."

"Any day would likely be a bad day for that, brother," said Crow. "I might hear it too. Up there's a little beach. We should tether her to something, then venture out a bit more."

"And then we'd have to cut the rope and lose it?"

"No, we'll paddle back, loosen the rope, repeat the same 'til next time we find a beach. Precaution against disaster. Slows us down, but recklessness in darkness—"

"Invites a stubbed toe, yes. I remember Da saying that, too."

"I'd forgotten who'd said it. Sure it wasn't Mum?"

"Pretty sure," said Bear, hopping out of the boat as they drew close to the beach. "Toss me the rope. There's actually a good tree root showing its skin amid the rocks here."

They continued on as long as the rope would uncoil, which was a fairly long while, it being Crow's rope—well-made and richly bought from Bran. There were several coils left in the boat before suddenly the tension released.

"What's this?" said Bear, pulling at it. It came to him easily, then stopped, as if tethered again. He sniffed at the air. "Hey now, Crow."

"What?" she asked, turning around and setting up the oar across the boat's stern.

"Listen and smell."

"Yes. Something's got the other end of our rope?"

"Aye," said Bear, quietly. Crow unsheathed her sword and beckoned Hunter to move behind her. Bear stood back as well, crouched a bit but with his arms on either side of her, his staff held high.

"If ye speak, know that we are ready for ye," called Crow quietly. "You might take one of us, but you won't take all before we cast ye bleeding into this dark water."

They waited, listening, watching.

A second boat, carved as theirs, glided into view of Bear's staff's glow.

"Hold, Crow," said Bear.

Karúm's face, hooded, emerged from the shadows, and their rope was tied to her boat. She steered alongside them.

"Well, hello, Wayfinder," said Bear. "This is my sister, Crow. And my apprentice, Hunter."

"Well-met," said Karúm. "You've traveled *much* too far below. After I saw your tracks in the warrens above, I sent the first boat out, in hopes you'd discover it. When I heard you upon the water, I tried my best to hurry. I'm glad my timing was good."

"I thought I'd heard brighter water up ahead," said Bear. "We used the rope to be cautious."

"Yes, well," said Karúm, "you were correct. But it is necessary to navigate the loudwater in order to leave this river. It wanders for nearly a hundred miles and loops across itself. All other ways will merely circle you around and take you to paths leading to places you'd rather not see."

"She means to say, we're going over a waterfall?" asked Hunter.

"She generally says what she means, yes," said Bear.

"You'll pitch over it, then there's a good enough pool just below. The trick is to paddle hard right as soon as you land, so you don't get sucked down into it."

"Yes, that sounds terrible," said Crow.

"It would be. The water's usually cold, and the beasts that live at the bottom are not to be trifled with."

"No trifling," said Bear, his eyes wide as the river picked up speed. "None, whatsoever."

"Then, once you gain the current that runs along the southern bank, continue paddling hard until you see the compass rock in the middle. Bear left after that, and that will take you out of the river proper. The stream continues on about two miles and banks at a grotto which is known by the *swarthe.* If we separate, I will wait for you there. Heed my instruction and you'll fair well."

"Yes, mistress," said Hunter. "Thank you for helping us."

Karúm nodded to him and paddled on, tossing Crow's rope into their boat. "A courteous human," she said in the darkness. "That's good news."

They glided on, carried faster by the rushing river. It seemed far too long a wait considering they'd heard Karúm's boat go over the waterfall and land with a great splash what seemed nearly an hour ago. Then the river slowed and became calm once again.

"Did we miss it?" asked Hunter, his voice echoing in the quiet.

"No. There've been no tunnels that we passed, I've looked," said Bear. "Just must have underestimated things. It's coming."

They paddled on, hoping to make up for the time and not have Karúm wait overly long at the grotto, but there was still no waterfall, and the river's currents were nearly still now. After a time, the river was as smooth as glass, and Hunter was asleep, curled in the bow of the boat.

"There was one thing I didn't leave back at Da's house," said Crow.

"Where are you keeping it, then?"

"It's at your house. Hidden."

"What is it?" asked Bear, watching the walls of the tunnel drift by.

"It's that book."

Bear looked at her. "That evil thing. Why did you carry it here?"

"It's the only real thing of value among Da's effects."

"What? Why?"

"He wrote it."

Bear sighed, staring at his sister. "Da never wrote a book, you know that."

"He wrote *this one*. The only one."

"That's why he sold books—the envy, the coveting of others' words."

"Even this book—he did not truly write. Not really. His hand moved the pen, but it was dictated to him, every night."

"That's ridiculous. Who could have slipped into the house unnoticed by Mum? Who told him the words, Crow?"

"I don't know. But I heard the voice of them sure as I can hear the water smack against this boat, right now. One night I heard it."

"And? What did you see?"

"Through the keyhole, nothing but our deranged father scribbling as fast as he could, and begging, cursing at the voice of the author that he was tired and he'd at least have a cup of wine, but his visitor did not let him rest."

Bear stared at his sister, mouth twisted in horror.

"There are dates, at the start of each passage. For thirty-seven years, it never let him rest."

The boat scraped upon gravel and came to a stop.

They sprang to their feet, looking around in a panic.

They had reached the grotto.

Bear stood and slowly stepped out of the boat, looking at Crow and she at him.

"Surely that can't be right," he said. Crow shook her head in answer.

Hunter roused from his curled nest in the boat and sat up. "I barely felt that at all."

"You didn't feel it, lad," said Bear. "Somehow we missed the fall-over."

"She didn't say there was another route."

"No, she didn't. Maybe this is a different grotto. But come out of the boat now, to the shore."

"So," said Crow. "Another approach is to get back in and retrace our route."

"If we were dealing with natural logic, I'd agree," said Bear. "But I don't think we are."

"No." Crow took Bear's staff, still grasped in his firm hand, and raised it higher so that it shone against the cave wall in front of them, and on the wide opening that was carved into the rock. "I don't think so, either."

The door was shaped like a giant mouth; the graffiti of teeth and lips had been scratched into the stone all around it, with chalk and charcoal. To the right of this mouth were two words, in the common tongue of the land above: NO GOLD.

"What is all that, there?" said Hunter, stepping out of the boat and walking towards the wall.

"Lad," warned Bear.

Hunter crouched, gathering something from the pebbly ground into his hand. He stood up and brought it closer to the light of Bear's staff.

The other two peered down at Hunter's hand. It was filled with small teeth; children's teeth.

He gasped and let them fall upon the beach.

"This place is evil," said Hunter, his voice trembling and high, and sounding as if he'd lose control of himself very soon.

"I don't like it either," said Crow.

"There *is* evil here," said Bear. "This is why pastors of Huil, Hunter, are not to be trifled with. We do much more than pick daisies and sit on mountaintops. We are here to rescue those who have fallen to the darkness. Including Huil herself."

They entered the mouth.

Bear took the lead, his staff shining dully against the close, dripping walls. Hunter was in the center, while Crow had the rear, her sword unsheathed and her dark eyes wary. The air smelled of death, not thickly but lingering, as a tomb smells even years after a body had been interred within. All along the curved walls were piles of tiny teeth, some blackened with gore.

Every once and again Hunter's breath hitched as if he were trying not to cry. Crow put her hand on the boy's shoulder.

"You will get through this, lad," she whispered. "This is not the end."

The tunnel made its slow way up from the river, curving to the right and steeply climbing until at last, after what felt like hours, it ended in an empty, round room. The floor was paved with black and broken tiles set in what was once a spiraled pattern. From the ceiling hung a thickly chained iron lamp; no light burned within its filthy glass. Directly beneath it was a circular drain.

"Be ready," said Crow.

There were two corridors leading away from the room in addition to the one from which they'd come.

"Always a choice," said Bear. "Would that we still had Karúm to guide us."

"Well, we don't. But we've got our wits. I'll take the right, you the left, sniff a bit, and listen."

Bear and Crow each stood in the entrance of the two corridors, listening, smelling the air, waiting. Hunter turned around to regard the passageway they'd just left. Suddenly there was a soft, scratching noise to his right. He turned.

A section of the wall to the right of the two new corridors was moving, just slightly, as if it were no longer made of stone but of black cloth. Hunter gasped and took a step backward. Great hands gripped his shoulders, and he cried out.

Crow and Bear turned to see two great creatures lift Hunter in the air, each holding one of his arms as his feet kicked and he screamed in pain.

"*We'll tear him apart*," said one of the brutes, his voice gurgling and wet and as deep as the tunnels were long. "*Lay down your arms.*"

"Aye," said Crow, laying her sword upon the ground. "We'll give you no trouble. Put the lad down, unharmed."

"Here's my staff too," said Bear, laying that next to Crow's sword.

The ogres jostled Hunter a few more moments, then dropped him, and he landed in a pile upon the iron grate, cowering, covering his head in fear.

"*Brave lad,*" said one of the ogres, his voice a sizzling hiss as he wheezed out a laugh. "*You are all so brave.*"

Crow watched them, her arms at her sides. Bear closed his eyes and moved his lips softly.

"*You,*" said the other ogre. "*Shut your mouth.*"

Bear continued to whisper.

The second ogre raised his naked leg and placed his bare, callused foot atop Hunter's head. "*Be quiet and still.*"

A pattering, slapping sound, as if a hundred palms were slamming skin against stone, could be heard echoing in the corridors behind Bear and Crow. Great swarms of rats burst forth and scrambled over the creatures like a dark, busy wave, biting and clawing. Crow and Bear ran forward and lifted Hunter under the arms, then turned and struggled to gain the tunnel on the right, escaping down it but a few paces when a third ogre appeared in the gloom and grabbed Bear around his broad chest and squeezed him. Bear cried out.

Crow took Hunter by the hand and led him back into the room to grab up Bear's staff and her own sword. The rats had vanished, and she and the apprentice were surrounded. She slashed at the legs of the other two ogres and, with Hunter right behind, made for the remaining tunnel, hearing the screams and cries behind them, growing fainter and fainter still, until there was only silence and the dripping of water from above, heading down to the black river.

###

They came earlier this time, it seemed.

Some of the children awoke, groggy, when one of the ogres opened the door to the cell and came in to heft Medie and Leisel from their places on the beds. Asher jumped to his feet and shouted after them but the door was slammed shut, and the cries of Medie and Leisel echoed on the other side as the ogres carried them away.

The other children woke and struggled to see what was happening through their sleep-murky eyes. Asher was shouting at the door, banging on it with his fists and yelling until he was hoarse, and then he was sobbing, and the other children were around him asking what had happened.

Far down the corridor, Leisel whimpered as he was carried in the ogre's arms. His face was red, his eyes were red, he was sniffling, and every once in a while he'd erupt into a full cry as the ogre tickled him and laughed that horrible wet, gurgly laugh.

"Shut up, you fucker!" Medie yelled at the beast, and she was put down on her feet.

"*Feissssty, so walk,*" hissed the voice of the one that had carried her.

"I'll walk if you put him down too," she snarled, her shoulders pitching up and down as she breathed out her wrath.

"*Fiiine,*" hissed the ogre, and Leisel was dropped to the floor.

Medie squeezed her way past her carrier and grabbed Leisel, holding him against her. "It's going to be all right," she whispered.

"No, it won't!" he wailed, and the ogren laughed again.

"Hush until we get where we're going," she said, her eyes a dark fury.

The ogres pushed them forward to stumble on the sand of the arena and lowered the gate.

"Just us?" whimpered Leisel. "But why?"

"Because, I imagine, they think you and I are the weakest. But we'll show them." Medie walked around the sand, looking. "Help me find anything long. A sword, a spear, a bone."

"Okay," he hiccupped, walking and looking as well. "Here's a bone." Leisel picked up what looked to be a femur, dried and bleached, and handed it to Medie.

"Good job. Now, watch the other gate for me and let me know when it lifts."

"There'll be that drum again."

"Oh, right. Thanks for paying attention, lad." Medie took the femur, and began to draw in the sand with it, her tongue jutting out the side of her mouth.

"What's that?"

"Not sure, but I was dreaming about it when they came for us."

Leisel studied the gate and jumped when the familiar drum beat sounded. "I think it's time. What are we going to do?"

"You, stand by me, behind me, beside me—whichever you like. Just do not leave my sight. You give me courage. All right, lad?"

"Yessim," said Leisel. "You're a brave *saylie* lass."

Medie smiled at him.

The gates lifted.

At first, she couldn't see exactly what they were, but then, after the roar and hoots of the crowd settled down, she saw them: a small regiment of tiny men with long faces, tall ears, clever hands and long feet, and keen, dark eyes fixed on them. Leisel trembled like a rabbit in the sights of a hound and pressed up against her.

"That won't do, lad," she whispered. "Watch them. Let's see what they're about."

"They're red-caps if they're anything at all!" he said, too loudly, and she noticed the change in the expression of the tiny men. The closest one flinched and snarled, and the one closest to him punched him on the shoulder.

"They didn't like that, Leisel," Medie said. "He heard you and he reacted angrily. They're most assuredly not red-caps."

The one that had heard Leisel's words hissed.

"Well, they're most assuredly upset with us!" said Leisel, pointing.

"Put your hand down," said Medie.

"They're coming this way and the crowd is cheering them."

"Let them come."

The men walked with purpose and swagger; the louder the crowd, the more animated the men became until they were balling their fists or pointing at Leisel and Medie and shouting. One of them even hopped up and down in rage.

"There are ten of them," counted Medie.

"A crowd of small kids can bring down one bigger kid. I've seen it happen," said Leisel.

"I know. Just wait."

The men had crossed more than half the distance now. The sigil that Medie had drawn in the sand was but a few yards from the closest goblin's feet.

Medie took a deep breath and got on her knees, bowing her head and kissing the sand.

The crowd screamed with delight, and some of the little men laughed and pointed.

Medie stood up, wiped the sand from her lips and raised her arms, just as the first three men crossed the sigil. The sand on either side of them rose up in great sheets as it had done to the small boar, but this time, the grains spun about the men's legs and torsos, then became still and immovable. They were encased; only their heads were free.

The other men rushed to see what had happened to their cohorts, and they all spoke together, the trapped men struggling and cursing. The remaining seven turned and ran at Medie and Leisel.

Medie pushed Leisel behind her, and together, they took a few steps back before Medie raised her arms again and pushed forward with open palms. A wall of sand rose and stood between the children and the men.

"Stay back!" she shouted. "Or the same will happen to you as what did your fellows."

The goblins waited, the tops of their disheveled heads visible beyond the wall of sand. The heads gathered together. Moments later, one man climbed over the wall and slid down to the other side.

"Will ye let 'em go when this is through?" he growled at Medie.

"I would be happy to. But let me ask you this—what is the crowd telling you?"

The man looked at the faces above on either side, and frowned. "They's telling us to gut you and break yer bones, because that's what's you'll be wanting to do to us."

"Do I look to you like I could do that? Like I'd be wanting to?" asked Medie, her chest rising and falling with her breath, her eyes wide.

The man shook his head as if a mosquito had buzzed too close to his ear and leaned closer to stare at Medie.

"Nah. Ye look like a little girl. And he a little boy. What the fook're you doin' here, then?"

"Trapped—same as you. I'm Medie Kieren. My uncle's the pastor of Huil on this mountain, and this is Leisel, a good boy from town. They took us."

"Took ye?" The man turned to look at the crowds, who were now booing and throwing globs of feces at them, which fortunately missed their marks and landed in the sand. "Them bastards. They took us too—said there was a mine down here."

"There isn't?" asked Medie.

"No. There's only death, to amuse the king. We been down here a long time."

After Medie and the tiny man had spoken some more, the man climbed back over the wall, and Medie raised her arms to let the sand barrier fall with a soft *shift* at the goblins' feet, but then the little men rushed the children, arms raised menacingly, shouting terrible things, and Medie raised her arms once more so that the entire floor rose up like a giant wave and fell upon the small men, burying them completely.

She turned in the direction of Bran-Nokken and bowed.

The gate behind them slowly opened.

Medie and Leisel were pushed back into the cell, and as the door clanged shut, the nearest ogre leaned its scarred and bulbous face close to the bars, and hissed at them, "*Parlor tricks are good enough for this day, but never do them again, girl.*" The creature shambled off, leaving the children to themselves once more.

"What happened?" asked Asher, his eyes puffy and his face streaked with tears.

"They would have had us kill other prisoners," said Medie. "What do any of you know about goblin men that work in mines?"

"Knockers," said Gareth. "They're called knockers. My da says some of the men in town brought them with them from up north when they came to live in Delster. They thought there was some sort of mine here once, but it ran shallow. Men came to Delster seeking gold, but only a tiny bit was found, so they looked to the river instead and just made a life there. But the knockers, they'd have stayed in the mountain, I imagine."

"But then *he* took them," said Leisel.

"Yes," said Medie. "I think so."

"Why'd you have to kill them?" wailed Leisel, crying again, his shoulders shaking as Asher held him.

"No, no," said Medie, wiping Leisel's face. "I didn't kill them. They're fine, I think. Me and the main man, we came up with an idea. They're good at digging, and remember I said the floor is just a false thing and there's a tunnel below? The knockers maybe had time to dig away, and so now—at least, I really hope so—they're free."

The children settled down after a while, now that Medie and Leisel were back. In time, food was brought to them again, and clean water, and so they ate and eventually, fitfully, slept.

Medie was woken by the feeling that a face was watching her, inches from her own. She opened her eyes to see the shimmering outline of Sanandra.

"What is it?" Medie whispered, sitting upright.

The body curled against hers on the crowded bed, and Medie put her arm over her, carefully, and imagined stroking her hair. She could hear soft words inside her head, but they were as close as if someone was whispering them in her ear.

"He desires you."

Medie gulped; her heart beat faster. "What do you mean by that?"

"He said something, before the other one could snatch me and tear out my heart. The fallen king."

Medie tried to calm herself, but the panic disregarded her attempts and rose anyway. Her heart felt as if it were in her throat. "What did he say?"

"He said, 'Devour her.'"

"I don't understand!"

Someone in the room said, "Shh, quiet."

"I'm sorry," whispered Medie.

"I think he wants to keep you, now."

"Well, then I must away. We must all," said Medie.

"Yes, yes you must."

"We will try at first light, whenever that is. When the others wake."

"He asked my father to bring me here. Because my grandmother knew magic, and so did I. My da wanted to be rich. They enchanted him."

"I'm sorry. I'm so very sorry, Sanandra."

"I had a body, and he took it."

Medie looked at the form of the ghost-girl and shuddered with fear.

"He ate it while I watched. I was floating above, and I watched him eat my flesh and my bones."

###

He was in a room, in full darkness. His boots were gone. He sat up and felt a manacle around his bare ankle, tight and painful. The flesh had been pinched when they'd closed it. From this ran a thick chain, and he followed that chain to a plate set in the stone wall. From there, he crawled, until he found the metal of the door. He stood up, balancing on one foot while the other was held away, behind him, by the chain, and he felt the tiny window in the door, barely enough to fit his hand through, and then he fell back.

He crawled more, in the dark. Found the bucket of water and smelled it, tasted it with one finger. It was silty but fresh. He found a long bone—possibly from a man or woman, possibly from a child, he couldn't tell—and pushed it away from him in the darkness. The floor was covered with straw, and the straw smelled of death.

He felt around a little more, the terror of his blindness and what might wait for him in the dark threatening to choke him, steal his breath, and his shaking hand came to rest upon a small pocket-blade, folded into its wooden handle. He took this and crawled backward to sit between the bucket and the iron plate in the wall, easing his manacled leg out in front of him.

He tried to calm the panic flapping in his chest like a spooked bird. His eyes were wide open but he could see nothing, not even his hand in front of his face. He carefully eased the blade out and felt for the hinge of the manacle, working the knife between it. He tried again with the manacle's lock; the results were the same. Bear slipped the knife into his pocket and took a deep, trembling breath.

He began to whisper the long, complicated spell of *garner light*, under a thickness of emotions, until the words began to resemble tiny hands forming a protective cage around his heart, shielding it from the fear that longed to strangle it.

"...and on a circle of grass, to which the sea has carried me, atop the white rock, beneath the shade of the wizened trees, there is a stone. By the stone stands a cormorant, and it watches me with livid eyes, and from its breast a single white feather lifts on the softly blowing wind, to my palm, and I grasp it, and as I grasp it, I also bend down to the pebble, and I reach for that in my other hand, and above me, the sky gains the visage of the five kings who once ruled this land, and they—"

Suddenly Bear was seized with a cough, a wracking, wet-sounding spasm that shook his body, and he lost the focus on the spell.

He opened his eyes, not wanting to but unable to stop himself from the reflex to do so. Keeping his eyes closed was exhausting. Opening them was panic-inducing, maddening. He blinked, and blinked again, lifting his hands to his blind orbs, rubbing them as if to regain some amount of sight, but there was such an absence of light in this place he could see nothing at all.

He started to breathe faster, his heartbeat quickening.

"Is there no one to come for me?" he called out weakly. The sound seemed muffled; the room was smaller than he'd imagined it to be.

"Is there no one?" he called louder. "*Why have you taken me?*" He tried to stand, but his legs wouldn't hold him, and his mouth was as dry as the stone upon which he sat. *"PLEASE."*

He focused his breathing, his body trembling with near-total terror and despair, but in time his breath came even again, and calm. He closed his eyes.

"On the seventh road from the sea of glass, there is a hidden ridge, amid the herds of goats and sea-birds that gather there. The road leads up to the mountains, and on the third peak, there is a bald bedecked with wildflowers, and a path that winds amid the stone."

He had tried to empty his mind through the weaving of the spell, and at last, he was coming around to the last of its verses. Just as he became aware of this, a voice spoke in the thick dark, and the spell popped like a soap bubble, and was gone.

"You cannot read yet you were a bookseller's son," said the voice.

Bear startled, kicking his heel against the floor, turning to the sound. "Who's there?"

"Answer me, because I want to know. What kind of imbecile refuses to learn to read when he comes to maturity in a house filled to the rafters with books?"

Bear turned, on his hands and knees now, trying to find the source of the voice.

"That prayer you've been attempting for the better part of two days—if you could read, and write, you'd have committed it to memory and you would likely be out of here, or at least, not going blind, as you are now. It's an interesting trick of the brain. The mind processes language first when it hears it, next when it speaks it, and then a third time when it writes it down, and so on. You've sentenced yourself to death, *sirrah*."

"Why do you assume we had books at home?" asked Bear, crossing his legs in front of him, gingerly holding the manacled ankle, reminding himself to close his eyes.

"Every bookseller does."

"Good theory. When one is sprinkling crumbs to the ducks, when one has a loaded flintlock. What are ye after?"

"Delight."

"Well, you've come to the wrong place. I'm far from delightful."

"Then I'll leave and return you to the silence."

"Wait!" said Bear, turning his head and opening his aching eyes to try to see anything at all in the darkness. "Don't go."

"Answer the question."

"Because I hated him."

"So you punished yourself out of hatred for somebody else."

"That's all he was, my da. That's all he existed for. He was barely a man, but that he could squeeze out the seed of his children from his balls. That doesn't make a man. All he lived for was books. So I didn't take to reading them."

"Why did you hate him?"

Bear groaned in the darkness. "This cuff is causing me great pain."

"I don't care. Why did you hate your father?"

Bear folded his arms, staring out at the voice, wherever it was. "Because of what he did to Crow."

"Did he kill her?"

"No."

"Then why the grudge? She lives. Is she happy?"

"I don't know. Crow just…*lives.* I can never tell if she's—well no, I suppose. When she's fighting, she's happy. Satisfied, would be a better word."

"And where does she fight?"

"Wherever her goddess leads her to do so."

"And where is she now?"

Bear opened his mouth to speak, then stopped.

"*Where is Crow, now*?"

"Well," said Bear, his voice hoarse, rough, quiet. A tear welled up to rest upon the curve of his eye. "I guess this is where you leave me in the darkness."

There was a sound like a breath in a tunnel, blowing out a flame or scuttling leaves as on a late autumn day, and then again, as before, there was silence.

Bear's head slumped and his chin touched his chest. His lip curled in despair, trembling, and his entire body shook as he wept, breaking the thick, infinite silence with wracking sobs, then shouts of anguish, and then, finally, screams.

###

"We have to find him," said Hunter, pulling at Crow. He'd refused to move from the spot before the open-mouth door, back at the beach where the swan-boat was still tethered.

"We will," said Crow in a quiet voice. "We—" She stopped and listened. "I hear the loudwater. I hear it, lad."

"It's a trick. Everything down here is mad and wrong. It's all as twisted as the roots of a tree."

Crow let the boy go and walked to the water. "Yes," she said. "That's true." She pointed to Bear's staff on the sand. "Can ye make that work?"

"I don't know," he said, taking it, regarding it mournfully. "Suppose it wouldn't hurt to try."

"No, I'd doubt it would hurt at all. Huil's magic is not of the nature to bite. Just try it, son."

Hunter held the staff close to him and kissed the beryl at its top as he'd seen Bear do so many times. He closed his eyes and muttered quiet words, then took a deep breath, and opened his reddened eyes.

The beryl was glowing faintly.

"Good job," said Crow, looking back and smiling. "Now, can you try to encourage it to glow more brightly?"

"Sure," said Hunter, taking another deep breath. "I will try."

He closed his eyes again. As he spoke, the beryl warmed as if a flame had been lit within it, and the light it now cast illuminated the beach, and the boat, and the softly lapping water of the dark river. Crow guided Hunter—his eyes still closed, his lips moving in prayer—to the water's edge and gently lowered the arm that held the staff so that the light shone down against the water's surface.

"And there it is," said Crow, looking at the dark shadow of a mouth below the bobbing boat.

Hunter opened his eyes and squinted, puzzled. "There what is?"

"The tunnel we need."

###

It took Crow the better part of the day, or night—neither was sure of the time anymore—to convince Hunter to dive after her into the sump of the hidden passageway, but at last she'd been successful, and as he swam, the apprentice held Bear's staff so that it cast its golden light upon the walls of the underwater tube. When they both emerged from the surface into a smaller cave and beside a larger beach, Hunter laughed, swimming to the gravelly shore and standing upon it, his clothing soaked but his courage seeming to be restored.

"See now?" Crow said, taking off her boots and pouring the excess water onto the fine gravel. "Nothing to it."

"I thought we'd see terrible creatures down there," laughed Hunter.

"Nope," said Crow. "Just little critters such as this one." She reached down to scoop up a tiny, white crawdad, its delicate legs reaching to crawl across her hand.

"So pale," said Hunter. "Nearly clear."

"Without sight, there is no color," said Crow. "Or rather, there's no need for such variations. And now—are ye very cold? I don't know what I could use to spark a fire, but I don't want you getting run down by the shakes after we've took up the path again."

"No," said Hunter, stooping to pick up a red-hued stone from the beach and putting it in his pocket. "I feel fine."

###

"Can you see it, in the space in which I've kept it?"

He trembled, and his thin, black tongue swept across cracked lips, running around the two fangs, worrying the cracked tip of the one, slipping back along the dry gums. Useless tongue, tasteless, speechless, ever wishing to savor something once more. But he'd only eaten meals of mundane flesh for so long, and very few of those, besides. The Voice rested over his milky eyes like a cool, silk veil, and he breathed the sweetness of the scent of it, and saw.

"It is not for your tooth, my King. For its magic is bespoken."

He roused, vicious with fury, his mind wheeling back into the spaces in which it liked to hide when he seethed, and he pushed the Voice off him, his ancient mind growling low, his silent voice like the *shikashikashik* of a rattlesnake's tail, chittering upon his useless tongue, his cicada-husk mouth.

"Do not worry, precious lord. I am keeping the creature of Huil for the secrets it hides. And its line has begat a child, sweet and lush, whose magic is ten times more potent than his."

The rage scuttled down to a dust that coated him, and he stirred upon it, a silken bed, and his fever-pitch desire roused, weary.

"I feel your hunger and your thirst. They will be sated soon."

###

"It's time, Medie," said Asher, coming to sit beside her.

His cousin hadn't stirred, or slept, or eaten when they'd brought the plates of bread and pork and bowls of water. She stared straight ahead, eyes unfocused, mouth slightly open.

"Time to come together and talk about what's next."

Medie's eyes closed for just a moment and her head snapped to one side; Asher reached to catch her as she woke.

"What is happening to you?"

Medie looked at him. "I'm too afraid," she said. "To do—"she began to tremble violently "—anything but wait for them."

"Oh, no, lass," said Asher. "We're not going to wait. We're going to act."

"What will it matter?" Her voice was small and still again. "They will catch us."

"*Persistence!*" Asher shouted, and Medie jumped, her eyes suddenly pin-sharp with focus, locked onto his own. "You will get up, you will come sit with us, and we shall, right now, devise a plan. Even if that plan is to *wait* for them and beat their ugly ogre-heads with our boots and our bowls until they run away in terror, leaving the gate open."

Gareth came around and knelt beside them. "You know what?" he said. "That's not a terribly bad plan."

"And they'll stomp us into jelly," said Leisel. Jumps High yipped and nodded her head, and the children looked at her.

"They've learned more and more of our language," said Medie. "You can just talk to them for most anything now, like I said."

"I wouldn't be averse to plucking out their eyes, and stomping *those* to jelly," said Gareth.

"Yeah? You ever reached in a man's eye socket and dug his eyeball out by the roots?"

Gareth was quiet, then muttered, "No."

"That's right, no," said Asher. "It's not easy. It's disgusting. And if you panic midst-pluck, you're gonna get the beating of your life from the one whose eye you meant to remove."

"Oh yeah?" asked Gareth. "And how do ye know that?"

"My Auntie Crow. She's a paladin of Babcath."

Unison sounds of astonishment and praise arose from the circle of children.

"She teach you any fighting moves?" asked Leisel.

"Not yet, but when I finally make it home, you'd better believe I'm going to ask my da to ask her to."

Medie got up and walked to the wall, leaning her head against it.

"Oh say, Asher. Your cousin's losing her wits finally. I hate to tell you," said Gareth.

"He already knows," said Leisel. "He went over to her while she was staring off."

"No," said Asher. "This is different. Medie?" He got up and walked to her, and she put her hand up for him to wait.

The others heard the tapping like hundreds of hammers, like teeth gnashing at the bones of a stone giant.

Gareth pointed to the wall to the right of Medie's head. "Step back, it's cracking." But no one seemed to hear him, so he shouted, "Get back!" and reached to pull Medie away.

A three-foot-tall crack, only a few inches wide, appeared in the wall to the right of Medie's face, and a tiny hand shoved its way through and reached out to touch the tip of her nose. She screamed.

The children pressed against the back of the opposite wall, Medie included, and watched the cracked wall collapse into smoking, powdery chunks as tiny men pushed and grunted through the spaces to finally stand before them, each brandishing keen, tarnished hammers.

"My apologies for the delay, junior folk," said the one who'd touched Medie's nose. "After this lass enabled our escape, we had to find our equipment. So if ye don't mind waiting just a bit longer, we're fixing to edge this tunnel out and see you up to the surface, back where ye belong."

Leisel made as though to cheer, but Asher clapped his hand over the boy's mouth.

"Shh," said Asher. "Time enough for that when we get where we're going."

With a scraping and a thump, a large, squared-off piece of the wall slid forward to settle on the floor, then a similarly-sized piece above it fell loose and was pushed out.

"It's not heavy, kids, help get tha' first piece outta the way, if ye please?" said the knocker, and they rallied around the chunk, grabbing at it and moving it a few feet to the center of the room so that the second piece could be pushed by the other knockers.

"Good job! Now listen. It's close quarters in there, so I don't want ye to be frightened overly much, but the lads are digging as they go and, of course, Bum, Fuck, and Twaddle are likely on their way back here to see about the ruckus we've caused, so ye can't dally. All of ye come along right now, and cover yer mouths a bit so ye don't breathe in the dust!"

"What's your name, sirrah?" asked Gareth, bowing to the little knocker.

The knocker's small face stretched in a huge smile. "Well, if ye don't favor yer grandpapa, so courteous. Name's Cefin. I'm the foreman of this gang. Come along now! Time's wasting, as it's wont to do."

The children ducked down and stooped into the opening in the wall, reaching up to judge the height of the tunnel and finding it was quite a bit shorter than they were. So, bent and reaching out with their hands in the darkness, they made their way out of the cell, Cefin taking up the rear and encouraging them to move forward and follow the sounds of his people's hammer strikes.

After a nervous, hectic time, they felt the tiny hands of the goblins ahead of them reach and grab at their clothing to stop them. Cefin edged his way past the children to see, then turned around to call out to them in the darkness.

"There's a drop up here, leads down to the river. We don't want no part of that, kiddos. That river's magicked rather hard by old Bran-Nokken. It don't flow right at all and would deliver us right back to him should we try it. Besides, we're without a proper boat and I don't much like swimming."

Leisel giggled in the darkness; Gareth shushed him. "What?" said Leisel. "He's funny."

"We're going to make our way around this drop, and the ledge is a bit narrow," said Cefin. "There are five holes along the wall, and we are aiming for the *fifth* and *last.* Do not go into a hole unless a knocker reaches for ye and pulls ye *in it.* Understand?"

"Yessir," said the children; the *reffke* barked.

"Walk with your feet firmly planted, yer backs to the wall, have your hands feeling the wall. We've no rope, but we'll keep ye steady."

Some of the knockers came back into the tunnel where they waited and positioned themselves so that the line was as such: knocker, child, and so on, with Cefin back again in the rear to shout orders and encouragement. First, Asher stepped out onto the ledge and was overcome with apprehension. The sounds of the rushing river and the cool, wet air that met his face made him feel as if he'd pitch over and fall in, but the knockers before and behind him held onto his trouser-legs, and he began to step slowly to the right, edging his way around the ledge. His back suddenly felt nothing against it—it was the first hole. Then he felt the second and kept going, taking tentative, trembling steps.

Next was Gareth, then Leisel, then the *reffke* children, and finally Medie, who was whispering to Sanandra.

"Who ye talking to, lass?" asked Cefin.

"My friend, she's behind you," said Medie, taking confident steps along the ledge, faster than the others had been.

They were in a small, freshly dug-out room now, and the air was thick with sand and particles. The children were coughing.

"Take a head count then we move on!" said Cefin, and the children felt their arms or the backs of their legs tapped by small hands.

"I count five," said a knocker.

"Eh? No," said Cefin. "Count again. That ain't correct."

They counted three more times. Medie was gone.

###

For miles, she had followed the ill-formed creature as it went about its business in the dark of the ruins of the kingdom of ogres. Karúm had seen drawings of what the ogres looked like once. They were, at the start of their line, somewhat handsome in a ruthless, predatory manner. Seeing the shambling brute in front of her, Karúm wondered at how such a strong line could fall to this—a misshapen son of a misshapen son, half-witted and reeking, confused in the retracing of its own ungainly steps.

She watched it worry over which direction to take for over an hour, lost in the crossroads of the tunnels just above what was once a great shaft that fell deeper into the ground, too deep even for dwarves or ogres, or anything that came from the origins of sun or moon to navigate. It was there that she saw the master scribe emerge from another corridor and call to the ogre, assuring him that whatever work had been done was good and proper, and that great plans were underway and great rewards would follow. Satisfied, the ogre trotted off, and Ygull made his quick way past Karúm, not noticing her crouched upon a ledge in the thickest of the shadows.

She followed him back to the outlands just beyond the *swarthe* city and knew she had little time left to act. Ygull was winded; she supposed his frenzied pace had been because of fear, but now he stopped to catch his breath, leaning his thin hand against a wall that dripped with moisture. Karúm could see him gasping, see his silver-touched crown and cheeks in the gloom-light as she stepped out into the middle of the corridor in full view of him.

"You think I cannot see you there?" said his lilting, madness-touched voice.

She waited.

"Come close, and I will be merciful," said Ygull.

"Well, all right," said Karúm, taking a few more steps towards him. "Here I am." She watched the elder *swarthe* walk to her, sword in hand. "Are you to challenge me? I'm not even a warrior."

"That's unfortunate," said Ygull. "An unfair fight shames the loser. You will not find yourself in heaven, come too long."

"Ah," said Karúm. "I suppose you're right."

Ygull walked to her, a grin upon his thin lips, and swung his sword arrogantly, sweeping it wide. Karúm stood still until the arm was in reach, then pivoted to grab Ygull beneath the shoulder and by the wrist, stepping forward hard against his knee to push it back against itself until he fell. She stepped upon his forearm as if she were breaking a glass, but he reached for her with his free arm even as he shrieked in pain.

She slipped a loop of the rope from her boat around the free arm's wrist and kicked the sword away.

"Get up," she said, yanking the rope to tighten it while bending down for the sword and tossing that back behind her. "I can't tie you up if you're sprawled on the stone like an upended beetle."

"You will rot in the deepest cell," said the scribe.

"No, I won't," said Karúm. "Nor will I see heaven this day."

###

The villagers of Delster woke to find the storm had soothed itself. The winds had settled and the snow was falling quietly from still clouds in a fish-scale sky. The bright, white light shone through the windows of the Silver house where the snow reached just past the lower sills of the first-floor windows.

Four ventured out into the street—Zahsie, Wystan, Alaric, and Martin. After walking only a few feet into the waist-high drifts, Alaric remarked, "This is rather pointless."

"Would that we had snow-shoes," said Martin.

"I actually have a pair," said Zahsie. "Well…they're my husband's. I wish I had more than just the pair, but."

"It'll do," said Wystan. "May I borrow them? And you can all stay warm inside. I just want to scout the street and see if we've got any more trouble."

Properly shod, Wystan wandered the street alone, taking awkward steps upon the strange landscape of the snow drifts. The road looked like a frozen sea, its waves captured by the cold. He made his way to the town commons and climbed up upon the shouting floor to look around.

"Oh, Donnir," he said. "What disturbs Ye so?"

The snow had lent such a peace to the air, and he found it truly beautiful but wished that he was viewing it from a proper cozy home nestled in mountains that understood such weather, and celebrated its regularity with traditions of comfort and cheer, instead of poor, sodden Delster trapped beneath a power and a fury that it did not understand.

He eased his way off the thickly blanketed platform of the shouting floor and landed on a drift not three feet from the platform itself, then walked further into town, towards the river as it flowed, framed between two houses. The homes were no longer the violent chaos of the day before, when chopped-off ice lay in piles like broken glass on the porch and along the ground. Now, they were once again neatly sealed beneath sparkling, rounded blankets of snow.

Coming out from between the houses, Wystan saw the river, still moving, with chunks of ice and gray bones of branches floating past. Beyond the river, the orchards stood hunched like cursed bodies, all with strangely benign and beautiful white caps of snow. He stood there at the bank, watching the trees, for the glare of the landscape had tricked his eyes, and he thought he'd seen movement beyond and amid the twisted, stunted trunks. Something was watching him.

"Well, even if you're there, ye've got no bridge, so there you'll remain," said Wystan. As he spoke, a small, dark figure slipped out from behind a tree as if it had heard him and stopped, boldly watching him. It stood as tall as a young child and was hued in shadow-smoke and soil, so dark Wsytan could not see the eyes nor the face particularly well; just a slip of coal come to life against the stark leavings of the early spring storm.

"Why don't you come to the water," said Wystan. "Go for a swim."

It began to approach the river. Would that he could see its eyes, he was certain they'd be fixed upon him, but he still could not make out the face and was sure it had nothing to do with the creature's coloring. Alaric was nearly as dark in shade, if not hue, and when he watched Wystan from across the room, Wystan could clearly see the man's intent, his intelligence—even desire—in those deep-brown eyes. But this thing—surely it was a thing and not a man, woman, or beast—simply had *no face*, only a constant flux of shadow and flicker where a face should be. It edged closer to the water, still.

"Come to it," whispered Wystan. "Touch it."

It hunched suddenly, arching its back and tucking its head against its chest as if enraged or in great pain.

"You heard me."

It stood up straight and halted its steps.

"Do as I bid you."

It turned as if to retreat from the river, then looked around its shoulder at him.

"Come back to the river. Cross it. Swim lively so you can wring my neck, creature," said Wystan, coming closer to the water's edge and holding his arms wide.

The thing turned and made haste to the river, where it knelt at the water's edge. It hesitated, but then Wystan saw something akin to a mouth open and snarl or possibly hiss at him. It reached for the water with one long digit and touched the surface.

"What are you about, evil thing?" whispered Wystan.

From the spot the creature had touched, a ribbon of ice began to crack along the top of the river's busy caps, crackling and breaking and floating away before reforming and growing thicker until it had made its way several feet across the waves.

"It won't work," said Wystan, to himself. "The river will wash it away."

The jagged line of ice had made it halfway across, but Wystan could see the creature trembling, vibrating against the white which framed it, bent even more as if it were in agony.

The line of ice was coming closer; he could hear it now, crackling like a fire when pine needles were thrown upon it. Wystan began to back away from the river, clumsily in the snow shoes.

At last, the creature fell back onto the snow and scrambled to regain its feet. It was holding the hand that had touched the water as if the limb had been struck, and it lurched away, back among the apple trees, not turning around to look at Wystan as it fled.

"Hallo! Lad!"

Wystan heard Alaric's voice calling to him from the street and hurried as best he could over the drifts to find the dwarf standing atop wooden shutters, strapped to his boots with rope.

"See that? A human would never think of that," Wystan said, smiling and walking closer to him.

Alaric scowled and pointed at the snow-shoes. "What're you wearing, then?"

"Surely your people made these."

Alaric shook his head. "No. It tends not to snow belowground."

"Elves, then."

"Usually elves don't need them. Being rather light."

"Your good friend, Bear—"

"Has broken with that tradition, yes."

Wystan gestured towards the river. "We should get back. There's mischief afoot, and waddling out here like two drunk ducks is likely the poorest choice after what I've seen."

"Let's get back and you can tell me," said Alaric.

They returned to the Silver home, and after freeing his feet from the shoes, Wystan regarded soberly the men and women sitting in the kitchen.

"So what'd it look like?" asked Thomas. Three other men were assembled there, as well as Mink, Zahsie, and Else Tucker.

"It's difficult to say," said Wystan. "Just a very dark thing, and I could see absolutely no face upon it. Couldn't see the eyes, nor the mouth, nor even hair. No clothes."

"As dark as 'im?" asked one of the men, pointing to Alaric.

"As dark as the absence of light," said Wystan, folding his arms. "It was neither man nor *swarthe*. You want to turn the cart around from the conversational direction that you're taking."

"Oh yeah?" said the man. "Or what?"

"I'm not from here and I don't give a fuck about the consequences of tossing you out there in the cold with whatever evil waits," snarled Wystan.

"First off," said Zahsie, coming to stand between the two men. "Nobody tosses anyone from what is still my kitchen. Second, sit down, both of you, and stop acting like children. Actually, to be honest, most children would be better behaved."

Mink came to Wystan, putting her hand on his chest. "The only evil-doing will be out there, at least, until we figure out a way to stop it. Let's not bring it into our hearts, in here."

"Don't tell me, mistress," said Wystan, slowly taking his seat. "Tell him."

"I didn't mean to insinuate," said the man. "Just asked a question."

"We're not fighting *men*," said Zahsie. "I can't tell you exactly what we're fighting, but I know, in my heart, it's not men or women, and I think you all know that too."

They sat there, the villagers, Mink, and Alaric, and Wystan glaring at his teacup, in silence. The wind had picked up again. The storm had almost risen back to its previous fury.

"Running out of water," said Mink.

"For now, I think it's best if we all stay inside," said Thomas.

"And if the house freezes up again? We'll need to fetch water," said Zahsie.

Zahsie and Mink left the kitchen to go back out into the cold, heading to the river with two empty buckets, and were nearly swept away by the gales of wind. The snow, however, had stopped whipping down from the sky, so, with good visibility and struggling steps, they made their way to the swiftly moving water's edge to fill the buckets. One woman watched the road from the mountain while the other scooped the water, and when they were finished, they followed their boot-prints back to the house.

The air was rent with a shrieking cry, carried long and loudly over the cruel wind.

"There's something outside," said Mink breathlessly as they came into the kitchen, water sloshing onto the floor from the full buckets.

"Did you see it?" asked Wystan.

"No," said Zahsie. "We heard it. When ye were up at Pastor Bear's, did ye hear anything like a screaming?"

"Yes," said Alaric. "Trees breaking, ice cracking, and what sounded like wind that screamed."

Thomas began to weep quietly.

"Come now," said Alaric. "It's not over. We haven't given up the fight yet."

"And it hasn't given up trying to fight us either," said Zahsie.

"Let's muster who feels able to stand and get what weapons we've got, and—"

"More protection against the cold as well," said Mink. "It's gotten even worse out there, with that wind."

"Zahsie, if you'd be so kind as to grab any more hats or scarves—hell, bedsheets'll do at this point—and Alaric and I will see about weaponry. Thomas?" asked Wystan, coming to the man. "Do you think you can help with bolstering up these windows? There's shutters outside that have fallen, and there's tables inside."

Zahsie stopped and looked at him.

"I'm sorry, madam, but at this point, I'll build you all new tables and chairs and shutters, should we make it through this alive."

She nodded to him, though her face was pale, and she hurried up the stairs.

Four went out in the street, balancing atop the shimmering, ice-encrusted snow drifts. No one else dared face whatever new horror was coming for them. Wystan, Alaric, Hugh, and Gailen stood heavily dressed, scarves tied about their cheeks, holding axes and blades—Gailen, a pitchfork—and they waited.

Tall, wiry shapes stalked at the road's distant edge, just before it curved to wrap around the mountain and thread its way up through the woods to Mink and Bear's houses. They seemed creatures built of white sticks, perhaps birch trees that had come to life and grown legs, with faces as dark as the thing Wystan had seen spooking amid the orchard trees. These new devils walked with purpose, taking long strides and pushing their strange, long feet down through each snow drift, crushing the ice to powder. Every once and again, the long, white heads would look to the sky and scream.

"We need to meet them," said Wystan, his hands shaking as he held an axe, Bear's sword sheathed from a belt cinched about a thick coat. "We cannot fight them here in front of this house. If we fail, and they break the walls..."

"I cannot take a step," said Hugh. "I feel frozen to this spot. Not intending to make jokes at this dark hour, of course."

"I share the same plight," said Alaric. "We must take courage in each other."

"Yet we are still here," said Gailen. "I've barely the courage to stand and look."

Then Wystan was running away from them, slipping and stomping across and through the snow drifts, his axe held high, bellowing at the creatures in the distance.

The other three begrudgingly followed, jogging toward that which they'd only ever imagined in nightmares.

###

"I have to find her!" yelled Asher, slapping at the hands of the tiny knockers who sought to subdue him.

Cefin, quick as a snake, grabbed the young *saylie's* hands and, with strength greater than his size, held the boy still.

"Lad," he said.

"I don't want to hear it," weeped Asher, sitting down on his heels upon the cold rock.

"But ye have to."

Asher sobbed, gasping a shuddering breath. "I know."

"We can find her. I've got a hundred and ten men. I'll send twenty after her. We're *good* down here. We can see in the dark and we hear like dogs. *You*, sir, have to get these other young ones up to the surface. My ear to the ground, there's a lot of trouble up there, and that includes some grown ones and your kin as well. So it's time to be a man, lad. Time to stop yer feelings because they're getting in the way."

Asher's tears streamed more freely, looking at the goblin in the midnight light.

Cefin wiped at the boy's face with a tiny thumb. "They just get put aside. Until ye can deal with them some other, better day. I'm not saying to erase them, because ye cannot."

Asher's breath hitched, but he quieted.

"They kept my men and I in metal boxes hung from the ceilings of a huge cavern," said Cefin. "For almost twenty years. I counted. Did I despair? *Often.* But my men looked to me for reassurance. For the will to go on. And now we're free, and I, too, want to cry, but there's still not yet time for tears." Cefin walked away to consult with his men, and Gareth scooted over to Asher.

"You know, he's right decent about things."

"Yeah," said Asher, sniffling.

"Doesn't change the fact that he's as tall as a cat, which is weird when he's giving us advice."

There had been four tunnels leading away from the small room to which the children had been led. Knockers had been flooding the corridors as well as the room for a better part of an hour, by Leisel's counting. Gareth had asked him what he was saying, whispering in the dark, and that's when they'd learned of his habit of counting the minutes on his hands and on the ground, tapping the moments in hopes to manage them.

"How long we gonna stay here?" Gareth asked of a passing knocker, and the goblin scurried away from the boy's reaching hands, muttering in some tongue the human couldn't decipher. "Are they quite rude, then?"

"No," said Asher. "They're busy. I thought your da worked in a mine?"

"He did. As did my grandpapa."

"So you'll know that if someone pesters someone who's working, they tend to get pushed aside?"

"True."

They sat and watched the knockers come and go, and finally Cefin came to stand again before Asher, Leisel, and Gareth. The *reffke* crouched beside the three boys.

"So, here's the thing," said Cefin. "Gonna be a moment or two before we can make for the surface."

"Why?" asked Leisel.

"There's traffic in the main corridor that connects all those four tunnels."

"There are four?" asked Gareth, squinting in the gloom.

"Aye," said Cefin. "There are four. And the ogres what run this warren are on the move. We don't know why, but we can't risk being seen by them."

"Okay," said Asher, "but if there are ninety of your men here still, plus four of us, can't we just overtake them?"

"No, lad," said Cefin. "I'm afraid it's not as easy as that. There's deep magic at work here. That old king, Bran-Nokken? He was a terror in his day, but he's next to dead right now. And something's kept him going well beyond his years—and that *something*...well, it's what's running the place now. And we best not let it know we're here if we aim to escape."

###

For hours, they sat in the coal-black dark, waiting. Asher felt his eyes growing heavy, and he lay down upon the stark rock, his hands beneath his face, cupped. He felt Gareth curl up beside him, and soon the others were joining them, cold and exhausted.

"Hey," whispered Gareth. "How many in your family?"

"What?" said Asher, for he'd dozed off, and he thought groggily, "Entire?"

"Well, I mean, that you know of."

"My da's got three brothers and five sisters. Got my grandparents. Beyond that, don't really know."

"Really? I know almost near everybody this side of the Bran valley."

"Must be nice."

"Not as such. Most of them are daft and irritating."

Asher laughed. "Well, okay."

"Who's your favorite?"

"My da, of course."

"No—I mean, obviously. Besides your da?"

"Hmm." Asher stifled a yawn and thought a moment. "Besides my Aunt Crow, I guess, my Uncle Genet."

"Why do they have all critter names?"

"My grandfather was a mad genius."

"Oh."

"Yeah."

"So, what about your uncle do ye like?"

"Well, he's a sellsword. Aunt Crow's likely better, but he works constantly while she just serves her goddess."

"I'd actually think a goddess would be a more demanding customer than people?"

"I would too, but it seems to not work that way. People have less a tap on nature and the big picture. My uncle is constantly at war—other men's wars—and mostly what he does is rescue the innocents trapped in the middle."

"Really?" Gareth sat up a bit.

"Yeah. He doesn't make a big thing about it. Tries not to get caught, because that's not what they're paying him for. He sees to it that any innocents he finds get a safe passage out of the troubled lands in which he's fighting."

"Wow."

"I know."

"See? That's a real hero."

Asher sighed.

"What's wrong?"

"I always wanted to be just like him, to be honest."

"You still can. You are, actually. You've gotten us this far. We couldn't have done it without you."

"That's what I mean. He comes home once every few years. I saw him at the last reunion. He makes it seem so easy, but it's not. I've been trapped down here, trying to figure things out, trying to not be scared. I thought I wanted to be a hero, but now that I guess I am? By my uncle's standards? I wish I'd ever just be a regular man."

Gareth nodded in the near-darkness. "That's very real. But I doubt that any of us will be regular after this is over."

"Time to go, kiddos," said Cefin, coming back into the small room. "The hullaballoo seems to have diminished, so we'll be grabbing this chance to get gone while the getting's good. This here—" he presented one of his workers, a red-bearded knocker "—is Harold. Yer to follow him, and there'll be more of my men behind you, guarding against any sneaks that might see to slowing you down. I want you to go as fast as you can without stumbling. And Harold's in charge—do as he says, please."

"What about you?" asked Gareth. "Where are you going?"

"Gonna join up with my boys who went after this one's cousin. I'll see ye all up at the surface, where I hope we'll be met with a fine, spring day."

"Well," said Asher, "I hope that too."

"All right. Let's get on with it. See you kiddos later. Be brave!"

"Yessir."

"Yes Mr. Cefin."

"Thank you, sir."

Harold led them swiftly down the last corridor on the left, and they crouched as they hurried, until that passageway met up with the larger tunnel beyond it—nearly as large as the one Asher, Medie, and Jumps High had taken down into Bran-Nokken's domain what seemed like months ago but was surely only days. Then they were jogging along with the knockers, the *reffke*'s steps springy and light, the boys panting but keeping a good pace. The corridor snaked around to the right, then back around to the left, and finally began to climb.

"We're going up!" said Gareth, his hand on Asher's shoulder for guidance.

"Yes, I know," said Asher, though his voice was grim.

"They'll find her," said Gareth. "I can feel it in my bones."

Suddenly they heard Leisel trip and fall with a winded *oof*, and the other boys stopped and turned. Asher could see in the gloom the *reffke* help Leisel to his feet.

"He all right?" called Harold.

"Yessir," said Asher. "Only there's…"

"What is it lad?"

"Something on the ground."

The boys knelt and put their hands on the thing that Leisel had tripped over. It was a leg bone, long as a full-grown man's. Asher could discern in the near-black many, many such bones, as well as smaller ones. There were also skulls.

The knockers could see them now, too.

"This is a bad place," whispered Leisel.

Suddenly a mournful wail broke the heavy quiet, and the children jumped as the knockers spun around, hammers at the ready.

Leisel pushed through them all, listening.

The wail was answered with a bark, and then the bark replied to by a series of yips.

The *reffke* were sniffing the air, their tails waving from side to side, and soon they were calling to the sounds in soft, encouraging barks and yips.

"This is too much noise," hissed Harold. "We don't want to call any trouble."

"They're locked in cages!" called Leisel, and he'd somehow disappeared from the corridor.

"Hey now," said Harold, pushing back to where the children were standing. "Where'd that boy get to?

"This way," said Asher, pointing to the *reffke*, who had slipped away too, down a narrower passageway that led off the main corridor. The boys and Harold followed the fox-children, and the tunnel curved down again, then turned sharply to the right.

"I don't like that we're going *down*," said Gareth.

"Nor do I, but…" said Asher. "Oh."

They had come out into a room nearly as large as the fighting pit. All around them were cells similar to the one they'd been locked in by the *nicht-ogren*, but with entire walls of bars instead of a simple door. And within these cells were dire beasts, larger than was typical, and of all sorts and kinds: badgers, raccoons, possums, even foxes. Dim torches sputtered along the walls.

"We have to get them out," cried Leisel, going to each cage, reaching his hands in.

"Don't!" called Asher, but he saw that the beasts were kind or, at least, weak enough to be docile. They nuzzled their snouts against Leisel's reaching hands, and the cries of them rose up once again.

"We'll have to get them out or that ruckus will bring back the ogres, Captain," said another knocker to Harold, and with that, the goblin-men were climbing the bars of the cage-walls, digging and tapping with their hammers at the seams. One by one, the walls of bars fell, and the beasts hurried out, jumping and pawing at the knockers and the children with feverish excitement.

"All right now," bellowed Harold; his voice astoundingly deep and rich for such a small fellow. "Time to move."

It was a chaos, the larger group funneling back into the smaller passageway to head back to the corridor, but in time, all beasts, knockers, and children had regained the main corridor and were heading up. All but Leisel.

"Damn it," said Gareth. "Come on now, Leisel."

Asher turned, and they could see Leisel coming, a young badger cradled in his arms.

"I think its leg is broken," he said. "I'm gonna carry it up and my da will mend it."

Asher nodded but turned to the darkness from which they'd climbed. A thick scent was hurrying towards them.

A black-feathered arrow appeared through Leisel's chest just above the silvery fur of the badger, and a crimson that was black for lack of light began to spread across the boy's shirt. His mouth gasped a breathless *O*, and his eyes widened then fluttered beneath his long lashes, and closed as he fell.

One of the knockers aimed his hammer for a point in the darkness and whipped it towards the unseen foe. Asher heard a terrific shout coming from down the corridor.

"*You horrible shit. Cracked my eye,*" gurgled a wretched, familiar voice.

"Pick up your lad and fly—we've got to go," said the knocker.

###

He to whom the crown had stained blinked his gluey eyes and regarded the child on the ashen floor below his feet. His breath shuddered, for his belly and brain felt hollow and empty, but the ghostly fingers soothed his head and traced his naked spine, calming him. The child was slowly waking up. She had retched in her sleep, and a pool of fluid spread out beside her head. The bitter herbs of the tea had nearly poisoned her to death, but thankfully, she'd survived those dreams, those torments, and was here before him. Her magic spanned out in each direction from her like the wings of heaven, freely, multi-limbed, glorious; his eyes could see the aureate keenness of its glow.

He thought that it would taste like honey, once her flesh was pierced by his teeth.

"She will come to you," said the Voice. "You must let her. To riddle her with fear will sully the meat and the magic."

The heartbeat quickened, and he saw that she could hear that. She struggled to her feet. Dub and Dother had torn away her clothes.

"Help," was the mouse-squeak, so small, so at odds with the greatness of her power. "Please?"

The ancient hand gripped the calcified, smooth-as-marble edge of the ledge he lay upon, pulling the bent and bloated body closer, the lank hair hanging down, the ghostly eyes watching her stumble in the somber torch flicker. The nails, curled and black, tapped at the wall's edge, and he thrilled to see her spin about, listening, struggling. Yes, what was that? Girl? Mouse? A rat? A stray thing in the darkness, perhaps?

"Shall I call to her, my beloved master?"

Yessssss breathed out every thought and cell of hunger within Bran-Nokken's atrophying soul.

###

Her throat burned and caught as if she'd swallowed bones, and it felt as if one or two remained there, poking the flesh of her insides. She was naked and burning with fever, so confused and full of sorrow at the sights she'd seen. Even before them, she felt as if at any moment she would open her mouth and wail again and again until she died from misery. But she did not wail and she had not died.

The ogren had lifted her away, and she'd been jostled by their quick, heavy steps, over the shoulder of one like a sack of grain. As they ran, they'd torn at her skirt and her blouse, plucked her shoes off her feet, and even her stockings; she'd shrieked and cried, and maybe that was why her throat hurt her so, but no. No, it wasn't.

They'd taken some tube, a soft but thick hollow reed fixed to a funnel, and shoved the reed into her mouth and down her throat just a bit, then drained a flask of horrible, bitter drink into her; she'd thrown it up almost immediately once they took out the tube, and so they did it again, and that time, she'd managed to keep it down.

The poison had made her legs feel like stone, and she'd fallen to the floor, where her eyes were suddenly robbed first of color, then of sight completely, and her face felt as if it was a sheep's bladder filled with air and would pop—hot and tight and painful. Drool poured from her mouth like she was a mad dog, and she tried to scream, but only strangled, little squeaks would come out of her hurting throat. The last she'd remembered before sleep took her was clawing at the floor of the room, hands and feet like a cat having a dream.

She had so many dreams.

She dreamed that she was a kite made of her own skin stretched over her own bones, flying over a ruined land of charred homes and torn trees. People were being lashed by cruel chains, the sky was purple and gold, and lightning was spinning in a wheel around the sun.

She dreamed she was a small mouse who'd eaten her way into a loaf of bread, but then the bread was being sliced up on a plate, and in the last thick chunk, she'd hidden and was watching a great mouth below ready itself to eat the bread and her.

She dreamed she was a broken, ruined thing that could never see the light of day, because he couldn't walk, or crawl, only be carried by the devil that sang to him, and so in his house, which was his grave, he slept fitfully, dreaming of better days while he sucked on the bones of those who had come down into his lair and had never found their way back.

She stopped pacing.

Medie crouched down, hugging her knees, for she felt eyes upon her and she was bashful in her nakedness.

It was then that the potion met its purpose within her, and she closed her tearful eyes one more time.

When she opened them, it were as if someone had placed a hundred candles in this miserable cell and she could actually see his miserable face—even the dark thing that clung all around him like a coat of shadow, a hungry wraith.

She stood before him.

"You hear me," said the whisper.

"I do," said Medie.

"Obey us and come to him."

She held her arms down, hands open, fingers spread apart. "Why would I do that?"

"Because he wills it, and when he touches you, he will imbue you with power you could never hope to obtain as a mere mortal *saylie*."

"I am not mortal," said Medie quietly.

"Oh, are you not?" asked the Voice. "What trick have you learned to give yourself forever life?"

"Well," said Medie, "a better trick, at least, than what you've been whispering upon the ears of your thrall."

###

Bran-Nokken could hear her derision and arrogance but could not tear his sight away from the glorious fans of arcana lifting up and out from her small form. She was so bright, humming like a tuning fork, trilling like a songbird's call in this dark, forgotten place that was his ruined kingdom. How he yearned for even just a drop of her blood, just a taste; how like an elixir that would be.

His heart spasmed like a toad in the hand of a child, and his body ached with desire.

"Come to him," said the Voice, putting all of its mind to the task.

###

Medie's eyes drooped, flickered shut, and she stumbled; the spell-sleep swift and heavy. She found she could not fight it.

###

"*I have found you.*"

Bear shivered in his fitful sleep. He imagined a young girl's voice, calling to him from within a sunlit garden.

"*I have found you, Pastor Bear.*"

He curled his body tighter against the wall, bidding the strange voice away.

"*Wake up.*"

He sat up and put his hand over his eyes—this was the only way he could open them and not be punished by the impenetrable dark of the room. He listened.

"*I am here.*"

"You are not," he said quietly, his mouth utterly dry, his throat painful. "You are another trick of the thing that torments me."

"*No, sirrah. I promise. I am Sanandra Gunther. Open your eyes, please?*"

"I will not. The darkness pains them."

"*Sirrah, I am not of the darkness.*"

Bear opened his hand a bit and saw between the fingers the faint glow of a person-shaped outline standing before him. He moved his hand away and saw her, as if she'd been traced by the phosphorescence of cave lichen or faerie flies.

"Is it really you, little one?" he asked, his voice a husk of a whisper.

"I lived in the house beyond the briar hedge," she said, and her voice was clear now, as if she were standing there in the room. "My father heard the Voice call to him, and it bade him tie me to the Very Old Tree, and when the ground opened up, the ogren took me to him."

"To whom, kind one?"

"To Bran-Nokken. The King of the Dark."

Bear brought his manacled ankle closer to him and rubbed the bruised flesh. "Why, Sanandra? Why would they do that?"

"He has lived long past his time, he has," said the ghost-girl. "The Voice can play tricks on people, make them see things, hear things that aren't real. It lures people down, deep far down, so that Bran-Nokken can feast upon them. But the flesh of plain men and woman doesn't stay in his belly."

Bear watched her glowing form with rapt attention. "Gods," he whispered.

"Only those who are magical remain within him and grant him life continued."

"My girl," said Bear. "Are you the reason Medie came down here?"

"Yes," said Sanandra. "And Medie's the reason I've come to you now."

He pulled at the manacle, digging his fingers under it, trying to break the hinge, cutting the edge of his thumb on the metal and shifting over to his side, frustrated, winded.

Suddenly something in his pocket was pushing into the flesh of his hip, like a finger jabbing, a reminder.

"Oh," said Bear, his voice trembling. "Oh, you stupid man." He removed the package from Zahsie Silver and unwrapped it: three slender locust branches, tied with a braid, and at one end of them, a thick glass globe. "Okay, then," said Bear. "What am I supposed to do with—"

The sticks felt warm in his hands, and he could *see* them. He could see.

He inhaled deeply, then breathed out onto the charm cupped in his hands, thinking *grow, grow little flame.* The globe burst into light as if it held a wick and oil, and he'd struck a flint stick upon it.

There, just beyond the span of his legs, lay an iron key. Just *right there.* For all the hours or days he'd sat in the dark, it had been there.

He unlocked the manacle and stood, tenderly balanced with most of his weight off the once-chained ankle. He hobbled over to the door and tried the key on it; it would not fit. The door held fast in its wall of bars.

"That is fine," said Bear, taking a step back and closing his eyes. "On the seventh road from the sea of glass, there is a hidden ridge, amid the herds of goats and sea-birds that gather there. The road leads up to the mountains, and on the third peak, there is a bald crown, bedecked with wildflowers, and a path that winds amid the stone. And on a circle of grass, to which the sea has carried me, atop the white rock, beneath the shade of the wizened trees, there is a stone. By the stone stands a cormorant, and it watches me with black eyes, and from its breast a single white feather lifts on the softly blowing wind to my palm, and I grasp it, and as I grasp it, I also bend down to the pebble and I reach for that as above me the sky gains the visage of the five kings who once ruled this land and they smile upon me.

"And their crowns shine with the light of the midsummer sun.

"And the rains fall from the blue sky, and each drop is as a spark from a blacksmith's fire.

"And I cup my hands to the falling rains, and as I command them, so do I command the fire!"

The door made a sound like a tree being felled, cracking and slowly breaking, and the rusted metal pulled inward as if made of cloth, then burst outward in an explosion. Bear cried out from both the shock and the success of it, then held the globe-kin to see into the corridor and carefully stepped barefoot over the shards of twisted metal there.

He followed the corridor down, his eyes blinking at the suddenly returned ability to see, now that there was light, and his lips whispered constant prayers to Huil, *lead me there, take me, lead me.* The corridors twisted down and around so many times he'd no idea where he was going but felt his heart jump as if pulled along by a string: *turn right, this way now, turn left, keep going.*

He stumbled into the small room and saw the bloated, gray-skinned thing with its long, black tongue, lapping at the blood pulsing up from Medie's wrist.

Bear gasped, and as he did so, he felt the wild, overflowing power of Medie's unbridled magic crackle down his throat, into his belly, spinning in his chest like a fire-wheel, let loose by the poison and filling the room, pushing against the walls, filling each living thing within and squirming around in their bellies, in their souls.

Bear gasped again and backed up, blinking against the intrusion. He saw the room fully now—roots hanging as it was beyond the *swarthe* kingdom when the floor collapsed, and this room, too, was unsteady, trembling with the combined weight of all of the bodies.

"Medie!" Bear called, still in the spell state from his own magic that he'd cast, still humming with the combination of his own power and of his niece's, and his voice sounding like a blast from a great horn, shaking the dirt like beads upon a drum skin. "We have to leave this place."

He took a step towards Medie, and the king of the *nicht-ogren* shot him a murderous look, his lips still pressed to Medie's bleeding wrist.

Bear bowed his head and whispered hurriedly, feverishly, and the trembling grew more violent as the roots hanging from the ceiling curled around his limbs like seeking snakes. His heart hammered in his chest with the vibrancy and adrenaline of the aspect he was calling into himself. Huil came down into him, and his form towered over the ruined ogre-king like fate itself.

Bran-Nokken, having had his small blood-supper, tried to stand on his own feet to face the pastor, his belly slung low, his bowed legs well-muscled and stout, and he swung a fist the size of Delster's bell at Bear's head.

Bear-become-Huil caught the fist and ripped it asunder, throwing fingers, flesh, and bare bones down onto the blackened floor.

###

"Uncle!" screamed Medie, for she at first could see his face, just before the ancient ogre had slipped down from its soiled ledge and caught her by the arm. The king had sliced her skin with his sharp, yellowed teeth, and she'd fainted, and he'd caught her, his arms cold as a worm's skin, his muscles trembling at first, then strong as a snake's.

She'd lost her footing and hung there in Bran-Nokken's arms, feeling her lips grow cold and her face heavy as before, when she'd been forced to drink the poison, but this was a different heaviness. It felt like sleep, like sleep as thick and certain as a winter's storm, and she was slipping blissfully away.

Then the seal was broken, and she fell, landing on her hands and knees on the rock, and she'd skinned herself. This was enough to snap her out of her fugue.

And there was Uncle Bear, before the roots rose up from the floor and covered him completely and he began to tear Bran-Nokken into gray, bloody pieces.

The shadow-thing had also crept down and was edging around the wall of the room as if it were an actual shadow of someone who was not here, not really. Medie saw long, clawed hands reaching for Bear, and she ran to the wall and slapped the hands away, the poison elixir still in her blood enabling her to see great golden sparks fly as she struck at the thing, and she heard it cry, its voice petulant, shrieking.

"Away, you foul thing," she wheezed, still struggling to catch her breath in her light-headedness, but her magic swirled and snapped all around her as if she wielded twin flails, and she struck at the Voice again and again, until it slipped away from the room, weeping as it fled.

"Uncle," whispered Medie, and she slid back to the floor, for all the room was spinning and she couldn't fight the sleep that covered her like blankets of snow.

###

They ran in the dark, the knockers, the boys, the *reffke*, all the freed animals, silently though sometimes one of the children would cry out in anguish, and this would elicit a firm push from a knocker against the back of a leg, or a pull on the hand. They had to keep going, and they did, going for miles until they stumbled, and then they ran some more, until the knocker in the lead had hurried back to meet them, shouting.

The smell of turned soil burned their noses, so used to the cold, dank air of the underground they'd become. Then there was the smell of clean snow and of stark, wild air. The light was growing up ahead, the light of the above-world, the light of the white sun.

"Stop," called one of the knockers. "Tear yer shirts. Cover yer eyes. It's a snowy mess out there in the Up, and ye'll blind yerselves against it."

Asher and Gareth were holding Leisel's body and gently set him down. They tore at their shirts and wrapped the cloth about their eyes. They tore more pieces for Jumps High and Quickly, who, after gently setting down the baby badger, did the same.

"It's the last," said the closest knocker. "We aren't goin' with ye. But be well, lads and lass. Was an honor to serve ye."

Asher hugged the knocker and began to softly cry, and then Gareth was weeping, too.

"Go on now, before ye run out of time. Also, I'd prefer not to cry m'self in front of the other lads."

Asher and Gareth gently lifted Leisel and followed the knockers up, and Jumps High and Quickly came behind them. Suddenly the Great Old Tree was ahead of them, and the light was shining through their bandages like airy fire as they stumbled out into the blinding day, into the snow, with all of the animals trampling over the ground and over the mountain, away to whatever sanctuary was available to them.

Hunter was there, by the tree.

Asher and Gareth ran to him, talking at once and crying as he looked at the body of Leisel in shock. He gathered the small boy into his arms as the two older boys told him everything that had occurred, and he listened, his hand against Leisel's golden head.

###

Crow had followed the ogren for the better part of that day, walking in silence behind their slapping steps, holding to shadows as they turned about, momentarily confused in their direction, sniffing the air to remind themselves of the proper path.

"Dumb as a dress on a horse," she muttered, sliding down to rest in an alcove while they argued.

"*You're always wrong,*" hissed the one whose voice reminded Crow of a hot weapon being dunked in a blacksmith's tub.

"Just got turned about. Today is a trouble and a bother. I lost an eye! Those horrid, little men."

"*You, are a trouble and a bother. Ought to slit your throat and toss your fat carcass to father.*"

"I'm not the one who dabbles in spells, dear," gurgled the taller ogre. "It's not me he'd ruther eat."

"I should hamstring both of ye," whispered Crow. "So you can get out of my way."

"What's that?" said the taller of the two.

"*I heard nothing.*"

"Nor did I, but I smell a beastie."

"Ach," said Crow, standing up and walking into the middle of the passageway. "Honestly, I just had a bath in the river."

"*Wring its neck, Dother,*" said the whispery, shrieky one.

"Magic it fast, Dub," said the gurgle-voiced one.

"Well," said Crow. "So the short, fat one—you're called Dub. And the taller one that sounds like he's got a potato jammed in his throat—that's Dother. Good to know."

"Shut up, beastie. We're about to squish ye to jelly," said Dother.

"That seems unlikely," said Crow, and she unsheathed her sword.

The *nicht-ogren* laughed, and the sounds combined were like the hiss of a great cat and the dribble of water upon clay.

"Which one of us will be run through first?" asked Dother.

"Which one of ye would like to be?" asked Crow, waiting.

"*You do it*," said Dub. "*I'm tired from the walk.*"

"Fine," said Dother, and he walked past the other ogre, sniffing at the air, squinting with his remaining eye. Crow ran at him then, sword pointed at him, and he snatched at the hilt and her arm, pushing her down onto her back. He laughed, standing over her, a gruesome bridge of flesh.

Crow slipped a dagger from its sheath, hopped onto the balls of her feet and sprang upwards like a cat going for a dish on a shelf, straight into his bare belly. She stood up fully beneath him, shoulder against his immense weight while he screamed. She hefted him over to fall on his back, stomped on her sword to flip it just into hand's reach and hacked down at his throat once, embedding the blade deep against his neck.

She slid it out from the mortal wound and ran at Dub.

"*Ayeee*," he whisper-shrieked, raising his hands at her and wiggling his thick fingers. He backed up a few paces then looked down at the dagger stuck deep into his chest. "*Now I am angry with you, horrible beast.*"

"That's fine," said Crow, and slid down in front of him, slicing hard across to amputate his left leg above the ankle.

###

The goddess had left Bear's body as suddenly as She had claimed it, and the air resounded with a great *crack* as if lightning had struck stone. The first things he saw were his hands, shining with blackening blood and strings of gore. Then he saw Medie, a tiny puddle of crimson seeping from her wrist. "No," he stammered and took off his shirt. With his teeth, he tore the sleeve that was the only part of the garment unsullied by Bran-Nokken's offal. He wrapped the wrist so tightly that the hand began to purple, and he lifted her to him and fled the room.

"Do you know where you're going?" asked Medie, her arms around her uncle's neck as he ran in the darkness.

"Wish I could lie and say I did, but I don't," said Bear, his breath coming in gasps, his legs shaking. He'd been without water for he knew not how long, and food for even longer than that, but the momentary aspecting of his goddess had imbued him with some energy; a small surplus of that now helped him go on.

"Did they hurt you?"

"They did," said Bear. "Not my body, though."

"No," said Medie. "They don't hurt one's body, unless they're eating it." Her head lolled back, and she was unconscious again.

There ahead of them, the light of Zahsie's charm reached something large. Bear stopped.

"No," he whispered. "Fuck. Please no more."

"She's gone," said a thick, hateful voice in the darkness.

"She's alive, just resting," said Bear.

"No," said the voice, and its owner came closer. The third *nicht-ogre* came into murky view. "Your goddess. Is gone, from you."

"Maybe she is," said Bear, easing Medie down onto the ground. "Maybe she isn't." He stood there, watching the brute, who was easily three hands taller than him. "But you know who is gone?"

The ogre's eyes squinted at him.

"Your king. And your king's master."

The ogre sucked in its breath as if a rock had hit it square in the gut. *Oof.*

"You killed them," it said.

"She and I did. As well as she." He gestured to Medie, "So you've no business anymore here. Go along home to wherever it is they build useless, irrelevant creatures."

"I was born in these caves. I shall not abandon them or he whose service I was born into. I've met that boy of yours—you smell nearly alike. I will kill him, after I kill you."

"Wrong. You're about to die here, as your father did before you," said Bear, and regretted his brashness, but he was exhausted and still buzzing from the interaction with his deity.

"Will I, now?" growled the ogre, who took another step forward, then stopped, turning to look behind him.

"Shame to waste all of these perfectly tomb-sized cells ye got laying about," said Crow, far up the corridor, in the dark.

"Shame," said the ogre and notched a black-feathered arrow into a bow he slid off his shoulder. "It would be that." He let the arrow fly.

"No!" cried Bear, his throat cracking with anguish.

In the distance, Crow screamed, and they heard her small body fall to the floor.

"That was easy," said the ogre. "And now for you. I'm all out of arrows, but I doubt I'd need them anyway. You don't look like the scrapping type."

"Do I not?" said Bear, assuming a fighting stance, arms wide.

The ogre gurgle-laughed. "No, you don't."

There was a sound like stone scraping upon stone, and the ogre looked down at his feet, and so did Bear. A small, curved blade came skittering down the tunnel, passing between the ogre's feet and stopping at Bear's, who picked it up. "Well."

"Won't help," said the ogre, reaching for him.

Bear brought the knife around to slash across the ogre's forearm, then stabbed upward. The ogre hissed in pain and struck out to punch Bear, who ducked his head to the right a bit too slow and caught a glance of the ogre's huge fist along his jaw, but Bear swung the blade around and punched through the ogre's bicep with it, then pulled it out and, ducking low, slashed it into the ogre's ribs. The ogre kicked out, and Bear caught the brute's heavy foot, then tried to duck again as the ogre brought down both fists upon his shoulders. Bear dropped the knife and fell, raising his arms to protect his head.

"I'm bleeding," said the ogre, "but you're about to be dead."

"Doubtful," whispered a voice behind him, and he stood up just as Crow's sword pierced his neck. Suddenly, there was a red slash at the center, and his life's blood sluiced out of his throat like water from a hand-pump.

Bear kicked away from the fountain of gore as the ogre fell, face-first, hands reaching and clawing until he stopped moving altogether.

Crow hurried to Bear, checking him, moving his lips away to see his gums, opening his eyes forcefully, pinching the skin of his arms.

"Ow," he said. "What're ye? Thought you got shot."

"Ye been too long without water. Take some of mine. Medie—how are you feeling? You look somewhat gray."

"They fed me poison," she said, her voice rough.

"What?" said Crow.

"I'll have to get her to Zahsie," said Bear, "when we get home. I don't think it's aiming to harm her permanently. It's dark magic, but it only sought to… I can explain when we—" He slipped backwards, leaning against the wall, panting with exhaustion, Crow's water-skin in his hand.

"Let's just get you both home."

"And her, too," said Medie quietly.

"Yes, Sanandra too," said Bear. "Help me up now. I've got a bit of strength left in me, and I mean to call Huil one more time today, so she can perhaps show us the way out."

"I've actually brought Her representatives," said Crow. "At least, they should be here soon."

In the distance, the sounds of tapping welled up like an arena of voices, echoing down the tunnel walls like rats running. Bear stepped back, but Medie took his hand.

"That's them," said Crow.

Out of the gloom and coming into the shimmering, green-gold glow of Zahsie's globe-kin, Cefin the knocker appeared, looking up at Crow with a wide smile.

"I'm pleased," he said. "Ye done well."

"Of course I did," said Crow. "Now, one last favor exchanged—lead us up to the surface, and you and I can be fully paid towards each other."

Cefin winked, his long nose crinkling against ruddy cheeks. "Wish there was still a bit of debt to be edged off," he said. "Wouldn't mind walking the caves with a capable warrior such as yerself."

"Well, all right, then," said Bear. "That's my sister. And…I'd much prefer getting angry about this conversation *aboveground*, little man."

"The tall are always in such a hurry," said Cefin. "Long-legged man's disease."

"By the way," said Bear as they followed the knocker foreman up through the corridor, "have ye seen my staff?"

"Hunter's got it," said Crow.

Medie stumbled, and Bear handed the globe-kin to Crow, hefting the girl up in his arms. "That's fantastic. Did he merely carry it—or did he wield it?"

"Made it shine like the sun. You'd have been proud, brother."

"I *am* proud," said Bear. Then he stopped.

Crow stopped as well, and the footfalls of Cefin also halted in the gloomy distance.

"What?" said Crow.

"It cannot be," said Bear so wearily it sounded as if a cry would escape his dry lips. "Damn it to the center of the world."

Cefin came jogging back, his eyes intense with focus. "I've only got a skeleton crew of my men left with me. Ye know what's blocking our path to the upside?"

"I do," said Bear. "Alps—am I correct?"

"You are," said Cefin. "A big ol' swarm, and they get nasty in large numbers."

"I'm aware."

"There are two choices that I can see." The roar of frenzied footsteps and the shrieking, howling of the alps was getting louder, beyond in the dark. "We all fight them to a man, and maybe we have a chance at weakening them enough to get past and make a decent run for it."

Bear and Crow looked at Medie, who had fallen asleep.

"Or I leave you with two of my men, who can dig ye out and around, closer to the opening to the ground, while the rest of my men and I hold the alps back."

"The swarm sounds large," said Bear. "There could be a hundred of them."

"It's fine," said Cefin. "We're not overly concerned." The knocker kept glancing back over his shoulder, and his men were shouting to him.

"Brother," said Bear, going down on one knee while still holding Medie. "I won't ask it of you."

"I won't ask you to risk the life of this precious child," said Cefin. He turned and whistled. "*Hans! Turil!*" Two knockers came running out of the darkness, their small chests rising and falling, their eyes wild with fear. "Dig these people up and out. Try to meet up with the main tunnel so ye avoid the root systems that're close to the surface. *Go! Hurry.*"

The two knockers nodded and motioned for the group to step aside, then raised their hammers and struck the stone wall in unison.

Cefin bowed to Crow and Bear. "Swift journey to the light," he said. "To battle I go." He turned and raced away, disappearing from the light of Zahsie's magic in fractions of a moment.

Crow and Bear dropped to a crouch, following as closely behind Hans and Turil as they dared, for the hammers struck hard and fast, clanging and pinging now against rock so hard that sparks flew; the knockers threw soil behind them as swiftly and industriously as gophers or moles. Great roots slapped Crow and Bear against their faces; beetles crawled away in the half-light.

Medie stirred in Bear's arms. "Remind them," she whimpered, twitching.

"Remind them of what, girl?" asked Crow.

"About the bottom—about the shaft going down."

The knockers ahead kept at their work.

"Oy," said Bear. "Gentlemen."

Hans stayed his hammer and turned toward the large elf. "We are not gentlemen, but speak, *saylie*."

"She knows the ground. She can see it. The girl, she's speaking about a shaft going down. That supposedly you know about."

Hans dropped his hammer. "By the iron, yes."

"You can get past them," said Medie. "Past the alps."

Hans looked at her, his eyes widening in astonishment. "By the gods. My master and the lads have forgotten. They might survive if I get to them in time."

Turil came to his brother then. "Go. I can work faster. If you can save them, you must try."

"All right," said Hans. "Dig for glory, brother." He squeezed past Bear and Crow, running back into the dark that led to the main corridor.

###

Zahsie stood in her son's third-story bedroom. All of the other rooms were occupied with her neighbors, and the snow had covered up the windows completely, up past the first floor. Through the flurrie which had begun to buffet the town once more, she saw them coming down—small things, barely darker in color than the snow itself but moving swiftly in a chaos of limbs, clambering down the rough road from the pastor's house, gaining the road to town in moments.

Gailen's arm was broken, and Hugh's mouth was stuffed with a rag for two of his teeth had been knocked out, but the men and women of Delster had beaten back the long-legged things that had stalked down the street that day.

The villagers were all still asleep, and Zahsie didn't have the heart to tell them yet another terror was coming. Regardless, she left the room to rouse the able-bodied and sniffle back tears while she hurried down the stairs. She ran into Wystan, who'd woken and was standing in the front room by the window, but the window was covered with snow and ice, so he couldn't see what was coming.

Zahsie babbled to him, her words a jumble, and when he'd finally calmed her, they could both hear the sounds of the newest terror scrambling outside, like the sound of whips upon horses' backs, a crack and a whispering. Wystan pelted up the stairs, shouting for all who were able to awaken and fight.

Soon after, nearly all of the surviving villagers of Delster were in the street, having slid down the snow drifts from the second floor windows to stand on porches, or atop the roofs of homes that had been freed of ice, pitching stones, tools, chairs—anything they could find at the creatures of ice and snow that were swarming into town. Some of the fiends hurried; some jerked, crept, stalked, reaching with long fingers to break windows or slowly tear roof shingles and pull apart porch columns like rotten twigs. One long-legged creature, similar in shape and nature to the things the four had fought the other day, caved in a man's chest with its foot; another had thrown a lad of fourteen against the side of a house, and the villagers were carefully lifting him, trying to get him to safety. Still more creatures ran like rats up the walls of houses and dug at the rooftops, burrowing down into the home as if it were a molehill.

Within the Silver home, the youngest of the children watched in horror from the third-story window as their parents, friends, and neighbors struggled in the street like sparrows fighting off hawks and eagles with their small beaks and tiny claws.

There came a sound upon the howling, snow-choked air, a sound of hundreds of feet pounding against the frozen road, and the villagers saw in the distance a great blur of darkness against the white. Many cried out in despair.

"It's the end! We're finished now, surely!"

But then faces appeared in the galloping darkness—faces of beasts, quick and cunning, and most importantly, *natural.* Badgers and hares, possums and raccoons, deer and foxes, and even a bear all ran straight toward the ice-creatures with purpose and snarls and fangs bared.

"Get out of the road!" yelled Wystan, and he and Alaric ushered the villagers back to the relative safety of Zahsie's house, though some hopped up on the neighboring porches to watch what was about to occur.

The animals swept down upon the snow-creatures, breaking some of them as a strong hand breaks an icicle, but most of the monsters turned tail and began to run towards the village commons, the animals in quick pursuit.

There, behind the great herd of beasts, were Asher and Gareth, each riding atop two unnaturally large badgers, hooting and hollering and driving the others forward.

"Well," said Wystan.

"Enterprising lads," said Alaric. "*Oy!*" he shouted to the boys, who turned their badgers about with fistfuls of fur.

"Hey there!" shouted Asher. "We've come to help."

"That's great, and ye know how ye can help?" said Wystan. "Drive those creatures straight into the river."

The boys turned their badgers back and rode off, shouting and calling. As the men watched, the crowd of beasts rallied and flanked the snow-creatures and drove them through the narrow alley between the two houses through which Wystan had wandered the other day. He and Alaric jogged around to the back of the Silver house as the animals of the mountain surrounded the snow-beasts, narrowing the gap until the monsters were forced into the swiftly moving currents of the river.

With cries of rage and terror, each was swept under by the dark water until the only sounds remaining were the yips and growls of the animals and boys, and then the lonely cry of the wind.

###

Bear emerged from the cave, which was not so much a cave as it was a mouth of the land, a violently opened seam of the dirt that stretched as if it were yawning, and he, Crow, Medie, and the ghost-girl slipped out onto the snow. Just before they could turn and thank Turil, the earth fell back together like a heavy carpet dropped upon a floor, and the hillside was again smooth.

Before them was the great tree where they'd found Medie's necklace. Bear walked to the tree, slipping in the deep snow, and fell to his knees, his large hands against the black bark as he prayed. Crow wrapped her coat around Medie, and they both put their arms around Bear to lend him warmth; he was still naked above the waist.

He called out:

Sul, sem uira sul
kem tara nain,
kem basa min,
emtala tir go faih
sul
sul
em tara
min ehta faih.

Bear slumped against the tree, his arms around it as if in an embrace, and slipped out of consciousness. The falling snow at last turned into a gentle, steady rain.

In the Year of Late Snow

THE CURTAINS WERE pale and still, though the window was open. He could smell the soil and the green come into the room like the smell of good food from a warm kitchen. As he watched, the white curtains turned from blue to golden, and he knew even in his sleep-heavy state that the sun had moved out from behind a cloud outside. His dark eyes focused a little, and through the delicate pattern of the curtain, he saw small ovals of sky. His ears suddenly became unstuffed with dreams; he could hear the day clearly, and it was filled with the shrill notes of jays and of the gulls that coasted above the river.

A fluttering at the window made him lean upon one elbow; a tiny goldfinch landed upon the windowsill and cocked its head. The curtains lifted up again on the fingers of a warm wind, and the bird flew away.

Bear looked down at himself. A new, clean shirt covered his body. His hands were bruised, but he moved his fingers and they were unbroken. His tongue felt as if it had been replaced by the drying hide of a hunter's best catch, but he looked, and there was a tin mug of water at his bedside. He drank it down.

At the window, the curtains billowed all around a tiny form. He tried to force his eyes to focus better, but they were still sleep-clouded and strange. A small child seemed to be hiding amid the fabric and the light, then it was gone.

Pulling the bedsheets from his legs, Bear swung himself around. A pair of trousers sat neatly folded on the bedside table, as well as a new set of suspenders. After using the chamber pot, which someone had thoughtfully brought to his room, and pulling on the trousers, he looked for his boots. *No, that's right.* The belowground fiends had stolen those away.

"How am I supposed to get a new pair of boots, my size, unless I walk in my bare feet all the way to Bran?" he muttered.

It was then the events of the past week hit him in the chest like a flurry of punches, and he stumbled back to the bed, sitting on its edge and hanging his head. "I failed them. They didn't deserve what they got. No matter how mean-spirited or unkind. Nobody deserved that. And here I am, complaining over a lost set of boots."

"Hello?" called a voice from the other side of the door.

Bear looked up but didn't answer. He reached for the tin cup; he'd already emptied it.

"Brother?" said a small voice from the hall.

"Minny?" He walked, stiff-legged, to open the door. She was there, smiling at him, and he embraced her. There, too, were Alaric and Wystan, and behind them, Asher. Bear saw his boy and, gently pushing the others aside, lifted him into his arms.

They walked with Bear down the stairs, helping him balance his weight, for his feet were cut and bruised, and he sat in Zahsie Silver's kitchen. They brought him a plate of breakfast as well as a pair of boots, a gift from the milliner, who'd survived. Bear would have to wait for the swelling in his feet to go down, but they were fine boots, and very close to his size. The pants, shirt, and suspenders were tokens of her appreciation as well.

"You said your prayer and by my reckoning it was three hours past noon when the rain fell," said Crow.

"That's very close to the hour when the animals came into town and drove the monsters into the river," said Wystan.

"And us," said Asher. "We did it too."

"Yes. Bear, you should know—your boy's taken to riding giant badgers."

Bear listened and watched them talk while he ate, making noises of surprise and encouragement.

"Where do ye find a giant badger anyways?" asked Thomas, leaning in the doorway, smoking a pipe. "How'd they grow 'em that big?"

"Ogre-magic, ach," said Crow. "Now none of ye'd better hunt those beasties after they saved your town."

"Ah, now there's a conundrum," said Alaric, sitting down with a plate of biscuits that Zahsie had pulled from the oven. "Wonder how long that's going to keep."

"As long as we live," said Zahsie.

Bear suddenly tapped his trouser leg, feeling for something that wasn't there. "I found a knife," he said. "It was in my pocket."

"I have it," said Alaric, reaching into a pocket of his vest and placing the blade on the table. "The initials *OC* are carved into the handle."

"Oliver Cook," said Thomas. "By name and trade. He'd go with the bigger boats, the ones that had a crew and had need of one."

"Is he the fellow who went missing a year ago?" said Bear.

"Aye."

"Constable said he'd gone looking for gold. I found this deep under the mountain, in a locked cell where the ogres'd thrown me. There were bones in there, but I don't know if they were his. Still, Milo will want to know that I found Oliver's knife."

"Milo is gone," said Zahsie. "Died in the storm."

Bear looked at her and gasped, then covered his face with his fists, rubbing his eyes.

"I'm sorry," said Zahsie.

Hunter came into the kitchen, and his mother stared at his feet in horror, and then so did everyone else in the room.

"Wha'?" he said.

"Her floor," said Crow. "Your boots."

"Oh, well, I mean…it's a river of mud out there," said Hunter. "What's wrong with Pastor Bear?"

"Just getting caught up on things," said Bear. "Don't worry about it, lad."

"Take them off, and get the mop and a bucket," said Zahsie. "*Now.*"

"I survive and come home, and this is the thanks I get," said Hunter.

"It's how they show you they love you," said Bear. "Get used to it. So…" He slowly reached for a biscuit from Alaric's plate to sop up the gravy on his own. "How long did it take for the snow and ice to melt?"

"Dawn," said Crow. "The wind stopped and the rain came down, and by dawn, it was all gone."

"We should call for a pastor of Donnir to come through and counsel with you," said Zahsie. "After—" She covered her mouth.

Hunter leaned the mop against the wall and put his arm around her. "Shh, Mum. All right now."

"Yes," said Crow. "Ye've got your dead to bury—once the ground dries up a bit. You'll not be alone. We'll help."

"Has your husband returned yet, Zahsie?" asked Bear.

"Not yet," she said, and her pale eyes seemed haunted with worry.

"Give them time," said Tom. "The storm might have made its way down to Bran for all we know. That's a hard current to fight. Let's give them the rest of today before we panic."

"Who's got panic left in them?" asked Wystan.

"I might have, just a little bit," said Zahsie. "Now, if you'll excuse me, I have to see to Medie." She took a tray laden with cups, a tea-kettle, and some dishes with herbs and slowly made her way upstairs.

"May I come?" asked Mink.

Zahsie paused on the stairs. "No. It's best that ye don't. It will be okay, dear one. She's in good hands."

The others sat quietly and let Bear eat, and Alaric and Wystan too. Then Hunter and Asher announced they were hungry as well, but after time, the villagers left the kitchen and it was only Bear, Mink, Alaric, and Wystan at the table. Asher, Hunter, and Gareth had holed up in Hunter's room.

"I wonder if there's whiskey," said Bear, looking sheepish.

"It's noon," said Wystan. "Not that I'm against what you're proposing."

"It's not my kitchen," said Crow.

"I'm sure she wouldn't mind," said Alaric. "I spied some above the bread closet."

Crow was up and on tiptoe in a moment; Wystan grabbed cups from the wash-sink.

"It's fine," said Mink. "I'm sure it's fine."

"I'm sure you're sure it's fine," said Wystan. "Lord knows with what we've been through."

"Ye should know," said Crow, lifting her cup. "My brother's been through the most."

They looked at him. Alaric frowned. "I'm so sorry, Ursoon."

Bear scoffed. "No, come on. There's no need. A bit uncomfortable, it was. Nothing more."

Mink's eyes narrowed at him. "Stop doing that."

Bear looked at his sister. "What? What's this now—you're gonna get angry with me because I won't accept pity?"

Those at the table were silent.

Bear set down his cup. "Well, fuck pity. I don't want it. I don't deserve it. If I were a better pastor of Huil, this wouldn't have happened. I almost let the entire mountain get poisoned by that *thing*."

"You killed the king, Bear," said Crow, in a deep, calm, slow voice that seemed of an age much older than she was.

The others looked at Crow.

"He killed Bran-Nokken. The last king of the *nicht-ogren*."

Alaric gasped.

Wystan stood up from his chair, and Bear regarded him. The man came to Bear, and bent on one knee. "Look," he said. "You'll not get my pity if ye don't want it. But one thing you're gonna have, whether you want it or not…"

"Yeah?" said Bear, sipping his whiskey, his dark eyes watching the man with skepticism.

"My undying respect, sirrah."

Bear regarded him for a time. "Well. All right. But please, get off the knee. *Please.*" He looked at the others. "I just want things to be…normal again. Also," he said, spinning his cup about and catching it, "I just realized. I think I haven't had a smoke in a blessed week."

###

Zahsie sat by the bed and said quiet words of a tongue Medie couldn't understand, while lifting pinches of herbs from the dish and letting them fall into a cup, then lifting the heavy kettle and pouring the water from it over the herbs.

"Please," said Medie. "I can't drink it. I don't think I can ever drink tea again. I thought it was tea that they were giving me, and then the straw, that reed that they…and then I…" She started to sob, and the tears turned into wracking coughs. She put her arm across her mouth to keep from retching.

"No, no," said Zahsie, and her voice was soothing and calm. "No forcing, and you wait. The magic comes first, then this little tea, and it will smell and taste like your favorite flowers. Trust me, girl. I aim to make you well." Zahsie put her hand gently upon Medie's forehead and spoke quietly. "*Siwin eh haa, soroyu fech, kala fech il ein soroyu, ensel, saba ta.*" As she said the words, she moved her hand from Medie's forehead to her cheek, then to her other cheek, then took the girl's hands in her own. "Breathe deeply."

Medie took a deep breath, afraid she'd cough, or gag, but suddenly she could smell the delicious air of the warming, growing soil outside and the plants, and the sweet, greening scent coming off the budding trees.

"Once more," said Zahsie.

Medie did.

"Now, I will hold the cup to you, and if it, at any point, smells distasteful, you will simply shake your head *no*, and I will take it away. Does that sound reasonable?"

Medie nodded, regarding the cup of steaming liquid as if it held boiled frogs.

"Here we go," said Zahsie. She lifted the teacup and brought it closer to Medie's lips, then waited, holding it there so the girl could inhale its sweet fragrance. "How is that?"

Medie nodded again, licking her lips nervously.

"Let's try one sip."

Medie leaned closer to it and put her mouth against the cup's rim as Zahsie slowly tipped it, the rosy liquid leaking into Medie's mouth, just a bit.

"Good?"

Medie nodded once more, then reached for the cup, drinking it down, sip by careful sip.

###

A week had passed, and those who lived in the village had returned to their houses, though Bear, Asher, Mink, and Medie remained at the Silver home. Zahsie's furniture was none the worse for wear, and so she generously released Wystan from his oath to build her new pieces. Alaric bid farewell and took Wystan to visit the *swarthe* city. No one begrudged their absence from the funeral arrangements of the Delster folk who had died; both men had fought bravely for those who were not their kin, and they were thanked for their efforts.

It was agreed to forgo the burying of the dead for the more ancient practice of releasing their spirit-souls by fire, though the problem of erecting enough pyres upon which to properly burn the bodies was a daunting one, and while it had been suggested that the homes of the dead could be torn down, plank by plank, such was the tremendous nature of that solution it was instead decided to leave their homes intact and to take wagons to the forest's edge and pull deadfall out past the northern edge of town, beyond the orchards, to the fallow fields. Seven pyres were lit, husbands beside wives, mothers with their babes in their arms, and by the fifth night, they were ready to send them all to the heavens. The survivors of the winter of Delster in the Year of Late Snow, as it was to be deemed, gathered around the flames and stood in silence, and Bear said these words:

"We beg of thee, Great Ones, take these innocents into your lands and allow them to cultivate a field where it is always summer, where the sun is golden and the rain, silver. Let them feel no more pain, but let them feel their connection to us, who still regard them with honor and with love. We must always see to our own, and I believe that we have done that."

Bear turned from the unlit pyres to the people of the town, and said, "When you see to your own, the Great Ones will see to you. I consider each and every one of you to be my own. We stand together in this time of mourning, and when the tide turns back to times of joy."

They lit the fires then, and as the smoke reached up into the reddening dusk, the boats of many fishermen who had set out the day of the first storm could be seen coming home, their dark shapes drifting slowly upon the mirror-like surface of the river.

Zahsie and Hunter Silver stood at the shore as Ives Silver and Timothy Wayne steered their boat in to land.

Hunter's father jumped out of the boat and tugged it in, tying it tightly to the mooring. He came to Zahsie and gathered her to him.

"I'm so sorry, lass," he said. "There was a terrible storm."

###

The other day I got to see Jumps High and Quickly again, and they brought their mum along. My signing is terrible, still, and I didn't have Medie with me, but I was able to decipher, I think, their mum's name. Bright Eyes, or Big Eyes—not sure which, but definitely something to do with her eyes. She was heavy with child, too, which is exciting. More reffke on the mountain. I hope to meet up with them again. They're excellent fellows.

Medie's at home. She won't ever come with me—says she doesn't trust the mountain. I'm here upon it now, actually, high above the town in this place where five great stones form a little ridge, and there's a proper comfortable fallen tree that I sit on. It's likely the most beautiful place I'll ever see.

I like to sit up here and just be still. And listen. I often hear the turkeys making their way up the hill. I hear a bird's chirp echoing up the mountain, and it sounds like a sharp bell under water. The leaves shiver, and it sounds like waves on a sea, or at least what I think that sounds like from Da's stories.

What sometimes chills me, though, the way the air and the sweat on your back will chill when a cloud slips in front of the sun, is that suddenly I know what's down under my feet, below the leaves and beneath the soil. Down there is an entire world of darkness. Some of it is simple and plain and good, like the homes of the badgers and the moles, or the deep lakes where creatures swim and sleep, and of course the land of the swarthe, which is beautiful and of peace, but…some of it, a great portion of it, is not dark for lack of light, but for lack of good. And it's right there, right now as I sit, writing this diary passage. It's down below me. Maybe terrible things are happening to someone there, right now.

For the rest of my days, I will always know, despite all the good in the world, there is that darkness, hidden, but waiting.

– Asher Kieren's journal, Midsummer,
in the Year of Late Snow

Epilogue

Wystan belched as they gained the hill overlooking the source of the mountain's swiftest stream. Alaric chuckled at him.

"Climbing. It makes things rise."

"I've been behind you all this time. I wholeheartedly agree."

Wystan looked at Bear, who seemed oblivious to the banter. "Not worried about me, delving into the *swarthe-land* for so long?"

"Worried? No," said Bear, leaning against a tree to catch his breath. "Envious, yes. You will see such beautiful things, richness of nature and culture."

"If he leaves his quarters, that is," said Alaric.

"Brother," said Bear. "This is a new side of you. I've never known you to be so casual."

"Even old dwarves can learn new things."

Wystan winked at Bear. "I certainly hope that's true."

"Don't believe him; he's not much older than either of us. But I'll take my leave of you both now. Crow and I have to plan our trip to the city. Take care of our father's estate."

"Listen," said Wystan. "Before you go."

"Yeah?" said Bear.

"I remember all that you said, that night in the kitchen, about your family."

"Oh," said Bear, looking down at the leaves beneath his boots.

"No, it's all right. I mean, it's not *all right*. But I just wanted you to know—if the rest of your family is anything like yourself, and Mink, and Crow, well—you did real good, despite the man who contributed to the making of you. I'm sorry, I don't mean any disrespect. Just, I wanted to say…well-met, Bear. Thank you for taking me in. I'm forever in debt to you."

"Brother, any debt has been paid, thrice over," said Bear. "Only, when you return, say hello to Medie. You're in her heart."

Alaric walked to Bear, studying his face, then embraced him. "Be heartened by the fact that you are not alone on your path. There are many who love you, Ursoon. And if you've need of me, or this wayward cur, it is easy enough to call for us. We'll break from our holiday to come to you and your kin."

Bear looked at Alaric, holding the man's arms with his own, and said nothing, but nodded to him, and to Wystan, and turned to take the long walk back down the mountain to his home.

###

"He's so full of sadness. I wish we could do something," said Wystan.

"It has to be lived out," said Alaric as he led Wystan down the mossy bed of the smaller stream that once ran parallel to the larger. Just ahead, the land rose up, and great tendrils of vine and shaggy moss hung over a great door, but to Wystan's eyes, it was only rock carved with sigils.

"What do ye mean?"

"Every pain needs to be worked out, worked out of the soul by time. Time and patience. Like, say, a splinter in the skin."

"But that I just cut out with a knife tip."

"Not everyone has such a knife tip for a heart. Or…sometimes, a pain lays itself upon the older pain, and then again, until there are so many wounds working their way through the flesh it becomes impossible to remove them all. And so you carry them."

"I suppose."

"Well, you lived for ten years as a dog. That doesn't trouble you?"

"I suppose," said Wystan again. "I mean sure, it does. But the point was, I was *alive.* I was grateful for that. And there was a solution. I just had to be patient."

"Not everyone sees their solution so clearly."

"True. The witch spelled it out for me."

"Yes."

They stood at the door, and Alaric turned to Wystan. "You can't see the portal, but if I touch you while you look to it, you'll be able to see."

Wystan reached out his hand. "Fair enough."

"I could take your hand, but I prefer to do this." Alaric reached for Wystan and, putting his dark hand around the man's golden neck, drew him close and pressed a long, slow kiss upon his lips.

While Alaric kissed him, Wystan opened his eyes and glanced towards the boulder. A white door, outlined every few inches in sullen, gleaming squares of mica and buttons of pyrite, came into focus as if he'd just woken from a deep sleep and was seeing the daylight gleam out across everything, sharpening the landscape.

Alaric stopped his kiss and looked at him. "I won't be jealous of the fact that you are awed by *swarthen* architecture."

"That's good," said Wystan, still staring. "Because I really cannot help it. How does one open it?" He walked to the door, looking for a handle or a pull.

"I walk towards it, you walk closely behind me," said Alaric. "Are you ready?"

"So ready," said Wystan. "And listen." He came around to stand beside the dwarf. "Thank you. For this honor. I'm serious."

Alaric smiled. "I know."

###

They walked towards the door, and as Alaric neared it by inches, the white wood became a sheet of water, a clean waterfall raining from the ferns and vines above. Wystan paused, but Alaric pulled him along, and as they walked beneath it, they were not dampened by the water but were instead refreshed, as if they'd woken from a restful second-sleep.

"Look into the shadows," said Alaric. "Tell me what you're able to see."

Wystan blinked. His eyes were, in fact, watering, as if he'd just been swimming. "I can see…" He stared ahead at the tunnel winding its way down into half-light. "The walls, and the floor."

"What do you not see?"

Wystan looked again and gasped. "Torches. I think? But no, I don't actually see them, or any light source, at all."

Alaric smiled. "Yes. The water-door will give you that gift—for a while. There are other such places within the city where we can take you if the sight begins to dim. Not that the city is devoid of light, but gray-sight helps."

They walked down the corridor together then, shoulder to shoulder as the passageway was wide.

"I do have a question," said Wystan.

"I'm sure it will be the first of many. Ask me, and me alone, so you don't appear too discourteous, but I will always endeavor to answer them."

"Why do you never call your city by its name?"

"Ah," said Alaric. "A good question. And we have a very specific reason." He led Wystan around a rising stalagmite of calcified quartz. "Our city's name is secret. It holds great power, as you can imagine. It goes unspoken so that we may exist apart from many of the troubles of the greater world—the shadows that plague humans and elves will rarely touch us. Our borders are not protected, but they are unnoticed. We live in a glamorous pocket of a very unglamorous world, and I hope you know to which meaning I'm referring."

Wystan chuckled, gesturing to himself. "Hello," he said. "*Was a black dog.*"

"Yes," said Alaric, stopping at the top of a long, narrow series of stairs. "Of course you know."

"Who among the *swarthe* knows the name, actually?"

"I'm not really sure."

"Do you?"

Alaric turned to him, tipping his head slightly, watching Wystan with curious eyes. "One day, but not today, I may well answer that for you."

"I'm sorry," said Wystan, shifting on his feet, embarrassed. "That was too much."

"No, it wasn't." Alaric squeezed Wystan's shoulder. "I will tell if you ever ask me anything that *is*, but odds are, you won't. One of the things I find appealing about you is your boundless curiosity. And lack of guile."

Wystan smiled again. "That reminds me."

"Yes?"

"Do you all have a library?"

Alaric's laughter boomed and bounded across the rock walls.

###

"And what of these ghosts that haunt this place?" said Mink, sitting in the front room of the Silver home. The carpets had been beaten free of the mud that was tracked in during the storm; the windows' shutters opened to the spring air and the light. Curtains blew inward with the heady, scented wind, and a small, yellow moth flew in and settled on the rim of a sugar bowl, balancing. Zahsie gathered it in her hand and walked up to the door; Mink got up to open it for her. She set the insect free.

"They walk," said Zahsie, returning to sit on a wicker chair. "And some have gone to the sweet-land, home. But many still walk."

"What can be done for them?"

"They first have to want anything done at all," said Zahsie, poking at the tea leaves in the bottom of her cup. "If they were bitter unbelievers in life, they're likely wandering, aimless spirits after death. Not everything rushes along on its road as it should. Some things linger, and some things fester."

"Like the mountain," said Mink, shuddering.

"Yes."

They sat in silence, listening to the shout of a wagon driver as his cart rolled past, the jingle of the horses' tack, the rolling wheels.

"Do you ever tire of living in town?"

"Did you?" asked Zahsie.

Mink leaned back into her chair, stretching her legs out in front of her. “Sometimes.” She reached up and re-gathered her hair that had come wildly loose from its tether, as it tended to do. “There was constant noise, unlike the nice lull you get in Delster an hour before the sun has set. Yet the buildings were built higher. There were places a woman could travel, alone, to be with her thoughts. Pockets of tranquility.”

“There are those here too,” said Zahsie. “But I understand your meaning. Here, we rely on the judgment of neighbors. In a city such as Bran, you rely on the judgment of the law.”

“Would that all adhere to the laws. There are no universal laws.”

“But there are so many different universes.”

Mink sat up, yawning. “Do you think so?”

“It’s not for me to determine,” said Zahsie. “It’s not an opinion. It’s something I know is truth.”

“Then there will never be unity, or peace, if that’s the truth.”

“Another truth. How’s your house, these days? A shame such a good, old place had to take such a beating.”

“Bear put shutters over the windows that were broken, for now. Said he’d see about taking the intact panes out of the briar-hedge house and setting them in mine before the cold comes. I’ll make do, just like my beeswax candles when they run out. I’ll get used to an airier, darker house, like everyone else.”

“He’s a good man, your brother.” Zahsie got up from her chair, and reached for the tray. “Are you needing anything else?”

Mink shook her head, yawning again.

“You need air and outdoors,” said Zahsie. “Let’s walk.”

“Where?” asked Mink.

“Beyond the orchards, I think. I’m not in the mood for rude stares and half-whispered comments.”

“I do not enjoy the river docks either.”

###

"Not all humans are bad, you know," said Zahsie as they walked past the remaining occupied storefronts, homes, and workshops of beaten-down Delster.

Mink nodded, pulling her shawl around her small shoulders.

"I know that's probably an awful thing to say. I'm sorry."

"It's all right. You're a very good person. I'm thankful to know you."

"It doesn't mean I should be up on a stump braying like a mule about *not all humans*."

"Well, no. You shouldn't."

"Thank you."

"For what?" asked Mink, glancing at her.

"For being so honest. So strong."

Mink shrugged, smiling a little. "I can't help that, and that's the truth. Our mum fought so hard, and I saw that. I guess I'm more like her than I ever expected to be."

"What did she fight for?"

"Her life. Our lives."

"Against who? Your father?"

"Yes."

They reached the commons. The mud of the road had dried enough to prevent boots from sinking into it, and tiny sprouts of green had risen up, also spots of vibrant purple—pansies—taking their turn beneath the sun to herald the season. Mink stooped to pluck one white pansy from the ground. She tucked it into her collar. "It's so silly."

"What is?"

"How men and women squabble and fight over appearances. Even beasts do not do *that*."

"No, but they do try to be the best of their kind. Biggest, top of the hill."

"Why is nature so ferocious?"

"It is and it isn't. But then, we notice the worst of it more often, I think, and why wouldn't we? It's terrifying. My mother used to tell me, 'every field you see is a killing field.' And she was right.

Beneath our footsteps, things are consuming other things. That is nature. Rise up, get hungry, seek a meal, take away."

"Or be taken away," said Mink.

"Or that, yes," said Zahsie as they passed one of the homes of the dead.

"We're rather grim today, aren't we?" said Mink.

"Yes," said Zahsie, taking Mink's hand. "We should try to lift our spirits above all that's occurred."

"We can try, at least."

"Okay. Have you ever seen the mill?"

"Can't say that I have, no."

"They don't use it anymore, though they could if we got another wheat farmer come to Delster. But the wheel turns. It's lovely. We can sit there and watch the river, away from the town and its eyes."

"Sounds good to me," said Mink.

"I'm glad to have met you. Glad I was able to help your girl."

Mink stopped walking, and turned to Zahsie and gathered her close, embracing her tightly. "I am so very glad, also."

###

The day they readied the cart to set out for Bran, the winds were whipping the trees in a green fury, and petals and pollen were swirling down like dusty rain upon the fields and the garden. The porch roofs were yellowed with it, and Mink's eyes were pink and puffy.

"What you need," said Crow to her as Bear came out of his house with bags and boxes to set on the cart, "is an apiary here. Ask Zahsie who she knows. Some honeycomb made from the same flowers that're troubling ye and you'll be back to yourself in a week, maybe less."

"Okay," said Mink, sneezing again.

Bear came out one more time with a long bag of his tools and implements and stopped midway between the house and the cart. "I'll be drunk and staggering," he said. "And where might've you been, yellow mister?"

There was Leiben the tom, sitting on the cart's bench, cleaning his whiskers.

"Well, good!" said Mink. "Because the mice have not waited for him and are busy conducting their springtime affairs."

"He'll roust them out thoroughly," said Bear. "Don't worry." He walked over to his sister, hugging her tightly, then walked back to the cart. "Asher!"

"Oy," said the boy, peering out from his bedroom window. "Ye leaving now?"

"What's this *ye* business?" said Bear.

"Sorry." There was a thundering of footsteps down the stairs and Asher came running out to give Bear a great hug. "Been hanging out with Gareth and the lads. Town's rubbing off on me."

"Don't let it *stick*," said Bear. "Or at least, only show it off in certain company. Not your father's, in other words."

Asher rolled his eyes.

"I'm glad you're friends with them, lad. Really I am. Be useful to your Aunt Mink, okay? As well as to your cousin."

"Yessir," said Asher.

"Good boy," said Crow, ruffling Asher's hair before climbing atop the wagon's bench. "You goin' to ride with us, Leiben?"

"Oh dear, no," said Mink. "Let me fetch some butter, coax him away."

"He has ridden with me all the way to town before. He likes the breeze," said Bear.

Mink came back out onto her porch, set down a dish with a spoonful of butter and began to *tsktsktsk* at Leiben, who luxuriantly leapt from the cart to saunter over to her.

"All right," said Bear. "One more hug for the road." Asher threw his arms around his father. "Love you. Will miss you. See you in about two months' time."

"I'll miss you too, Da. Love you too."

Bear bade Walter head for the road down to town, and as they passed the little path towards the briar hedge and Sanandra's house, he and Crow saw Medie, still as a stone, between the goldenrod and the rushes that had sprung up around the spring head, watching them go by.

They were quiet, Crow and Bear, though the cart brakes were not, squealing and protesting all the way down the switchback road, and when, at last, they reached the main highway, they stopped at the old, worn sign that pointed north towards Delster, and south towards Bran.

"I haven't left this town, Crow, for nearly fifteen years."

"It'll be good for ye. Have you cleared everything with the boss?"

Bear chuckled, turning Walter to the right, toward Bran. "Yes. Why I have so much luggage."

"I was wondering about that, figured you'd tell me."

"I'm to meet up with the Deacon of the Branwin Chain, as soon as I'm able."

"Nonsense, he gave you a date."

"He did."

"But?"

"I've personal business to attend to."

"Bear Kieren," said Crow, laughing loudly, spooking a pair of greenfinch who'd been hopping along the roadside foliage, watching them. "Ye loathe Da, and ye love your order. Why put him off?"

"I don't particularly enjoy Deacon Milic."

"I'm flabbergasted."

"No you're not."

"I am!"

"There has never been a gast amongst your flabbers since ye turned your horse cart into adulthood."

Crow hauled off and punched Bear so squarely he scooted sideways on the bench.

"Ow," he said, chuckling. "That actually hurt." He glanced at her.

"Never heard my nethers called *flabbers* before. That's a good one. I'll have to use it at some point in the future. So...what about him do ye not like?"

"He's a pompous ass."

"Ah, well, that was easy."

"He does not care about *people*, at all. Not at all. Huil is a giving goddess; She is not aloof. But Her deacon is. Oh so very. I'd like to punch him like ye just did me."

"I'll bet you'd like to do it harder than that, brother. Be honest."

"True."

"Well, look," said Crow. "There're always going to be *asses*. In every calling, in every art, in every profession. Unless you truly live alone, on a hill surrounded by flaming sands, and then ye know what? You're yer own ass."

"I'd make a very fine ass for m'self if you must know."

Crow looked at him and shook her head, laughing.

"I can't ignore people, Crow. That's my problem."

She glanced at him, and nodded. "Go on."

"Leisel—little boy died in the tunnels. They carried him out. I didn't want the body to go sour so I buried him beside that ancient tree. And his mum, she came to me, after we'd gone back to mine and Mink's houses."

"I remember. And I remember coming out of the outhouse to see a woman and a little girl at your door."

"That was them."

"What did they want?"

"To see him. So I took them up. I carried the little girl. I'd have carried the mother too, but she was too proper, too of the old ways. We stopped often, for her to catch her breath. We got to the tree, and I asked her if she wanted him out of the cairn I'd built upon him, to bring him to the orchards. She cried upon my chest and said, 'No, I don't want him burned.' And I asked her if she'd like him buried closer to town where she could visit him. And she said yes."

"You carried that boy, two weeks dead, down the mountain?"

Bear nodded, and his eyes never left the road.

They rode to the deeps of the River Branwin, where the ferryman named Nedbalek was having a cozy nap beside his three goats. The goats were working hard at chewing away the creeping vines that had crossed the road and were making for the river. The cart wheels struggled across the ropey tendrils, and Bear hopped out to stay Walter by a tree stump, looping the rope to his harness and setting a rock upon it.

"He's that good, eh?" asked Crow.

"He is. And if it's wolves or thieves, I'd prefer he run."

"Our journey ends for a nap," said Crow.

"It doesn't. Same man was here, sleeping, when Solace and I first moved to Delster. Oy!" he called, and Nedbalek stirred, then hugged his hat to his chest even tighter.

"Sirrah?" said Crow, nudging the man with her boot.

"Fire! Foes!" yelled Bear.

Nedbalek sat up, drool whitening his beard. "Yeah?"

"We need to get across," said Crow.

"Just lemme piss first."

They waited, listening to the man drown the weeds with his water and go on with various groans of contentment. Finally, he emerged from the rushes and beckoned them to board the broad, sturdy barge tethered to a twisting root at the shoreline, after he slid a wide gangplank out from its deck to rest upon the damp grass. As he uncoiled the rope from the Delster-side of the river, he pulled the rope tethered to the opposite side, where the road continued on, leading to Bran.

"Hope ye don't mind," said Nedbalek. "The goats like to come with."

"Of course," said Bear. "It's no bother."

As they crossed the Branwin, its currents slow and lazy at this deepest point, the sun resolved to shoulder its way out from behind the heavy clouds, and the wind scuttled down to a humid breeze.

"It's not going to be easy," said Crow. "I want you to fix that in your mind."

"Already have."

"And I'm sorry for being away so often. For not being a greater part of your life."

"You don't owe me anything, Crow."

"I know I don't."

"What I do get, I'm grateful for."

"But that's just yer thing. That's yer problem. You take what you get and ye don't pitch a fit, as Mum used to say."

"It's not a problem. It's just my nature. It's me."

"I want for you to command what ye need. Sometimes, Bear. I feel that would be right for you."

Bear looked at Crow, her tiny frame clothed in her dark leathers, hood pulled over her head, keen eyes cloaked in shadow. "I will trust your counsel," he said. "And I will look inward."

###

Medie lay on the floor of what was once Sanandra's room, and she watched the late-day light filtering through the silken cobwebs of the open windows to the floor on which dust and snow stains swirled a random pattern, where she'd placed a wreath of honeysuckle and ivy, spiked with honey-locust thorns and specked with violets and trilliums.

"Give me your hand," she said to the shadows, but only the light answered, as it was that which surrounded the small girl shyly crossing the floor of her own room in incorporeal, barefoot steps. As if it were morning when her mum was alive. As if it were summer and the heat from the attic had woken her. As if she were alive and smelling a good breakfast from the kitchen below.

"Put the wreath on your head—let me help you," said Medie. She lifted it to where Sanandra's haloed face was, held it above her brow and smiled. "It looks beautiful on you."

The wind blew in through the bare windows and leaves scuttled across the floor.

"Are you ready to go home?"

The light dimmed briefly, and the small head tilted. Medie could see the eyes, tiny onyx-whorls of life, darken and shadow.

"No, no, sweet girl. This was home, but the greater home, the better place—is the sweet-lands. That's where I meant. One day, I will go there too, and we can see each other again, and we can dance and play. I will hold your hand, and I will see your smiling face. We can eat honeycomb and cakes, and have tea. Won't that be so good?"

The light shone fully around Sanandra now.

"I will help you."

Medie held the briar crown still. "I put the softer things in the middle so it would feel nice. The thorns are there so that nothing harasses you on the path upward to the sweet-lands. You must be brave. Can you be brave?"

Sanandra's aura shivered and danced, as if lit by fire.

"Repeat after me. *I go away, from the night and the day, to the up and away, to my ancestors, stay—I return to the forest, to the field and the home, I return to the lands where my ancestors roam.*"

Medie leaned forward, planting a kiss upon Sanandra's shimmering forehead, and let go of the crown.

It fell to the attic floor, and the wind spun the leaves about in a spiral all around it.

The aureate light of the spirit was gone, and the setting sun had drifted down from the window. The attic was in full shadow now.

The ancient tree whose bough had touched beneath the windowsill of the southernmost window scraped upon the peeling wood of the house. Upon this, a figure watched Medie with gleaming eyes.

But her own eyes were too wet with tears to notice, and she hurried down the stairs, through the empty house, down the porch steps and through the bramble path, to home.

About the Author

Deven Balsam is a single dad, resident DJ at Asheville North Carolina's oldest running gay bar, and new author of sci fi, fantasy, and speculative fiction. He weaves a bit of romance, horror, and spirituality into everything he writes. Originally a Yankee from the New York metropolitan area, he currently lives on a mountain at the edge of 250 acres of Pisgah National Forest, and that suits him just fine.

Website: https://devenbalsam.weebly.com

By the Author

Tourist Season

Three: A Tale of the Bookseller's Children

Beaten Track Publishing

For more titles from Beaten Track Publishing,
please visit our website:

http://www.beatentrackpublishing.com

Thanks for reading!

CPSIA information can be obtained
at www.ICGtesting.com
Printed in the USA
JSHW010827250819
1186JS00001B/2